What the Fireflies Knew

What the Fireflies Knew

a novel

Kai Harris

RANDOM HOUSE
LARGE PRINT

Copyright © 2022 by Kai Harris

All rights reserved. Published in the United States of America by Random House Large Print in association with Tiny Reparations Books, an imprint of Penguin Random House LLC.

Interior art: Wildflower silhouette © Karen B. Jones/ Shutterstock

Cover design by Dominique Jones
Cover illustration by Kaitlin Kall

The Library of Congress has established a Cataloging-in-Publication record for this title.

ISBN: 978-0-593-55658-0

www.penguinrandomhouse.com/large-print-format-books

FIRST LARGE PRINT EDITION

Printed in the United States of America

1st Printing

This Large Print edition published in accord with the standards of the N.A.V.H.

For my momma and my big sister.
For the three little girls who call me Momma.
And for my husband.
My definition of love was born with
and lives with each of you, always.
Keep teaching me how to love.

What the Fireflies Knew

January 1995

I was the one who found Daddy dead, crammed in the little space where my old bike's training wheels turned rusted. I hadn't ever seen a dead body before, cept one funeral when all I really saw was one dead arm folded cross a still chest, cause Momma ain't let me get close; and sometimes, too, in the cop shows Momma loved to watch before bed and I snuck and watched, pretending to sleep, tucked between Momma's bony elbow and fast-beating chest. But Daddy was different. His skin, once deep brown, had turned dull gray like the sky when it rains and rains, and the sun hides behind full clouds til it's too late to go out and play.

I was s'posed to be sleep, but I couldn't sleep, so I crept down the creaky stairs looking for

Daddy. He was always up late, too. I ain't scream at first, when I found him there, cold. I just walked back up the steps, quiet like Momma always taught me, and pushed open her heavy bedroom door. When I told her, she screamed, so finally I screamed. Momma screaming felt heavier, scarier, more real than Daddy laying limp in that little space beneath the stairs.

Momma called the police, and they came with loud, red sirens. One officer peeked into all our drawers and cabinets, while the other draped yellow tape around our whole house til I barely recognized anything. I sat wrapped in a thick carpet blanket on the hard kitchen floor, trying my best to listen, but only being able to hear once, just as one cop whispered, "another fiend," to the other. I ain't know that word, fiend. But I had heard Momma yell it at Daddy sometimes on the days the basement steps would rot with a sour stench.

PART I

June 1995

1

"We there yet?" My big sister, Nia, unbuckles her seat belt and lays cross the back seat beside me. Her skin shimmers in the sun from a half-cracked window, which lets a tiny breeze slide in that carries her cottony hair back and forth, up and down. People say Nia's the one who looks like Momma. They have the same oval eyes and mahogany skin. My eyes are rounder and my skin pale yellow, like the color of french fries that ain't quite cooked.

Momma ignores Nia's question. Probably cause it's bout the tenth time she's asked. My nose finds the smell of rotten banana and that's got me thinking back to that night, almost six months ago now. The smell fills the car, just like the stench in our old basement that stuck around even after Daddy was buried. I dig my hands into the seat cushions and touch something sticky, but it's more peppermint sticky than banana sticky. Days ago, laying with a book in the back seat, one of my favorite places now, I got interrupted by Momma and Nia, right outside the car door and yelling, like always. They ain't see me, so I crept out before they could, hiding the banana I was just bout to bite. I hid it in a perfect place to come back for later, once all the fighting finally stopped. But it never did, and now I can't remember where I put it. I rub my eyes as I look around. I wanna fall asleep, but now I'm awake and smelling that stink.

Nia don't look my way, just stares out the window, so I stare out the window. Ain't nothin' but flat green spaces. Cars speed by on both sides. I like that Momma drives slower than the other cars, cause then I don't get carsick. I count signs bigger than me as they blur cross my reflection in the car window. There's one for Toys"R"Us with a big picture of the new Easy-Bake Oven and Snack Center right in the middle. A NOW OPEN sign for a new restaurant called Ponderosa. And one with a picture of a bunch of kids playing with dirt, and words at the bottom that say: NEW NAME, SAME FUN. VISIT IMPRESSION 5 SCIENCE CENTER, AHEAD IN 28 MILES. I wanna ask Momma to stop—for the restaurant or the science center, mostly, but even a toy would do—but I know we ain't gon' stop. So I count and count and get to twenty-two, then I'm bored.

I find my book between the seat cushions and open to the first page. This gon' be my third time reading this book bout Anne, the Green Gables girl. I wonder what a gable is, and why it's s'posed to be green. I can't always understand the kind of words she's using cause nobody I know talks all proper like that, but in some ways, Anne is just like me, so it's my best book. Besides, even if I don't always get her way of talking, I like the sound of her words, all big and **eloquent**. Ever since I picked it from my school's Lost and Found, I been reading bout Anne and even learning how to talk like her. I ain't ever had too many books of my own, so when nobody at my school came for it, I did.

The sun was coming in at the window warm and bright; the orchard on the slope below the house was in a bridal flush of pinky-white bloom, hummed over by a myriad of bees. I roll the new words over my tongue slow like dripping honey. **Myriad, myriad, myriad. Orchard**, what is an **orchard? Bridal flush of pinky-white bloom.** Sometimes I try to use words like in my book, but when I do Nia teases me, saying I don't even know what I'm talking bout. But even if me and Anne don't look the same, we can still talk the same and be alike in other ways.

I read six more pages bout Anne showing up in Avonlea and tryna fit in where she don't belong; then there's a loud clanking sound and the car slows down. Momma mutters a bad word under her breath, the one that starts with **D**. I said that word once, just to test it out when nobody could hear me. It felt good. I repeat it now in my head like a silent chant, once for each time our car has stopped working—maybe twelve since we got it bout a year ago—but at some point, I stopped counting. Seems like our old Dodge Caravan—nicknamed Carol Anne like the girl in that scary **Poltergeist** movie—breaks more than it works.

"Nia, KB. Get out and push." We know what Momma is gon' say before she says it, so my seat belt is already undone, and Nia is halfway out the car by the time she finishes the sentence. We step out into the sun, at the top of a stubby hill where the smoking car is stalled. Back when Daddy used to push the car, his muscles would grow big as he pushed, sometimes even **up** a hill. I am happy we get to go **down** the hill, at least.

"This is stupid," Nia mutters, but I pretend not to hear. Instead, I keep quiet, we keep pushing, and Momma keeps steering and smiling.

Momma always smiles, even in the bad times. Her smile is like a gigantic, dripping ice cream cone, after I stuff my belly full with dinner. Even with a stomachache, I want that smile. I need that smile more than bout anything in the world, I think. Momma has different smiles for different things. This smile, when the car hisses and puffs and then stops, is squeezed tight cross her face like the drawn-on smile of a plastic doll.

"Ugh!" Nia groans from the other side of the car. I still pretend not to hear, wiping sweat from my forehead and squinting up at the hot sun as I take off my favorite rainbow jacket with holes where there should be pockets, then tie it around my waist. Carol Anne don't take too much muscle to push, probably cause we going down a hill, and also cause we ain't got much stuff with us. We drove straight from the Knights Inn that's been home ever since we lost our real house, before we even had a chance to finish crying for Daddy. Before this, we never stayed at a motel. It smelled like cigarettes mixed with fried chicken grease and sometimes we found bugs in the mattress, but it had good stuff, too. Our first day there, Nia showed me how to trick the vending machine while Momma talked to the man at the front desk.

"We got money?" I asked, eyes scanning back and forth. There was all kinds of good stuff behind the glass, like chocolate bars and potato chips, and even a toothbrush.

"We don't need none," replied Nia matter-of-factly.

"It's gon' give us stuff for free?" My mouth got

real dry thinking bout all the chocolate I could eat—one of them things we don't get a lot, but still one of my favorites.

"Nah." Nia put both hands up on the glass. "Unless you know the secret trick." She pushed her hands against the window, banging against it til down fell a bag of chips and two packs of gum. "Ta-da!" Nia stuck her hands down in the bottom and pulled out her stolen treasure, stuffing everything in her pockets before Momma could see.

"How you know that? You been to a motel before?" I tried to reach into Nia's pocket, but she swatted my hand away.

"No, KB, motels ain't the only places with vending machines." Nia dug in her pocket and snuck out two sticks of gum, passing one to me and popping the other in her mouth. "You ain't ever seen nobody do that before?" I shook my head, but Nia was already walking away.

Turns out, tricking that vending machine wasn't the only new thing I learned at the motel. They also had hair dryers that stayed stuck to the wall, and people in uniforms that would come clean your room every day. After the first time I let them in, Momma came home from work at the Chrysler plant yelling and said we can't ever let housekeeping do chores in our apartment. She likes calling it that better than the motel—we learned that the hard way—and even though I thought chores were over when we lost our house, still I did as I was told.

"Almost there, girls," Momma yells from the front seat. As we push the car, I dig my worn shoes in the dirt. Cept it's more like mud now, even though there ain't been no rain today. I look back to see my own small footprints beside Nia's bigger ones. The ground looks like it's decorated with big and small polka dots as my shoulder shoves into hot metal. It's a good feeling to help Momma, but every time I look over at Nia, she frowns.

"That's it, girls!" Momma sings as we finally reach the bottom of the hill. The car makes a loud **pop!** And then it's working again. Momma pulls on her braids as she waits for us to climb back inside. Nia's first, quick. I take my time, so I can catch Momma's eye in the side mirror. And there she is, just like I knew. First, one wink. Then, she blows two kisses. I catch the first and kiss it, catch the second and blow it back into the wind. Our special thing, just me and Momma. I buckle my seat belt beside Nia and try Momma's smile on her, but all it gets back is another frown.

Momma's watching us through the rearview mirror before she pulls off, and I wonder how we look to her, two daughters, one who smiles just like her, one who frowns just like Daddy. Either way, she smiles at us both the same before driving again, even slower now.

"Nia?" I tap her shoulder light at first, then harder. "Nia!"

"What do you want?" Nia rolls her freshly opened eyes.

"We there."

This is my first time visiting Lansing, Nia's second. Her first was before I was born. We have lots of family in Lansing, but we're here to visit Momma's daddy, who I guess we s'posed to call Granddaddy. Momma said we all gon' stay here for the rest of the summer, before school starts back. My eleventh birthday is bout a month away, and Nia gon' turn fifteen the week after. When I pointed that out, that these would be our first birthdays away from home, away from Daddy—Momma's smile disappeared, just for a second, but then it was back, pasted in place like somebody glued it there crooked.

Momma pulls into the driveway and Carol Anne groans, either from exhaustion or from the bump-bump-bump of the gravelly road. As she parks, I try to remember the last time I seen my granddaddy. It was years ago, probably when I was bout seven, back when I used to wear my thick hair in two ponytails parted right down the middle with Blue Magic hair grease making it shine and Pink lotion laying down my edges. It was Nia's favorite style, so it was my favorite style. Then Nia started wearing her hair in two different ponytails, one on top and one on the bottom like a unicorn. Back then, Granddaddy came to visit us once in Detroit, when there was a funeral for somebody on Momma's side of the family. I chew my thumb and try to remember the dead person in that casket. The dead arm laying on the dead chest that I could only see when standing on tip-toes. That picture fades now into the image of dead Daddy, but this was long before that. Back when I still thought dead people in caskets ain't belong to nobody. They were always just dead people, not nobody's kid or friend or daddy.

"Okay, okay, I'm up." Nia stretches and yawns. But I'm still stuck remembering the itchy lace dress I wore to that funeral, the dress that Momma loved, and eating the last piece of sweet potato pie before Nia could. I peek out my finger-smudged window at the little house squatting at the end of a long driveway. The biggest thing I remember from that other funeral was meeting my granddaddy. He wasn't bad, but he never smiled, and he never talked that whole day long. I decided he couldn't speak, like maybe he lost his voice in an accident. I imagined all the possibilities, til he finally grumbled hello in a voice low and deep as thunder.

"Come on, girls, let's get out!" Momma is cheerful, but Nia moans. Granddaddy's house will make the third place we've lived in the six months since Daddy died. The more we move around, the more I forget stuff. Like the pattern of my wallpaper in the old house on the dead-end street. I'm starting to forget what it feels like to have a home at all.

I swallow and fight back tears as I climb out the car, slow. Momma don't like it when I cry so much. And Nia teases me, calling me Crybaby KB when I do. The **K** is for Kenyatta and the **B** for my middle name, Bernice, which was the name of my daddy's grandma. Nia started calling me KB when I was a baby. I have other nicknames like Kenya and TaTa that I like better, but KB is the one that stuck.

Gravel crunches under my shoes and something rustles in the bush ahead. I search for the noise as we march up to the tree-shadowed house like soldiers, but don't see nothin'. Just before we reach the wooden porch, wrapped around the house and sloping in the dirt, Granddaddy comes outside to meet us. His skin is dark as a moonless night with hair brushed in black and gray patterns, and a heavy limp that dips and jumps and dips again.

"Why he so bent over and wobbly?" I whisper to Momma. She swipes me on the bottom and flashes me The Look. I been gettin' The Look from

Momma all my life—not nearly as much as Nia, but enough for me to know exactly what it's s'posed to mean.

"Hush your mouth," she hisses. I wonder why it's a bad question but know better than to ask. These days, asking too many questions is just as bad as crying.

"I bet he need a cane to walk, cause he so old." Nia is suddenly beside me and trying not to let Momma hear her giggle. I giggle, too, happy to get an answer, and happy it's from Nia.

Just like I remember, Granddaddy don't speak, only opens his arms to say, **Come on in.** Nia drags her feet as she walks, so I drag my feet, too. But Momma walks quick with her very best smile stretched cross her face. She is first up the steps, and is fixin' to hug Granddaddy, but he seems nervous and moves out the way. So she stands next to him instead, with that other smile for when she's mad but has to act happy cause we at church.

"You remember Nia and KB." Momma offers us up like treasures, but Nia got a hole in the knee of her pants and my too-small shoes are black with mud. Granddaddy looks at Nia first, then me. It's quiet, like a test. He stops on my face and looks straight way in my eyes. I wanna look away, but I notice his eyes got tiny spots of dark in the part that's s'posed to be white.

"Kenyatta," he grumbles. It's the only word he says to me that day.

The house is silent and smells like a mix between the old people that kiss my cheeks at church, and the tiny storage unit where all our stuff lives now. I'm surprised there's framed photos of me and Nia and Momma on the tall mantel. I wonder why Momma never brought us to Lansing before. I guess cause it's so far away. It took us two hours to get here, and another with pushing. I keep looking and see plenty of other pictures, but no more with us or Momma. Some of the people in the pictures look just like Momma, even though I don't know them.

"Let's take a look around," Momma says, but I keep my own pace as Momma and Nia and Granddaddy move ahead.

Next to the pictures on the mantel are tiny statues. They are all kids, weird-shaped but kids, with skin the color of tar and hair nappy like mine. Some are playing, some asleep, and some ain't doin' nothin' but looking. The one I like best is two girls, one braiding the other's hair. They both have pretty faces, like the singing angels in our church's Christmas pageant. I always wanted to be one of them angels, just like Nia was, but when I auditioned, I ain't get the part. Instead I had to be a goat, sweating in a fuzzy costume and peeking out at the angels, all with hair braided and tied in bows, and makeup they could wear just that day.

At the end of the room is a giant bookcase, and I stop to look, even though Momma and Nia keep on with Granddaddy to see the rest of the house. The bookcase leans to one side, like it might bend over from the weight of so many stories, with the leaning side propped up with a thick Yellow Pages. Beside it is a big raggedy couch, dirt-smeared red and with a big dent right in the middle, cross from a giant, muted TV with an antenna sticking out the top. At the motel, the tiny TV was impossible to turn on and fuzzy once it started, so I hope we can watch this one. It's a strange thing to be so important, a TV, but it reminds me of them late nights tucked in Momma's elbow, of **Scooby-Doo** and **Animaniacs** with Daddy on weekends before we even got outta bed. Him and Momma would make room for me right in the middle of the fluffy covers, and I would lay there til they made me get up, pretending to watch the bright images lighting up the screen. Truth is, I mostly just liked being right there in that small space where I fit perfect.

"Time to eat." Granddaddy is suddenly beside me, pointing to a square table in the dining room. We sit down without talking, Granddaddy and Momma on the ends, me and Nia between.

Granddaddy made hot chili with beans, and corn bread with a hunk of melting butter on top. It's a funny meal for a hot day, but I'm hungry so I slurp burning bites from my spoon. Then I ask for Nia's food when I'm done, cause she's barely eating. I watch Granddaddy as I eat, cause he don't eat, neither. He watches Momma. He watches Nia. Then he watches me. I lay my head down by my bowl, like when my teacher makes me put my head down in class for finishing my work too quick.

After I finish both bowls and Momma finishes one bowl and Granddaddy and Nia finish nothin', we all stay at the table. We don't talk, just sit. Momma and Granddaddy read the newspaper, even though it don't seem like Momma is doin' much reading cause her face keeps gettin' all scrunched up and sometimes her eyes stay closed awhile after she blinks.

"So, how is Sister Stephens?" Momma breaks the silence, setting down the newspaper and turning toward Granddaddy. "Still head of the usher board?" She clasps her hands together while she waits.

Granddaddy finally says, "Yeah," and nothin' else. Momma sucks her bottom lip into her top lip, just like Nia does when she's annoyed with Momma.

"Isn't it almost time for the big family picnic?" Momma tries again. She sits up taller and rests her elbows on the table, but all Granddaddy does is nod. Momma frowns, and they both go back to reading.

I wanna get up, but Nia stays put, so I stay put and count the statues I can see in the kitchen. Thirty-seven, then I'm bored. I try to make faces at Nia, but she's too busy rolling her eyes. Momma says one day when she rolls her eyes, they'll get stuck.

"Well, I guess I'll get going." Momma folds her newspaper and stands. Nia looks confused and then scared. I drop my spoon into the empty bowl and it makes a loud, metal thud. Granddaddy don't look up from his newspaper.

"Going where?" Nia asks. Momma don't speak, only looks at Nia, then me, with wet eyes. Nia says, "I'm going, too," and stands up. I stand up, too, but Momma shakes her head.

"You girls will stay here with your granddad," Momma says. "I have to go take care of some business." I look down fast, before Nia can see my tears. But then I see she's crying, too.

"But-but . . . when you coming back?" I wail.

Momma takes a breath and lowers her head. "I don't know yet, girls. But you will love it here, I promise."

"No, Momma!" Nia screams. She rushes to Momma, buries her face in the soft place in her neck. I ain't tall enough to reach that place and settle for hugging Momma's waist. We stay that way for a while, me crying and Nia begging and Momma rubbing our hair. Soon, Momma is kneeling, and Nia is crying, and I am rubbing both of their hair. Finally, we let Momma go. But we don't know why, and we don't know for how long. She grabs her purse and walks to the door with us following. Granddaddy looks up from the newspaper at last, but he stays at the table. Seems like now would be a good time for him to start acting like he cares, but he don't.

"One day, you'll look back and thank me for this time," Momma whispers, pulling me and then Nia into her arms for a goodbye hug before she turns and walks out the door. For a second, I feel like I'm back in that rotten basement again. First Daddy, now Momma. I squeeze my eyes shut and imagine myself leaving one day, instead of always being left behind. But even this makes me feel sad. I wanna cry again, but I stretch my face into a cracked smile, like Momma. I been cryin' or trying not to cry since the day Daddy died. Not no more. If Momma can fake a smile when she wants to cry, so can I.

Nia spots my smile, so I cross my eyes and stick out my tongue to make her laugh, just like on the nights when Momma worked late and Daddy was nowhere to be found. We'd watch reruns of **Good Times** all night and make each other laugh, and it wouldn't matter so much that the bathwater never got hot and dinner was cereal with stinky milk. Momma clip-clops down the steps and Nia snorts—not on purpose but cause it's a habit now—then we both giggle into the space between us, that special space where no matter how far we go, we can always get back. Stuck standing at the shut door we laugh and laugh, cause we know Momma's wrong. We ain't ever gon' be thankful for something so bad.

The sky that night is like fire-burnt marshmallows, with some patches too dark to see, but some patches that glow. We sit on the big porch, me and Nia and Granddaddy, none of us speaking. Back in Detroit there was always so much noise. I used to cover my ears with earmuffs, even in the summertime, and say over and over, **I just wanna be alone. I just wanna be alone. I just wanna be alone.** No matter how many times I said it, I never got to be alone. There was always somebody there, always so much noise. But now, ain't no noise. I'm still not alone, but feels like I am, here with Nia and Granddaddy and wondering if either one of 'em even likes me. I decide not to worry bout it, though, and just enjoy the quiet I always wanted. I open my book and peek at Nia, who got headphones in her ears, as usual.

She begged Momma for days after finding a new Walkman at the secondhand store, and now she listens to it nonstop.

Hours ago, before the sun crept into its shadow, Momma backed out of Granddaddy's graveled drive, no smile painted on her face, only a blank frown that spread to her eyes. She frowns so much now, and I know it has something to do with Daddy. And not just cause he died. She been sad since before that day. Some nights I'd hear her arguing with Daddy in a big whisper that crossed the thin wall between their room and ours. If I asked bout it the next morning, she'd keep humming and washing dishes and say I imagined it all.

After Daddy died, I looked up that word, **fiend**, in the dictionary. The first definitions I saw all made it seem like a fiend was some kind of devil. But the third definition down talked bout somebody who was addicted to something, which reminded me of a movie I once watched with Daddy. It was called **New Jack City** even though it took place in New York City, and it was bout gangs and a drug called crack and a guy named Nino Brown who sold it to people. I ain't sure why Daddy let me watch it cause the movie had naked people and guns and it was definitely not a movie for little kids. But when I found him on the couch in the basement and snuggled up next to him, he ain't make me leave.

Once I thought back to that movie, I figured out what the smell was, and what Daddy was doin' on them stairs, and how Daddy died. At least I think I know, cause I ain't ever ask nobody. But I think Daddy was doin' drugs, and kinda like the crack addict Pookie from the movie, Daddy did too much til he died. But there's still a lot of stuff I don't know, too. Like why Daddy ain't just stop doin' drugs if he knew it could kill him. And why Momma ain't do nothin' to stop him, or if she did, why it ain't work. Even Pookie tried to go to rehab, which I guess is a place for people to go and try to stop being addicted to drugs. Usually, I would ask Nia my questions. Used to be that Nia would tell me the stuff the grown-ups wouldn't. She was the one who finally told me the truth bout Santa, after I asked her why Santa forgot our house one Christmas. But these days, talking to Nia is like talking to a grown-up. And all grown-ups do is lie to me and treat me like a kid.

I pull off my gym shoes—damp now cause I ain't wear no socks—and stretch my legs in front of me, wiggling my toes in the cool night air. This summer, I'm gon' get Nia to start telling me the truth again. I bet if I figure out how to be her friend again, then she gon' tell me stuff and we can figure it out together. I bet me and Nia gon' fix everything, so we can all go back home.

Granddaddy stands up from his big rocking chair and slowly walks into the house. It's black dark outside now, so the words in my book disappear. I strain my eyes, try to make out anything in the darkness, but ain't nothin' to see, cept, barely, the leaves of a giant tree, stretching and growing and pointing in all directions. A strange noise like when the wind gets caught in my bedroom curtains makes me wonder if something is crawling nearby—maybe a raccoon? I ain't ever seen a raccoon, cept for when I begged Momma for a subscription to **National Geographic**. We couldn't afford it, but she found me just one encyclopedia at the secondhand store: animals starting with the letter **R**. I read in that book that raccoons have thumbs like humans and can turn doorknobs. After six straight nights of raccoon nightmares, I hid the book under Daddy's stairs, where I knew nobody would ever find it.

I shiver and stand, tryna think bout something else. But now my mind is stuck on that book. On raccoons and Daddy's stairs.

"Nia?" My whisper comes out more like a shriek. But Nia, still with them headphones on, don't budge. I creep closer. Her eyes are closed tight, and her head sways slow, back and forth, to a rhythm I can't hear. All I can hear instead is a bunch of noises I don't recognize. Too many noises I don't recognize. "**Nia!**"

Her eyes pop open just as I reach to shake her shoulder. She jumps, and her Walkman lands with a hard thud on Granddaddy's wood porch. "What'd you do that for?" Nia scoops up the Walkman and shoots me her very best mean face. I smile, even though it don't make no sense. Nia turns the Walkman over and over in her hands, but she can't find nothin' wrong.

"I just wanted to get your attention," I whisper. "You wanna go inside?"

"Nah, I'm gon' stay out here." Nia stretches her long legs out, crossing one ankle over the other as she leans back on the corner porch post. Her legs are thicker than mine, especially her thighs, but we both got the same little spots all over—not quite moles or freckles, but more so little brown speckles—just like Daddy.

"How long you think it's gon' be," I ask before she can turn her music back on, "before Momma come back?" I hope this might be my chance to get Nia talking.

"You serious?" Nia rolls her eyes, a half smirk cross her face.

"What you mean?" I say, slow, chewing the ends of my hair.

"Don't be such a baby, KB. Momma ain't coming back." Nia laughs but it sounds all wrong, more like a whine caught in the back of her throat. I can't tell if this is one of them times when Nia

25

says something mean just to mess with me, or if this time, it's really true.

"Yeah she is," I say, cause I can't think of nothin' better. Of course Momma's gon' come back. Nia goes back to her rocking and swaying as I count all the reasons in my head: **Momma, me, and Nia are a family. We barely even know Granddaddy. We got school again in the fall. We already lost Daddy.** "Why would you say that?" I ask, but Nia don't respond.

My mouth turns dry til my spit is a giant lump I can barely swallow. I want Nia to say something else. And I want her to come inside with me. I sigh and stand, mouth, "Good night," as I stumble cross the porch through the blinding dark, even though I know it ain't gon' reach her. I know I ain't gon' reach her.

Granddaddy's sittin' on the couch in front of the TV, but it's off. I wonder what he's doin', sittin' there all quiet. He don't say nothin', just stands and walks to the back of the house. I figure he wants me to follow, so I do. His quiet feels just as tiring as Nia's being mean, but right now ain't nothin' much I can do bout either one. I make sure to stomp as loud as I can, though, when I follow Granddaddy to a room back by the kitchen, a tiny room with a tiny bed. Ain't nothin' in the room but a bed and a dresser, with a pile of towels and two pillows on top, one for me, one for Nia.

Granddaddy nods—I barely seen he did it—then leaves. I think bout Anne from my book, realize that Granddaddy act kinda like Marilla Cuthbert, who ain't talk to Anne much at first. Problem is, ain't no Matthew Cuthbert here who's gon' talk to me when Marilla won't. Ain't nobody but Granddaddy.

I place my muddy shoes on the floor of the empty closet and hang up my rainbow jacket. I ain't got no pajamas so I keep all my clothes on cept my jeans, which I fold tight and set on top of the dresser. I'm s'posed to braid my hair before bed like Momma tells me to and like Nia taught me, but I just pull it into a thick, messy ponytail. Stupid Momma ain't here and stupid Nia don't care.

That night, I lay awake and listen to crickets. They make a rhythm like raindrops that reminds me of a day when flooded streets trapped me and Nia and Momma and Daddy together in the house for an afternoon. It was a Saturday, which was a day we usually spent apart. Daddy would leave early and, as usual, not say where he was goin'. Momma would do laundry all day, and sometimes go to the grocery store or secondhand store, depending on what we needed. That would just leave me and

Nia. Used to be, we would play house or school together, pretending to be teachers or students or mommas, but always still sisters, too, in any game we played. No matter what was goin' on with Momma and Daddy, we always had each other. But then it got so Nia would do her own thing, and so I would pretend to have my own thing to do, too.

But not that day. The rain started the night before, and by morning it was coming down in heavy buckets. Daddy tried to leave, but he opened the door and water from the porch rushed in and covered his feet.

"Maybe you don't have to go?" Momma whispered from the couch. And for once, that question ain't start a fight. Daddy stayed, and we played games and ate popcorn and watched movies all day. Even though I caught Daddy staring at the door a few times, he never left, not once. Momma covered his face with kisses every few minutes, I think to thank him for staying. They held hands, me and Nia shared a blanket and a bowl of ice cream, and nobody fought all day long. I thought we were finally fixed. But that night the rain stopped, and it all started again.

Granddaddy's little room for me and Nia is black dark, so I can't see nothin' cept the little bit of light peeking in from under the door. I imagine

Granddaddy sittin' on the porch, rocking and humming in the silent dark, and then I imagine Momma there, too, their knees touching, a smile lighting her eyes. I try to imagine Granddaddy without a frown on his face, but it's all I can see.

I still got a whole summer here with him, though, like it or not, so I try to start thinking of stuff to do. I wonder if Momma had adventures in Lansing when she was a girl. There ain't many adventures to have in Detroit, unless you count the times I bought lottery tickets for Momma. Momma don't believe in spending money on stuff we don't need, cept lottery tickets. She'd send me to the store with a ripped-out slip of paper filled with numbers, and instructions to tell the man at the counter, "A dollar straight and a dollar box," which made me feel like a grown-up. Kids ain't allowed to buy lotto tickets, but nobody ever stopped me.

I must've fell asleep, cause even though I don't remember her coming in, Nia's knee touches mine in the cramped bed. I can't see her, but she's snoring loud as our old, rusty lawnmower Momma taught me to cut grass with after she begged Daddy to teach me for months.

"Nia," I whisper in the shadowy room. I wanna wake her, make her explain what she said bout Momma. But she only snores louder. I ain't scared of the dark, but the dark here feels different, like it's wrapping my whole body in a hug that's too tight. In my head, I count the piercing cricket chirps. I wanna fall asleep, so I count and count. Seventy-six, then I'm sleep.

2

Granddaddy's house is quiet in the morning. When we lived with Daddy in the old house—dirt colored and rickety on a dead-end road—summer mornings were noisy: me watching TV, Nia complaining bout her hair or her clothes, Daddy still snoring, Momma humming and cooking buttery pancakes like I like. When Daddy woke, he'd tousle Nia's fussed-over hair, then spin me around like a carousel to the rhythm of his favorite Al Green records.

This morning don't feel like those. Granddaddy sits at the table quiet, drinking black coffee from a plain white mug. Nia don't speak, so I don't, either. She finds a box of oatmeal in the kitchen and makes a bowl that she puts in the microwave. I hope she makes me a bowl, too, but I don't ask.

Instead, I sit at the table cross from Granddaddy, watching him as he reads.

Granddaddy holds the edges of the newspaper tight in his thick, calloused hands. His eyes barely move when he reads, but I know he's reading, cause every so often he makes a small grunt in the back of his throat or nods. Nia joins us at the table with two bowls of oatmeal, one for her and one for me. I realize she got the same frown on her face like Granddaddy, and I giggle. Guess we really are family.

I scoot my bowl close and dip my spoon into the oatmeal. Nia made it with brown sugar and butter, just like I like. With Momma gone, I can't help but be happy that I at least have Nia. She does some things just as good as Momma. I smile at her, my way of saying thank you, but she don't smile back. I feel the start of tears cramming up into my throat, but I swallow them down, quick. When Nia wordlessly turns to grab more brown sugar from the canister on the countertop, I whisper instead, "You the reason why Momma left."

Nia turns around so fast she spills a little bit of sugar on the floor. "What you say?" Nia's head is tilted to one side and her eyes are squinted tight like they almost closed.

"I said," I start again, louder, "you the reason why Momma left." I say each word slow, so she can hear me this time. Granddaddy hears me, too, and lowers his newspaper, just a little.

Nia stands there for a few seconds not saying anything. I bet she surprised I said something mean to her for once. Eventually, she rolls her eyes and says, quiet, "You so stupid."

"Girls." Granddaddy finally speaks, folding his newspaper and placing it on the table in front of him. I think he's gon' say more, but he don't. Nia comes back to the table and slams her bowl down, hard. I laugh.

"You the stupid one," I say, feeling confident now.

"Kenyatta—" Granddaddy starts, but I keep going.

"You think you all that," I yell at Nia, "when you can't even get good grades in school. All you care bout are your stupid friends, and they dumb just like you. Even Momma don't like you, and she like everybody! Now I gotta be stuck here with him"—I glare at Granddaddy—"all cause of you!"

Nia and Granddaddy both stand up at the same time.

"Shut up, KB!" Nia yells.

"That's enough!" Granddaddy shouts.

Satisfied, I grab my bowl and leave the table. I bet Granddaddy and Nia watching as I dump all my oatmeal in the trash, one spoonful at a time. When I'm done, I don't even look back at them. I grab my book and my rainbow jacket, and I march out the door with a smile on my face.

With my book in hand for inspiration, I try to see Granddaddy's world the way Anne would. Everything comes alive as I find the right words to describe what I see. I tread through a patch of mud that covers my sandaled feet. Granddaddy's house is nestled right in the middle of a quiet street, with towering trees and only a handful of houses on either side. I imagine I'm an explorer at the start of a mysterious journey. Kinda scared and full of questions. There is a giant field in the back-yard, and I go there now, cautiously navigating knee-high grass and dodging bugs that fill the air with a whizzing noise like air pushing out of a bal-loon. I inhale the smell of fresh cut grass. Plants bigger than my head poke up from the dirt in crowded groups, like they ain't got enough space to stretch. A small, furry animal runs past me and up a tree. I think it's a squirrel, but it don't look like them squirrels in Detroit that steal your food if you drop it.

I continue through the squishy mud to the pond, where there's fish swimming in the murky water and frogs burping on top. Colorful flowers remind me of the rainbows in my books. Back at the dead-end house, we never had real flowers. Momma kept a glass vase on the card table in the kitchen, which mostly stayed empty. But sometimes she would fill it with plastic flowers from the dollar store. The petals on the fake flowers pulled off in mounds with a smell like rubber bands.

I pick a flower that smells like clean laundry and perfume. I pick another, and another. Even though I'm mad at her, picking flowers makes me think of Nia. She never liked Momma's plastic flowers and would hide them under the sink when her friends came over. I bet, if I picked the right ones and gave them to her, it might finally make Nia smile.

But then I remember yelling at Nia. Yelling at Granddaddy. Even though it felt good to take all my sad and turn it into mad for once, now I just feel kinda bad. Especially since I was s'posed to be tryna get Nia to be my friend again. I bet I just ruined that for good.

"We're going outside!" The voice comes from behind me, on the other side of the street, where a boy and a girl race down the porch steps. I stop looking for flowers and watch them instead.

The boy looks older than the girl, maybe even older than me. But not older than Nia. I watch as he pulls the girl in a bright red wagon. I always wanted a wagon like that one, but even after begging Momma and Daddy every year for Christmas we ain't ever get one. What we did get, one Christmas, was one of them Barbie Jeeps. It was shiny and purple and perfect. Well, cept for the fact that it was a hand-me-down from a middle school girl at our church and it ain't work no more, plus it was covered with old **Sesame Street** stickers and lots of rust. But we loved that Jeep like it was brand-new. We used to take turns pushing each other down the sidewalk, but mostly Nia would push me, cause when I tried to push her, we wouldn't get too far. But she ain't mind. We would play outside together every day, Nia pushing me in that old Barbie Jeep and me laughing til my face hurt.

The little girl is laughing now, just like that. She has golden pigtails that wave in the wind when the boy tugs the wagon. I wonder what it would feel like if I could touch her hair. Probably like rubbing soft yarn that untwists right in your fingers. Even though I been around white people before, it's never been this kind of white people. The few white girls at my school in Detroit wore their hair in cornrows just like the Black girls.

A shrill voice comes from the house and the boy and girl look back. A woman is standing on the porch, hands on her hips, yelling something I can't quite hear. I lean closer, make out a couple words. "Over there" and "careful." She points in the direction of Granddaddy's house. The boy and girl look unhappy or confused, I can't tell which, but head back in.

Disappointed, I look down at the clump of flowers in my hands. Things used to be so easy with me and Nia, back when we used to play together just like them kids cross the street. But ain't nothin' easy no more. I can't give these flowers to Nia. She ain't gon' smile, I know it. Silently, I take the flowers back to the field, scattering the rainbow petals on the grass like ashes. Daddy's gone, Momma's gone. Nia's still here, but she might as well be gone, too.

Later that day, I decide that there ain't much to do in Lansing. Especially since I been tryna avoid Nia and Granddaddy, which leaves me stuck outside with nothin' but my thoughts.

After what Nia said bout Momma last night, all I can think bout is gettin' back home. I don't know why Nia said what she did, but I know she ain't gon' tell me so I gotta figure it out by myself. I run back to the house and sneak inside. Luckily, Granddaddy must be in his room and I hear the shower running, so I bet Nia is taking a shower. I rush to the room and dig through my backpack til

I find my yellow spiral notebook that used to be for school, but I had some pages left over so now I use it to write down my ideas and my stories. But today, I make a list.

Back outside, I write in block letters at the top of the page: REASONS WHY MOMMA MIGHT NOT COME BACK. Then I put numbers on the left side of the page and chew the eraser on my pencil while I think. I want five good reasons, but I only end up with four:

1. She's mad at Nia for being so rude.
2. She's mad at me for crying so much.
3. Without Daddy, she don't wanna be a momma no more.
4. Without Daddy, she ain't got enough money to take care of us.

I think and think but can't come up with nothin' else to add. I read number 1 and number 2, then cross them both off the list. Ain't no way Momma left us here cause she was mad. She always tells us not to act out of anger, cause later you won't be mad no more but then it might be too late to fix the action. Then I cross off number 3 cause Momma loves being a momma. I know cause once I asked her if she could be anything in the world, what would she be, and she pinched my chin and said, "I would be this. Exactly this." Then she went back to humming.

That only leaves one thing: money. I circle it on the page again and again, til the words almost disappear. Of course, it's money. Money always keeps us from doin' stuff. Paying for field trips on time. Buying school uniforms that fit. Keeping food in the fridge. And now, it's why Momma had to leave us here in Lansing. **Right?** I need to find out for sure.

I jump up quickly and run back to the house. It's not til I push through the screen door and find Granddaddy sittin' on the couch, sneer on his face, that I remember the oatmeal fight. In the past bout thirty minutes, my excitement took me from sad to happy and back to kinda sad, but look like Granddaddy still stuck on mad. He glances up at me for a second, then turns his eyes back to the TV without saying a word. I don't see Nia, but I don't hear the shower no more, so I figure she's probably in the room sulking, just like Granddaddy. Good, let her sulk. I don't mind if she's still mad at me, but if I'm gon' get Granddaddy to let me call Momma, I might need to be nice to him. At least for now.

"Hey, Granddaddy," I say sweetly. He don't respond or even look my way. I try again. "Granddaddy?" I scoot closer, standing beside the arm of the couch. He still don't speak, but he presses mute on the remote. Now's my chance.

"I was wondering if it might be okay if—"

"Kenyatta," Granddaddy interrupts, finally looking me right in the eye with one eyebrow raised and his head cocked to the side. I can tell this ain't gon' be good.

"Yeah?" I whisper.

"Don't you leave this house without my permission again." He sets the remote down and folds his arms cross his chest.

"Well, I ain't really go nowhere, just out in the back mostly, and up front for a little but only to watch them kids cross the street—"

"What kids?" Granddaddy interrupts.

"Umm, I don't know," I stammer, "them white kids cross the street with the red wagon."

"Kenyatta, stay away from around that house."

"How come?"

Granddaddy's voice becomes somber as he sits up straight and uncrosses his arms. "Cause they don't like people like us."

"What you mean, people like us?" I hope it ain't a silly question. Maybe they don't like us cause Granddaddy and Nia both so mean.

Granddaddy is quiet for a while, then finally says, "Kenyatta, do you know bout racism?"

I shake my head, even though I heard the word before. A grown-up word that I pretend not to know so Granddaddy can explain it to me. All I do know is from what I hear other kids say. It ain't ever happened to me, but some kids at school say that white people sometimes do mean things to them just for being Black, like yell at them or call them names. But I wasn't ever really sure what to believe, since Momma never told me nothin' bout racism, and the one time I tried to ask Nia, she opened and closed her mouth once, then twice, before telling me to shut up and leave her alone.

"Well, I should start at the beginning, then. Back when I was growing up, a lot of the country was still segregated. That means Black folks couldn't be with white folks."

I nod, cause I remember learning bout Rosa Parks in school during Black History Month. We learned that she was important cause she ain't wanna give up her seat on the bus to a white person. After my teacher told that story, I asked her a bunch of other questions bout Rosa Parks, but she ain't seem to know much bout her, cept that one little ol' story.

"Even though Black folks was supposed to be equal," Granddaddy continues, "most white people at the time weren't ready to start welcoming Black people with open arms."

"So, what would they do?" I ask, shifting my weight to lean against the arm of the couch.

"Well . . ." Granddaddy pauses. "They would

do all sorta mean stuff, to let Black people know that we wasn't never gon' be equal, no matter what the law said."

"What kinda mean stuff?" I ask again. Granddaddy don't start answering right away, so I add, "Did any white people ever do mean stuff to you back then?"

Granddaddy clears his throat like he's gon' say something, but then he don't. Instead of talking, he keeps turning his hands over so that first his palms are up, then he flips them over and picks at his nails. He repeats this pattern three times, slow, but still don't speak.

"Granddaddy?" I whisper, which causes him to finally stop flipping his hands and look back up at me. "What happened?"

When I ask this, something in Granddaddy seems to soften, just a little. He sits up, sighs deep, then sits back again and folds his arms. "It was the first day of summer," he begins. While he talks, he looks up at the ceiling like the memory is up there, waiting for him to pull it down. "I was nothin' more than seven, eight years old. Me and my buddies, Lil Earl and Tyrone—we called him Head cause he had a big ol' head—was gon' go down to the store and buy some candy, cause we had earned some change doin' little jobs round the neighborhood."

At this point, Granddaddy sits up and starts to talk a little faster. "We was excited the whole way to the store," he says, "cause we ain't usually have no money to buy nothin'. This was gon' be a big day for us."

I look down at my hands, scratch my pointer finger with the nail on my thumb. Seems like this bout to be the bad part.

"But before we even got to the store, we was stopped by a white man who saw us walkin' down the street, talkin' loud and wavin' our coins in the air. He ran up on us and called us some thieves. Said we must've stole from somebody, cause he ain't ever seen no nigger boys with that much money." Granddaddy looks me straight in the eye now. "That white man took all the money we had worked so hard for, and ain't even look back when we all laid down, right there in the middle of the sidewalk—me, Lil Earl, and Head—and cried."

Granddaddy look like he might cry now, just thinking bout it. I try to imagine what it would be like to have something like that happen to me, but it don't seem like nothin' that would happen anymore. Still, I wanna make sure Granddaddy know I been listening, so I think and think of a good question to ask.

"Why you ain't just get some more money and

go back to the store?" I finally ask, cause I can't think of nothin' better. Plus, it don't seem like such a big deal to me to lose a couple coins.

Granddaddy sighs. I can't tell if he's disappointed or just tired. "Well, in the time after slavery, things was different than they are now. And not just cause of segregation. Black folks ain't have the same opportunities as white folks, to do stuff like go to school or get a good job. Back then, a lot of Black folks still worked for the white folks. Like my grandfather, he worked twenty-four years for a white man named Mr. Harvey." I clear my throat and he stops, but I ain't got nothin' to say yet, so he goes on. "He worked every day for Mr. Harvey, from sunup to sundown in scorching-hot fields with no shade and not much water. Then, at the end of the week, Mr. Harvey would give him seven pennies."

"Seven pennies?" I ask, curious. I reach into the small pocket of my shorts, where I got more money than that hidden, cause I found a dime earlier by the pond.

"Yeah, he only made pennies," Granddaddy says, then folds his hands, slow, into his lap.

Before we came to Lansing, I heard Momma call Granddaddy a penny pincher. And when I asked her what it meant, she said that he ain't ever gon' give nothin' away for cheap. I wonder if that's why Momma thinks he's so stingy with money, cause his granddaddy worked so hard for only seven pennies. Or cause when he finally made his own money, it got took by that mean white man. I wanna ask, but then Granddaddy turns the volume up and the sounds of **Wheel of Fortune** fill the room.

I stand to go back outside. I came in to ask Granddaddy if I could call Momma, but it don't seem like a good time no more. And what I really wanna ask now is if I can still play with them white kids, since I got this dime in my pocket; plus, things ain't even like that no more. But Granddaddy seems sad now, so I don't ask.

"Can I play outside?" I ask instead.

"Stay away from around that house," Granddaddy grumbles without looking my way.

I nod, even though Granddaddy don't see me. I can't tell if he's lost in **Wheel of Fortune** or lost back on that sidewalk with his friends. Either way, he don't move when I leave, not even a flinch when I let the door slam shut behind me.

Back outside, I find a spot in the middle of the grass out front and sit down with my legs crossed and my list unfolded in my hands. I think bout what I would've said if I had called Momma. I was probably gon' tell her that I know why she had to leave us here and it's okay. But then I remember her sad frown as she backed out the driveway. That same sad frown that I been looking at since the night Daddy died. I get that Momma is sad, but her sad is so big that it takes away from other people. Sometimes it feels like Momma's grief for Daddy keeps me from having my own grief for Daddy. I bet it's hard to lose a husband, but it's hard to lose a daddy, too. I guess she don't get that, though, cause her daddy been right here this whole time, and she barely even sees him.

I squint my eyes as the sun shifts higher in the sky. On second thought, maybe it's good for me and Momma to have this time apart. Maybe it's good I ain't call.

I fold the list into a tight square that fits in my pocket, then lay out in the middle of the green grass, not quite happy or sad. I count the long, skinny blades poking between my bare toes. By seven, I'm bored. I flip over and pretend I'm a swimmer in a deep, olive ocean. Then flip on my back and look at the sky. Ain't no clouds in all that blue. I close my eyes and listen to nothin'.

Then, the nothin' is replaced by the rattle of a too-loud car on the road. I recognize the sound immediately, cause one time the muffler in Momma's car went bad and when we drove past a school, a little white boy at the corner yelled at

Momma, "Turn that car down now!" Nia and me both laughed and laughed, but Momma ain't smile not once.

The loud muffler is right in front of Granddaddy's house now, pulling into his long driveway. I hoped for a second it would be Momma, sorry for leaving and ready to take us back home, but the loud muffler's roaring from inside a beat-up truck that might be even worse than Momma's old car, cause this truck is smoking and coughing and roaring up a storm. Just when I think it might explode, the engine stops and the nothin' fills my ears again. But now I am too curious to go back to nothin'.

Eighty-six steps til I'm standing at the passenger-side door. The truck's red, but the kind of red that ain't really red no more cause it's so peeled and chipped. I stand on my tiptoes. Inside, there are crumpled paper bags on the seat and a Bible with a bent front cover on the floor. The cup holder ain't holding no cups cause it's too busy with coins and candies and a foil-wrapped sandwich that's got a big bite taken out of it. In the driver's seat is a man with the darkest skin I've ever seen. He sees me staring and smiles. I run, fast, to Granddaddy's porch, but before I get there, Granddaddy is coming out, looking straight at the truck in the driveway. The man is gettin' out now with the bent Bible in one hand and the bit sandwich in the other, smiling with teeth so white they glow like Chiclets next to his jet-black skin. Even funnier is the way he walks, like he has a leg made of wood. He hobbles over to the porch slow, while Granddaddy waits and I am frozen.

"Well, hiya there," he says, tipping the hat from his head to reveal thin patches of hair speckled with gray. I think he might be tipping the hat for me, cause he smiles like I should know what to do next. But I just stand there.

"My name is Charlie," he continues, "and you must be Kenyatta." I frown at Granddaddy, who barely talks but somehow gave this stranger my name. I scoot closer to Granddaddy, even though he's really a stranger, too, wondering what he told this man bout me.

I nod instead of answering, and that seems to be okay with Charlie, who faces Granddaddy and adds, "Looks just like her." I guess he's talking bout Momma, even though nobody ever says I look like her. As I watch Charlie focus on gettin' up the three small porch steps, I wonder how he knows Momma. It takes him forty-nine seconds to make it up on the porch, plus I even counted with the Mississippi in the middle like Nia taught me.

"Come on in." Granddaddy don't waste no time with hello, just walks inside for him to follow. Charlie steps aside for me to go first. Nia's lucky not to have this strange man smiling at her and tipping his hat. I guess she's still in our room, mad. For a second, I wish that I ain't fight with her this morning. Having her here would probably be better than being alone. Then again, my chances of actually being included are probably better out here, with these strangers.

Granddaddy sits down on the couch. Charlie sits cross from him in a giant wicker chair that I ain't notice before, hiding in the corner. Granddaddy finds a Bible from somewhere and that's what they start to read. I wanna sit and read, too, but I only got my Anne book, which don't seem like a fit for the thick Bibles. So, I stand in the middle of the room and watch.

"Kenyatta." Granddaddy whispers my name in his crumbly voice and pats a seat beside him on the couch. I go to him, hoping he might talk to me now. He don't, but he does lay the Bible cross his lap so I can see it, too. I scoot closer to him as he flips to a page with the word **Job** at the top. I learned in Sunday School that you can't say it like if you have a **job** at McDonald's; the word is **Job** with a lot of **O** in the middle. But that's bout all I know.

Fifty counted seconds of silence pass before Charlie says, "Where did we leave off?" His Bible's open to the same page, with **Job** at the top.

"Chapter 2," Granddaddy starts.

"Verse 11," Charlie says, and then, even though I ain't sure how he knows it's his turn, Charlie starts to read. "When Job's three friends, Eliphaz the Temanite, Bildad the Shuhite, and Zophar the Naamathite, heard about all the troubles that had come upon him, they set out from their homes and met together by agreement to go and sympathize with him and comfort him."

I try to keep up, but the Bible's got such big and long names. I asked Daddy once why all the names were so long, but his only answer was a hearty laugh followed by taking the Bible away and hiding it in his sock drawer.

"When they saw him from a distance," Charlie goes on, "they could hardly recognize him; they began to weep aloud, and they tore their robes and sprinkled dust on their heads." Granddaddy clears his throat loud and Charlie waits, like they both know the rhythm. "Then they sat on the ground with him for seven days and seven nights. No one said a word to him, because they saw how great his suffering was." Charlie finishes and closes his Bible but keeps his thumb stuck in the pages. Granddaddy keeps his Bible open and watches Charlie, like he's waiting on something.

I wait, too. Soon, there's a low rumble beneath the sound of the clock that ticks from the wall. It takes me a minute to realize it's coming from Granddaddy. He's humming—a song, I think. At church on Sundays, when I was still a little girl, Momma would pick up the little book in the back of the pew. There were two books in every holder: the first, a Bible, usually with a black cover, and a second book with a red cover.

One Sunday, I tapped Momma after she picked hers up, asked, "What's that?"

"A hymnal," she whispered back, not taking her eyes off the words on the page, nodding toward the singing choir. "It's got the words to all the songs." Then she followed along, matching every note perfect. The song Granddaddy hums now sounds like one of those hymns from the red-covered book, even though his voice is lower and stiller than Momma's.

Granddaddy and Charlie start talkin' bout the Bible, and as I listen, I see more bout Granddaddy than I could before. I wonder if him and Charlie are friends. Maybe friends like Job's friends in the Bible that sit and don't say a word when Job is hurting. I wonder if Granddaddy is the one hurting now, or Charlie. But if there's one thing I've learned in my family, it's that when you hurt, you gotta ignore it and pretend it don't exist; otherwise it'll swallow you whole.

"Your turn, next time." Granddaddy speaks

this part loudly to Charlie and his voice makes me jump. I try to hide it with a big yawn, stretching my arms up in the air. Meanwhile, Charlie is turning pages in his Bible, quick, til he finally stops on one page that he sticks his finger in.

"We'll read from Proverbs next," says Charlie, and Granddaddy's pages are already flipping, "Chapter 13. Let's start with verse 7 and go through 11." It's easy for me to remember cause Proverbs was always my favorite chapter in the Bible, and 7-Eleven is my favorite store back in Detroit. We ain't go too much, but once Momma let me get my own Slurpee, and I mixed together every flavor into a drink that made my head cold and turned my tongue purple.

"One person pretends to be rich, yet has nothing," Charlie begins, "another pretends to be poor, yet has great wealth." He clears his throat and waits. Then Granddaddy picks up.

"A person's riches may ransom their life, but the poor cannot respond to threatening rebukes." Granddaddy uses his finger to underline his place on the page for me to follow along, which I can do easy cause Proverbs don't have so many big names, and most of the words I understand.

"The light of the righteous shines brightly," Charlie reads, "but the lamp of the wicked is snuffed out." Granddaddy nods, so I nod, too.

"Where there is strife, there is pride," Granddaddy reads, "but wisdom is found in those who take advice." The back-and-forth rhythm feels almost like a song, and I sway, just a little.

Then Charlie reads the last verse. "Dishonest money dwindles away, but whoever gathers money little by little makes it grow." Before, when they read bout Job, they did all the humming and talking after. But this time after reading, Granddaddy closes his Bible right away, so I guess they gon' talk bout this one next time. But I'm stuck thinking bout that last line. **Whoever gathers money little by little makes it grow.** . . . My thumb finds the folded list in my pocket, and suddenly I have an idea.

Charlie stands up and starts gathering his stuff, then Granddaddy stands up, slow, and joins him. They tilt their heads toward each other, and I perk up. I know this move. It's the way grown folks act when they wanna talk bout something without the kids hearing. So I do like I always do and pretend to not be paying attention. I pick up Granddaddy's Bible from the couch and open it to the middle, sticking my nose all the way in so the Bible covers my face. Then I pretend to read while they start to talk.

"Any word yet?" Charlie says.

I don't hear nothin', so Granddaddy must ain't answer with words.

"How's the treatment going?" Charlie asks next. I peek out from the top of the Bible and this time see Granddaddy shake his head.

"I don't know," he whispers, "she ain't been talking to me much."

"And the girls?" Charlie asks. I pick the Bible back up quick, scared one of them gon' look my way. After a long silence, Granddaddy finally responds.

"She ain't been talking to nobody much." He pauses for a while. Then finishes with: "I just hope this works."

My mind fills up with questions. Were they talking bout Momma? But what treatment was Charlie talking bout? And what does Granddaddy want to work?

"KB?" Granddaddy calls my name and I worry for a second that they caught me listening. But then he offers his hand out to me for prayer and I stand and take it, joining the circle with him and Charlie. My mind is spinning from what I heard, but I gotta pretend it ain't. So I listen to Granddaddy pray. Bout halfway through, I notice my head ain't spinning no more. Comfortable, I don't let go of Granddaddy's warm hand, even after the invocation fades.

Charlie says goodbye without ever closing his Bible, leaving his thumb stuck in the page instead. His red truck roars to life from the driveway and rumbles away. I think bout walking down the road a bit, just to see where he goes, which way he turns and how fast he drives, but I don't cause I ain't sure if Granddaddy gon' let me. I stay in the house with Granddaddy instead and trail him like a shadow, watching. It's one of my favorite things, watching, cause it's how I learn the stuff people don't want me to know. And since Granddaddy don't wanna talk to me much, I figure this is my best chance to figure out what's really going on with Momma. Granddaddy knows something that I don't know, and I plan to figure it out.

I watch Granddaddy's face, his hands, his feet. I watch the way he smooths the small pillow on the wicker chair where Charlie sat. I watch as he shuffles to the kitchen and fills water for tea in the heavy kettle that always sits on the stove. When I watch people, I'm looking at more than what they do. I look at how they do it, then try to figure out why. Ever since I can remember, it's how I learn people, especially since most times, people don't wanna tell me the truth bout stuff. I watch as Granddaddy puts the Bible back on the middle shelf of the large and leaning bookcase, still hovering in the corner like a secret. Granddaddy feels around for his house shoes. I see 'em peeking out from under the couch, but I don't say nothing. Instead, I check the books from spine to spine. There is one book that stands out, cause it ain't got no words on the spine, and it's thick like a binder. I bet it's a photo album. I stand up and walk over to the bookcase, trying not to look like I'm sneaking but also not tryna get Granddaddy's attention focused on me. My hands creep toward the photo album, and I just bout got it, when Granddaddy stops me.

"Kenyatta," he says, and I turn around quick. "Why don't you go on back in the room with Nia now?"

"Why?" I frown, disappointed that I ain't gon' be able to keep watching Granddaddy.

Granddaddy sits forward in his chair, and unlike this morning, he looks real ready to discipline. "Don't you talk back to me," he says, and that's all he says.

I keep frowning, but I don't speak again. Neither of us speaks, like we both tryna test each other.

"Go back there with your sister," Granddaddy finally says again, this time not a question. "You two need to figure out how to get along. And until you do"—Granddaddy pauses to kick back in his recliner—"you can use the time to get the place cleaned up."

I try to think of a comeback, but the look on

Granddaddy's face tells me ain't no point. Being sure to drag my feet the whole way, I walk back to the room to get ready for my next pointless conversation. The door is closed, and I stand outside it for a while tryna decide if I should knock or just walk in. At home, Nia always makes me knock on her door before I come in, and she yells at me when I don't. We used to share a room, til Nia turned fourteen and decided she was "too mature" to share a room with a "little kid." I snuck and listened when she whined and begged Momma, then pretended not to care when she moved all her stuff out of our perfect little room into Momma's old office that was cleaned out and repainted for the occasion.

But here at Granddaddy's house, this ain't really Nia's room. We're back to sharing, just like I wanted. I smirk and walk in without knocking. Nia is laying on the bed with her arms crossed over her chest, staring at the ceiling. At first, I think she's listening to her Walkman, like usual. But as I get closer, I notice her headphones sprawled cross the dresser. And Nia just laying there, listening to nothin'.

"Granddaddy said we gotta clean up," I announce as I plop down on the edge of the bed. Nia don't say nothin' yet, just keeps staring at the ceiling.

"Nia, you hear me?"

Finally, Nia turns her head toward me. I expect

her to look annoyed, but really, she looks kinda sad. "Clean what?" she asks, propping herself up on her elbow.

I shrug. "He ain't say. I think he just mad cause we fighting." I wait for Nia to say something, maybe offer to make up, but she don't.

"Okay," is all she says, before laying back down.

"Okay?"

Nia sighs. "Go ask him what we gotta clean, okay?"

"Fine," I say. I don't even know what I want from her, but I know it's more than this. I go back to the living room and find Granddaddy still in front of the TV but looking half-sleep.

"Granddaddy," I whisper. He don't move. "Granddaddy," I try again a little louder. He moves around a bit but keeps his eyes closed. "Granddaddy," I practically yell, and his eyes pop open, wide. He looks around for a second before his eyes finally focus on me.

"Kenyatta," he says, before clearing his throat.

"What you want us to clean?" I ask, shifting my weight from one foot to the other.

Granddaddy takes his time looking around. I don't think he even thought this through before deciding we needed to clean up.

"Ain't yawl kids ever had to clean up before?" he says with a scowl.

I shrug. Truth is, Daddy never made us do

much cleaning around the house. Whenever he was home, Daddy would do all the cleaning. He was the only person I ever saw who loved cleaning like it was something fun to do. He would always start by turning on music, and the music would always match his mood. When he was in a good mood, Michael Jackson or Prince would blare from the little CD player on top of the fridge, and Daddy would twirl around in the kitchen with his broom, trying out all his best moves on his favorite girls. On bad days, it would be Earth, Wind & Fire or the Isley Brothers singing sad love songs with Daddy quietly humming along. When Daddy was gone, Momma would clean, but with no music.

"Start in the kitchen," Granddaddy grumbles. "The cleaning stuff is under the sink." And with that, he lifts his feet up on the coffee table and settles in for another TV nap.

I take my time gettin' back to the room, cause I don't feel like dealing with Nia's attitude. I know she won't be happy with Granddaddy's vague instructions—instructions that will probably keep us cleaning for the rest of the day. This time, when I come into the room, Nia is standing up and looking out the window. The look on her face— a mix of missing something and tryna run away from something—makes me wonder if maybe me and Nia feel the same bout Momma leaving. But when she turns and looks at me, I'm suddenly too scared to ask.

"He said start in the kitchen," I say, and Nia nods. I follow her to the kitchen, where we pull Ajax, bleach, and sponges out from under the sink. I find a bucket in the very back, and Nia fills it up with hot water, dish detergent, and a little bleach. I guess she was paying more attention to Daddy on cleaning days than I was.

"You wash the dishes," Nia says, "and I'll start on the floors." I nod, and we get to work. What feels like hours later, after the sun has started to disappear from the sky and Granddaddy has fallen asleep and woken up three times, we finish. Between the two of us, we washed dishes, cleaned countertops, windows, and floors, and organized everything in the refrigerator and cabinets. Even Granddaddy would have to smile when he saw all the work we did.

"Done!" Nia announces with a smile, and I smile back. "We never cleaned that much before, have we?"

"Never," I respond, laughing along with her. I figure in both our minds we see Daddy sweeping the floors with his microphone broom. "And now I'm hungry."

"Me, too," says Nia, and then in a whisper, "Do you think he's even gon' feed us?" She crosses her eyes and puckers her lips to make a funny face, pointed right at Granddaddy, still in front of the TV.

I shrug, covering my mouth to hide my laughter.

"Granddaddy," Nia yells in a singsong voice.

Freshly woken up, Granddaddy responds quickly this time. "Nia?"

Nia looks at me and rolls her eyes. I'm holding my laughing mouth with both hands now and can feel the air pushing out through my nose. "We're all done cleaning. May we please have dinner now?"

Granddaddy don't know Nia well enough to know her fake sweet voice yet, so he sounds happy to hear her being so polite. "Gon' and heat up some leftovers," he replies proudly.

Nia sticks her finger in her mouth and mimics gagging, while she yells back to Granddaddy, "Okay, sounds delicious!"

I can't take it anymore and let out a tiny snort, but luckily Granddaddy has turned the TV back up, so I don't think he hears. While I start to put away all the cleaning stuff, Nia opens the refrigerator and begins taking out the pot of chili from yesterday. While she warms the pot on the stove, I sit down at the table and begin to count all the times Nia smiled today. I lose count at nine, but either way, it's probably more than she's smiled all summer so far.

"Hey, Nia," I call out cheerfully, "you wanna

play outside after dinner?" I start imagining all the things I can show her in the backyard, since she ain't been out there yet. I bet she'll like the flowers best, and this time, I won't throw 'em away after I pick 'em.

"Yeah!" Nia replies enthusiastically. Too enthusiastically. My smile slowly starts to fade as Nia turns to face me. "And you wanna braid each other's hair after, and be bosom buddies like Anne and Diana from your book?" Nia is using the same fake voice on me that she was just using on Granddaddy, and even worse, I almost believed it. Nia rolls her eyes before turning back to the stove to stir the chili.

Before Lansing, I made the mistake of telling Nia bout my favorite scene in my favorite book, when Anne meets her best friend, Diana. Anne knows they will be best friends soon as they meet, and I told Nia bout it to make her feel better when we had to move out of our house and she was worried she wouldn't make any new friends. "Don't worry," I said that day, "Anne thought she wouldn't make friends, either, but then she found Diana and they were bosom buddies right away, like that." I snapped my fingers proudly, even though Nia was barely paying attention, like always.

"We could never be like Anne and Diana," I say

now, crossing my arms on the table and laying my head down into my elbows.

"Let me guess," Nia retorts, "because we don't have a gable?" She snickers quietly, I guess reluctant to have Granddaddy hear us fighting again—which would surely mean more cleaning. At least we agree on something, cause I also don't want nothin' to do with Granddaddy now. Far as I'm concerned, I don't need Nia or Granddaddy. I don't need nobody.

"No," I finally respond, "we can't be like them cause I hate you, and Anne don't hate nobody." I stand up and start walking back to the room. "Plus," I whisper, being sure Granddaddy can't hear, "Diana ain't a bitch like you." I catch Nia's surprised gaze just long enough to wink at her, then flounce away.

For the next few days, Granddaddy and Nia don't talk much, so I don't talk much. We tiptoe around the little house like strangers, staying quiet and out of each other's way. And for once, I don't even care. I spend most of my time outside, where I can be alone. At some point, I even stopped wanting to talk to Momma, once I remembered how sad she's been lately. The only person I wish I could talk to is Daddy, and he's dead. Far as I care, everybody else could just be dead now, too. Starting with Nia and Granddaddy.

What finally brings me and Granddaddy together are the fireflies. On a night quiet like whispers, I lay cross the front porch reading. Nia sits on the steps, flipping through one of her grown-up magazines that she started reading last year when she left middle school for high school. A girl dressed in a bikini laughs from the cover. The one time I snuck a peek inside, I saw a quiz with the title, "Are You a Secret Bitch?" I quickly put the magazine back on Nia's desk, cause back then, I ain't wanna know the answer to that question. I smile to myself at the thought of using that word on Nia the other day. Guess her magazines ain't so worthless, after all.

Granddaddy sits in his rocking chair as usual, humming a song I never heard. I peek up at him from my book and he winks before going back to humming, a little louder. I smile, then settle back into the comfort of his voice, the comfort of the moment.

"Look," Granddaddy whispers after a while, breaking the reverie, "you girls see that?"

Nia pops her head up, so I pop my head up. And what I see is that the whole field that used to be dark is now sprinkled with light, like flames dancing a wild routine. Nia looks for only a second, then goes back to her magazine. But not me.

"What is it?" I ask.

"Fireflies," Granddaddy whispers. "I ain't ever seen so many all at once."

It surprises me that something so small can create something so big. Every time I think I see one, know exactly where it is, the light goes out. And by the time the light comes back, it's somewhere completely different, so that the fireflies dance and disappear right before my eyes. Granddaddy says some people call 'em lightning bugs, but **fireflies** sounds more magical to me. My palms itch as I think bout catching one of 'em. I wanna learn the secret of their light.

I run out into the field, clasping my hands around pockets of air that once were a firefly's hiding spot. But no matter how hard I try, I can't catch a single bug. Seems like soon as I spot one, it magically disappears. I wonder what the trick is, the secret that these little bugs keep as they disappear into the dark. I run and trip through the chilly night air, waving my arms wildly. No matter how hard I try, I can't figure out their secret. I hear a chuckle behind me and turn to find Granddaddy standing there, a broad smile planted on his cracked face. The first smile he ever gave me.

"Slow down," he says softly.

He takes my small hands in his giant ones and

slowly leads me toward a patch of light. With a silent flick of his wrist he uses my hands to circle a firefly, just before it escapes to the wind. I open my cupped hands careful, like I'm pulling a bow from one of them perfectly wrapped presents I get at church on Easter Sunday, then smile at the gift of light crawling between my thumb and fore-finger. The firefly came to me. Just like that, I had the secret right in my hands, and suddenly, it ain't seem so hard to catch. I look back to thank Granddaddy, but he's already started his slow retreat to the leaning porch.

Before Daddy died, he started tryna teach me how to play cards. It was our thing, just the two of us, cause Momma and Nia ain't like to play. The first time we played, Daddy found an old deck of cards in our kitchen junk drawer. The deck was missing a two of clubs and a jack of diamonds, but Daddy used the joker cards and an ink pen to make a whole deck. He started out by teaching me the easy games like tunk and go fish, but then we got to the good stuff. My favorite was speed, cause I loved tryna put my cards down fast enough to beat Daddy. But no matter how fast I went, I could never beat him. Til one day, Daddy whispered to me, **Wanna know my secret to winning speed?** I nodded so hard my eyes went dizzy. Daddy showed me the cards in his hand, all organized in perfect patterns. **I set my cards up before**

I put a single one down, Daddy said, showing me how it worked. **Sometimes, when you wanna speed up, you gotta slow down first.**

I feel the gentle tug of the breeze around my arms and find myself back in the field. "Thank you," I whisper into the wind. I pretend the words are smoke, watch as they spiral up past the stars to catch a kiss from Daddy, then back down to Granddaddy—again rocking and humming in his chair—to graze the soft place on his cheek, just above the chin. I hope, when it lands there, he knows it's from me. I think back to my Anne book; how I figured Granddaddy was gon' be like Marilla Cuthbert, who acted like she hated Anne when they first met. But eventually, Marilla loved Anne just as much as Matthew did. Maybe even more. Granddaddy rocks and hums, rocks and hums. Maybe one day he'll come around, I wish, just like Marilla.

I turn and glance cross to Nia, still in her same spot. She ain't even look up from her magazine, and I feel sad for her. I bet, if she had tried, she woulda loved the fireflies, too.

There's a long crack in the ceiling I stare at every morning. I fall asleep staring at the crack. I wake up and I stare at the crack. I ain't even sure what I like bout it, cept that it's the only thing in the tidy room that look like it don't belong. Everything in Granddaddy's house is in its place all the time. That's why I spend most days outside, where for once—with nobody else around and nothin' else to do besides what I wanna do—I feel like I belong.

I don't get to play outside in Detroit much, cause our dead-end street still gets lots of cars that play music so loud it beats in my chest like a second heartbeat. Ain't much to see outside even if I did, cause all the houses on my block got dirt in the front lawn where there should be grass or plants or flowers. I used to play in the dirt, making muddy sandcastles that looked like dog poop, til one day someone drove through our neighborhood shooting bullets that nicked two trees and left a permanent hole in our neighbor's front mailbox. After that, I stayed inside. But here in Lansing, outside is green and noiseless, and so being inside feels like choosing one scoop of ice cream when you could have a whole chocolate-sprinkled sundae.

A wind blows in from a window Nia must've opened. I pull the covers up around my shoulders and curl my legs til they meet my belly. It's been three days since I first saw 'em, but I can't stop thinking bout fireflies. My tucked body reminds me of catching that first one in my cupped hands. Since then, I been catching fireflies every night, sometimes with Granddaddy watching and sometimes on my own. Never with Nia. I watch her now cross the room, a familiar routine, as she stares at her face in the mirror, then pulls at her hair like she's tryna stretch it longer. When it don't stretch, she frowns.

Nia has the best hair I ever seen, curly and fluffy like a big ball of cotton candy. But she tells Momma she don't like it, cause it's different than the other girls' hair. I don't much like the girls with straight hair, though, cause they have hair so flat it just lays against their head. Nia's hair is alive.

"Hey, Nia?" I wait for her to look back my way,

but she don't. Just keeps staring at herself in the mirror. "I like your hair," I try again, this time at least gettin' her attention, but only long enough for her to frown.

"I don't," Nia whispers, but I can't tell if she's talking to me or herself.

Me and Nia ain't said nothin' bout the fight we had, or the word I called her. Still, I can't help but try to be close to Nia. And I wonder if she feels the same. She does sit on the porch while I'm outside now, but I ain't sure if it's to be close to me, or if it's just cause she don't wanna stay in the house with Granddaddy, who is still just as quiet and distant with Nia as ever. Either way, she sits on the porch all day with her headphones and magazines. But me, I explore.

I begin today clutching a book that I snuck from Granddaddy's bookshelf and climbing a tree that I decided yesterday would be my favorite tree. My tree's hidden behind two giant trees with leaves as big around as my hand. But my tree is better, cause even though it's small, it knows me best. I climb it, easy, even with the book in one hand. My tree has branches in a perfect row, like steps. Once I climb, I sit with legs dangling on either side of a wide branch right in the center. Sometimes I stay in my tree all day, just reading and watching and reading some more.

Since I finished **Anne of Green Gables** a couple

days ago, I been trying my luck with the few books on Granddaddy's shelves that don't look too boring. The book I chose today has a tattered brown cover, with its curious title stretched cross the front in block letters. **Their Eyes Were Watching God.** I picked it for that title, and for the picture of God—not like the framed Black Jesus hanging in Granddaddy's dining room, but more like the white God in TV shows—strangling a lightning bolt underneath. When I open the wrinkled pages, I can tell the book is for grown-ups, cause it's filled with tiny text and big words. But as I start to read, I meet a teenage girl with skin like mine and hair like Nia's, who's gotta figure stuff out just like us. I keep reading—even after the teenage girl becomes a grown woman with a mean husband—cause I feel like I know her, and cause I only have to skip over a few hard words along the way.

I read all 227 pages without taking a break. When I'm done, I go back and fold the corner of my favorite page, then close the book. Now I'm thinking a lot, bout Janie in the book who reminds me, in some ways, of Momma. In the book, Janie gets three husbands—the first husband picked by her granny, the second husband who's mean and tries to control her, then the third husband, Tea Cake, who's bad for her, but who Janie loves the most. Come to think of it, Daddy was probably Momma's Tea Cake, cause he ended up being bad for Momma in the end. But now I know it ain't that simple. Cause when Janie and Tea Cake got caught in a bad storm and thought they would die, Janie said to Tea Cake my favorite line of the book: "If you kin see de light at day-break, you don't keer if you die at dusk. It's so many people never seen de light at all." I wonder if, like Janie, Momma feels like all the bad stuff with Daddy was worth it, for the good.

Thinking bout it this way, I feel more sad for Momma than mad. Maybe Momma really is just like Janie, tryna take control for herself instead of always being controlled. This reminds me of the idea I got during Bible study, which makes me realize, I'm kinda like Janie, too. The whole book long, Janie was tryna find a way for herself, and now I'm tryna do the same. I reach into my pocket, remembering my list with the big circle around **money**, but it ain't there. Then I remember: it's in a different pair of shorts. I climb down and run to the bedroom.

The list is still perfectly folded in the pocket of my old shorts, wrinkled and dirty on the closet floor. I open and refold it, then place it in my new pocket. That Bible verse told me exactly what I needed to do, gather money little by little, and now it's time to do it.

The sun feels hotter than just a few minutes ago, so hot it could burn patches of my skin. It's like when kids put magnifying glasses over ants, cept I'm the ant, and ain't no dirt holes for me to run in and hide. Besides the trees—which I'm walking away from now—ain't nowhere to escape from the sun on Granddaddy's big, wide-open block.

In one hand I clutch the handles of a brown paper bag I found underneath the sink. When I would go to the grocery store with Momma and they'd ask her "paper or plastic," she'd always pick plastic, much to my disappointment, and we'd walk home with bags pulling on our fingers and in the creases of our elbows, plastic that would sometimes break as soon as we walked in the door, leaving all our groceries in a big pile on the floor. The paper bags always seemed stronger, richer. All the fancy people would pick paper and leave the store with arms full of crackling bags that fit snugly between their elbow and chest.

I guess Granddaddy's one of them fancy people, cause he got a whole drawer full of paper bags. I picked the biggest one, with a picture of a tree on the front and the little recycle symbol on the back. When it's unfolded, the bag is bout the same size as my backpack, and it's gon' hold a bunch of bottles, soon as I find some. That's my plan— collect bottles to take to the store for money. In Michigan, you get ten cents for every bottle you find, which I know cause Daddy would always yell at me and Nia if we accidentally put one in the trash. If I can find enough bottles, I can get enough money to get back home to Momma. I ain't sure what it's gon' be like to be back with Momma—especially with the way she's been since Daddy died—but it's gotta be better than being stuck here with Nia and Granddaddy. Back home with Momma, maybe we can try to be a family again.

The sidewalk on Granddaddy's street is strange, wide in some places and narrow in others, and it even, sometimes, disappears completely, leaving nothin' but grass and dirt and pebbles to walk on. My feet crunch and crunch as I walk on the parts of sidewalk that ain't sidewalk, looking back and forth for bottles to put in my bag. But ain't no bottles to find, just rocks and bugs and flowers. I count twenty-seven rocks, then eighteen of four different kinds of bugs—ants, bees, worms, flies—and finally fifteen flowers, which I can't help but stop and smell, one at a time. But I don't find even one bottle, even after walking all the way down one side of the street and back up the other.

Dragging the empty bag behind me, I make my way back to my tree and begin to climb. I'm just bout settled in my spot when I hear voices coming from cross the street. It's them white kids again. I ain't stopped thinking bout them since the first time I saw them playing with the cherry-colored wagon. They ain't got the wagon today. Instead, they draw pink and blue and yellow pictures on the sidewalk with chalk.

I hop down from my tree to get a closer look, but I don't dare go over. Not cause of what Granddaddy said but cause of how he looked when he said it. I know he don't want me to play with them white kids. And even though I got a feeling he's wrong bout them, I can already tell Granddaddy is stricter than Momma and meaner than Nia. I can't take no chances.

From my spot near the tree, looks like the boy is drawing a family—Momma and Daddy and son and daughter—while the girl draws a field of flowers. Looks like the flowers in Granddaddy's backyard, but I can't be sure. I imagine the kind of pictures I might draw if I could play with them. I might draw flowers, too, or my old house or old school or maybe even a picture of me and Daddy. Just thinking bout it makes me happy. Best of all, I would finally have somebody to talk to and play with. Somebody who wouldn't be mean to me or leave me behind.

I look around, then take a deep breath. Last I checked, Nia was taking a shower and Granddaddy was enjoying his regular afternoon couch nap. I might have just enough time to make it over there without gettin' caught. I don't wanna make

Granddaddy mad again, but I really wanna make some friends.

"Hey, can I play with y'all?" Somehow, my legs got me cross the street and standing in front of the white kids. They look up with mouths gaping open, like they don't speak English. I try again. "My name is KB. Can I play with y'all?"

Finally, after I count twelve seconds, the girl nods. Just barely, but enough. I offer her a smile but avoid looking at the boy, whose mouth is still hanging open. Up close, the girl's golden hair is no longer the color of the sun; it's more like the sunset, streaked with warm reddish and orange hues. And it's so long that it's braided into one long thick braid that wraps around itself twice with giant bows on the ends. The bows don't lay down flat; they each stick out like giant flaps beneath her ears. As she moves, I expect them to bounce up and down, but they stay stuck beside her head like they glued there. I decide to call her Pippi—since she ain't told me her name yet—for one of my favorite book friends, Pippi Longstocking. Cept she's blond-haired, blue-eyed Pippi, with a look in her eyes like she's scared and excited all at once.

The girl—blond Pippi—hands me a cracked stub of chalk, yellow, and goes back to her drawing. The boy is too busy watching me to draw. I think bout what I can make with yellow. I shove the stub to my nose and yellow dust floats in the air. I decide to draw a garden, starting with the sun. But when I see the garden in my mind, it has trees that reach their arms cross to each other and block out the light, so I use the yellow for a bird instead, that sits watching in the garden's tallest tree.

We stay there like that, not talking, just drawing, for seven pictures. I draw two of those pictures: my garden with the yellow bird, and a portrait of Momma. I try to draw her as best as I can remember, but the white kids don't have no brown chalk, so I make her skin yellow. Like this, she looks just a little like me. The girl draws four pictures. She don't spend too much time on any one. She draws the flowers, animals near some trees, a school, and something that I think is a little girl. But with two big boulders where there should be lips and a mop on her head instead of hair. The boy only draws the one picture, the family, which he ain't touched since I came over.

"Who's that?" the girl asks, pointing at my drawing of Momma.

"That's my momma," I answer shyly, "but I drew her a little like me." I smile and the girl smiles back. I think we might be friends. Even though I still don't know her name yet.

"Pretty," says the girl with no name. I feel proud when she says it, not cause she likes my drawing, but cause she thinks Momma is pretty.

"Thank you," I reply with a big grin. "What did you draw?" I point to the mystery picture that's either a deformed doll or a wild animal.

"It's you." She says it so sweet that I almost forget to be insulted. Almost. I look back down at the picture, at the too-big lips, thick nose, and nappy hair. Is this how I look to her? I force myself to smile cause I don't want her to feel bad.

"Oh," is all I can think to say. I go back to coloring my already finished picture.

"My name is Charlotte," says the girl, "and this is my brother, Bobby." She smiles. I wonder if she knows the drawing made me sad, but I figure probably not, cause now she's smiling big and sweet. But not the boy, Bobby. He squints like he's thinking bout something real hard. I think it's funny that I said my name so long ago, but just got their names now.

"My name is KB," I tell them again. I don't know what else to say. I wait, but they don't talk, so I pick up another piece of chalk and get back to work, pretending not to feel their stares.

"Give it, Bobby!" Charlotte's shriek interrupts my fake concentration. I look up and see Bobby holding the red chalk above his head, high so Charlotte can't reach.

"Come get it," taunts Bobby, waving the chalk. I wonder if I should jump into the argument, but I figure it's not my place. This is probably what it looks like to watch me and Nia together. I sit back and pretend not to notice as Charlotte's eyes grow watery, and Bobby makes up a silly dance that makes things worse. A part of me wants to cry for Charlotte, but the other part wants to laugh with Bobby. I guess there **are** always two sides to a story, just like Momma always says when me and Nia get to fighting over something.

"I'm going to tell Mom!" Charlotte stomps off.

Bobby considers her warning, drops the chalk, and yells, "Here, crybaby, take it!"

At the sound of Bobby's surrender, Charlotte returns, pouting. Then she picks up the chalk again like none of it happened at all. I watch the two of them for a few seconds before I go back to my drawing. I guess sisters ain't the only ones who fight.

Bobby runs off to the back of the house, kicking rocks as he goes. I worry that he plans to tell they momma what happened. But Charlotte don't seem to be worried. I study her as she concentrates on her drawing. Every so often, she chews on the ends of her hair. Seems like the more she concentrates, the more she chews. She wipes her skinny nose with the back of her hand as I memorize her eyes. I ain't ever seen blue eyes like hers before. They are swimming pools full with clear water that, if she blinks, will surely spill over.

"You done with the green?" Charlotte's question makes me jump. She don't seem to notice, stretching her hand out toward the stubby green chalk, which I was using to draw a vine.

"Sure." I hand it over quickly, even though I really ain't done with it.

"Do you like to read?" I ask, looking for a conversation to start. We ain't barely talked since I first came cross the street. Even though I like drawing with the chalk, I want us to be friends, too. Lansing's been lonely without any, especially since I ain't got Nia no more.

"Yep," Charlotte says without looking up, "I love to read."

I watch her for a few seconds, notice the way she scrunches up her face when she's tryna draw a straight line. "Have you read **Anne of Green Gables?**"

Charlotte quickly looks up. "No, but all my friends at school have that book!" Her response is more excited than I expect. She's smiling from ear to ear now. "I really, really, really want to read it! But my mom won't buy it for me. She says it's too grown-up for my reading level."

"Well, how old are you?" I ask.

"Ten," replies Charlotte.

"Me, too!" I exclaim. "But I'll be eleven next month," I finish, in my most mature voice. "So why can't you read the book, then, if we the same age?"

"I'm not sure." Charlotte stops to consider my question. Then whispers, I think to herself, "She never lets me do anything." Her head stays down after that. She looks sad now, with her head low and her tiny lips forming a pout.

"You can read mine," I say, quiet. I ain't sure I wanna offer her my best book, but now I've done it and it's too late to stuff the words back up in my mouth.

"Really?" Charlotte's eyes open wide and round like saucers.

"Sure," I respond, even though I'm not sure at all. Charlotte don't say thank you after that, but I can see the thank you stretched cross her face. I wonder if I have time to read my book one more time, before I give it to her. But I don't say that. I'm happy to have something that's like a treasure. My book helped me make a friend. A friend that likes to draw and read and has a mean older brother. Just like me and mean Nia.

It's funny, though, cause Charlotte's so much like me—same age, likes the same stuff—but when I watch her wipe her dirty hands on her clean shirt without worrying bout gettin' in trouble for dirtying up new clothes, we also seem real different.

Just then, Bobby comes back. He's changed into a new T-shirt with a big picture of Superman on the front and is carrying a large suitcase in his hands.

"What's that?" I ask, forgetting for a second that Bobby's been trying real hard to ignore me from the beginning. I figure maybe he'll start liking me if I say and do the right stuff, just like Charlotte did.

Bobby hesitates, then finally says, "Wanna see?" I nod enthusiastically and stand to move in his direction. Charlotte keeps drawing.

Bobby settles down on the edge of the perfectly cut grass, resting the suitcase on a patch of colored sidewalk. The suitcase is brown and tattered and ugly. But he carries it like it's important, so I'm anxious to see what's inside. He opens one silver latch, and next the other. Then creaks the lid open til the hinge clicks in place. I look eagerly, but ain't nothin' inside but a bunch of dirty-looking rocks.

"It's my rock collection," he declares proudly. I try to hide my disappointment by pretending to cough. "See, I've been collecting these rocks since I was seven." He begins pulling rocks from the pile.

I decide to take a closer look. There are big rocks and small rocks. Some that look like sparkly diamonds and others that look a lot like dog poop. I try to quickly count how many rocks he got. I count twenty-nine, then stop cause Bobby is looking at me funny.

"Can I touch 'em?" My question is cautious, but he responds with a smile.

"Sure." Bobby hands me a rock the size of a peach pit. Its weight in my hands is solid. I run my hands cross the face of the rock, which is smooth and cold like metal. But the underside of the rock is the opposite. Jagged with dips and dents and bumps. Where it's jagged, the rock is brown like dirt, but where it's smooth it's the color of half-burnt charcoal. I ain't ever seen a rock look like this one.

"Where'd you get it?" I ask.

"I found that one when I was nine," starts Bobby, "when I went away to summer camp for the first time."

"Summer camp?" I repeat as I turn the rock over and over in my hands. Each time it turns, it changes into something new. Up, flat and shiny. Down, coarse and dull. Up, gray like fog. Down, brown like mud. Up, beautiful. Down, flawed.

"Yeah," continues Bobby, "it's a science camp that I go to every year. But that year was my first. I didn't have any friends yet, so I kept to myself, mostly. Until I found this rock." He takes the rock from my hands and holds it up proudly. "This rock is how I made friends."

"Really? How?" I scoot closer. If a little, ugly rock made Bobby some friends at summer camp, maybe it can work for us now, too.

"Well, it was our third night of camp," begins Bobby's story. I settle in to listen, while Charlotte continues to color. "Like I said, I didn't have any friends yet. It was time for Campfire Circle and—"

"Campfire Circle?" I interrupt.

"Oh yeah," Bobby says, "it's when we would group off by age to roast marshmallows and tell stories and do other cool stuff by the fire. I was in a group with two other boys—Marty and Kevin, both third graders like me. They were already friends with each other, but not with me." Bobby is twirling the rock in his hands as he talks, like the stone can put him back in front of that fire.

"That night, I decided I didn't want to hang out with these boys that didn't like me. So when our camp counselor wasn't looking, I snuck away."

"Where did you go?" I ask, watching the magic stone spin in his fingers.

"I tried to go back to my cabin, but it was really dark and I got lost. I circled around the wooded campsite for what felt like hours, but I never found my cabin. Instead"—he holds up the rock triumphantly—"I found this!"

I wait for more, cause the way he tells the story, I can't figure why the rock is so important. Besides the fact that it can be pretty and ugly at the same time, ain't much special bout the rock.

"Well," continues Bobby, "it's actually more like this rock found me. I was wandering around in the dark, looking for my cabin, when I tripped over it. I landed flat on my face, got a bloody nose and everything." For some reason, Bobby seems happy bout this last part. I half smile, not sure if he wants me to be happy bout it, too.

"I was laying there, nose bleeding, feeling like an idiot," he continues. "Then I heard some voices getting closer. And when I picked up my head, Kevin and Marty were running my way! I guess they noticed I was gone and came looking for me. Anyway, when I showed them the tiny rock that had my nose bleeding into my camp T-shirt, we laughed and laughed for hours. I was trying to be so big and tough, but I guess this tiny little thing was even tougher." Bobby smiles at the rock. I smile at Bobby.

"That's incredible." I stare hard at the rock and try to imagine something so small doin' something so big. Like the fireflies, I guess. Tiny, little bugs with lights brighter than the whole sky, even when it's filled with stars. The fireflies were like Bobby's rock, in a way. Something small that had the power to bring people together. Bobby and Kevin and Marty. Maybe me and Granddaddy. I heard before in Sunday school that God puts little things along our path for when we need a push in the right direction. I ain't get it then, but it makes sense now.

"Yeah." Bobby smiles. "It is pretty incredible." I

smile, tiny, wondering why he's telling me all this now. He ain't seem too friendly to me when I first wandered cross the street, when he ain't even wanna look my way, let alone talk to me. But now he's being all nice and showing me his special rock collection. I've known since first grade that boys can be weird, and this boy ain't no different.

"Charlotte, you seen his rock collection?" I look her way and hope she might come over, so we can all play together. But she shakes her head soon as I ask.

"I've seen that stupid rock collection too many times! Boring!" She holds out the word **boring** so that it's more like two words, **booooar-innnnng!** Then she rolls her eyes and goes back to drawing. I feel bad for Bobby cause Charlotte's being so mean, but when I look back at him, he don't seem to care. He's too busy studying all his rocks, like he ain't seen 'em before.

"Check out this one," Bobby exclaims, "isn't it cool?" He holds a rock faceup in the palm of his hands, which he holds out to me.

I take the rock—smooth and dark and cool— then listen to a story bout Boy Scouts and first grade. Then another—chalky gray with sparkles along the edges—and a story of moving trucks and new schools and fear. For every rock, there's a story. I sit and listen and my fascination with rocks grows. I still think most of the rocks are ugly, but the stories make up for the flaws. Each story is full of so much life and memory. Just like the rocks, the stories ain't always perfect. But seems like just having all those memories, good or bad, is special by itself.

"Bobby! Charlotte!" The shrill voice comes from the porch and pops the bubble that we've been floating in all this time. Butterflies buzz in my stomach as Charlotte and Bobby's momma comes walking my way. Hair in a bun, clothes neat and pressed, with a look on her face like she's planning to yell.

But when she reaches us on the sidewalk, she don't yell. "It's time to come inside," she half whispers to Bobby and Charlotte instead, not once looking my way.

"Mama!" Charlotte yells. "This is our new friend, KB."

"Time to get washed up for supper," she replies, like she ain't hear Charlotte at all. She finally does look in my direction for a second, just long enough to focus on my ashy knees and nappy hair, before looking away. "Let's go." She walks back to the house without looking back, like she knows that Charlotte and Bobby will follow.

Charlotte is the first to move. She starts picking up the chalk and gathering it in the bottom of her T-shirt. Each piece of chalk adds a new color to the growing rainbow on her once-white top. I grab a piece of chalk that she missed by the grass and take it over to her.

"Here, you forgot this one." I wait for her to say something, but she don't. "I can bring the book over later, if you want." I don't even know if I'll be able to sneak back over here with the book, but for some reason, it feels like it's important to do.

"Sure!" Charlotte squeaks as the smile returns to her troubled face.

I smile back. I think we gon' still be okay. I wave as Charlotte skips to her porch, bouncing colored patterns against all the white.

"KB?" I almost forget Bobby is still there, til I hear him call my name all quiet. He's closed the suitcase, but he's still got some rocks in his hands.

"Thanks for showing me your rock collection," I start, since he ain't said nothin' else yet. I don't know what to do with my hands while I wait for him to talk. I put them on my hips, then run them cross my hair, then lace my fingers behind my back.

"You're welcome," he finally says, then gets silent again. I turn to head back home, cause he ain't talking and I don't want his momma to come back out.

"Here-you-wanna-have-these?" Bobby blurts the sentence out like it's all one big word. I start to ask him to say it again, but then he holds out his hand, where he's got three rocks. And not just any rocks. The prettiest rocks from the whole collection. Which ain't saying too much, cause most of the rocks was ugly. But not these. They sparkle in the sunlight as they rest in his palm. He inches his hand closer to mine, so I know he's tryna offer me the rocks. I open my hand and feel the weight of each stone drop into my hand like gold.

"You can start your own collection." Bobby smiles, so I smile.

"Thank you," is all I can think to say. I'm too busy thinking bout starting my own rock collection. Before now, I only tried to start a collection once. Momma was the one who gave me the first thing to collect. Dolls, three of them to start. A bald-headed Black one with an open mouth for drinking bottles; a white one with long blond hair and only one leg, after an accident when Nia dropped her out the car window and right into the middle of the road when Momma was driving; and my favorite, a dark-skinned princess who I named Nia, just like my Nia, and whose hair was plastic waves drawn on her round head. I ain't think it was so big a thing, the dolls, but when Momma gave them to me, she waved her arms and smiled real big, talking bout the dolls she collected when she was a girl just my age, and all the fun she had. She talked til her eyes were round and wet. I ain't get it, but when I showed the dolls to my friends at school, one at a time on show-and-tell days, I repeated Momma's words, that a girl and her doll are inseparable, and my friends tried out the new word on their own tongues, **inseparable**.

When we moved to the motel, all my dolls had to go to the storage unit with the rest of our stuff, so that was the end of my collection. But now I got a new collection. I got three rocks, and I'm in Lansing, where I can find more rocks—or anything else I wanna collect—and probably, somewhere to put 'em. And I got two new friends cross the street, best of all. Yeah, they momma was acting kinda mean, but I know that sometimes mommas do stuff we don't like and we gotta just go with it. So I ain't too worried.

"You're welcome!" Bobby has to almost shout that part cause he's walking up the three wide porch steps and into the house. I can't tell if he gave me the rocks cause I listened to all his stories and Charlotte didn't. Or cause he don't like these ones, or he got too many. Or maybe he gave me the rocks for the same reason I offered Charlotte my best book. Cause sometimes it's worth it to give something so you can get something. The first lesson I ever learned from Daddy.

Bout three years ago, when I was seven, Momma had to go on a trip to Chicago for work. She had been working at the Chrysler plant most of my life, but this was the first time they ever sent her anywhere. She said it was just for a boring convention, but still she spent almost a week perfectly folding all her clothes and organizing them in a little suitcase with flowers and rolling wheels.

Me and Nia had never been outside Detroit, so she let us come along. And Daddy, to keep an eye on us while she was working. I don't remember much bout the trip, cept we never really saw Momma. Me and Daddy and Nia explored the city all day long. Then, when we would get back to the tiny hotel, Momma would talk forever bout everything she heard that day and all the food she ate for lunch and how sure she was that she would always remember it all.

For our last day in Chicago, Momma promised that we'd spend the whole day together. All of us were excited. Even Nia. We stayed up the night before talking bout what we would take Momma to see and do. I made a list on the little notepad from the hotel, while Daddy and Nia yelled ideas to each other from cross our double hotel beds. But the next day, when I held up our list for Momma to see, she barely saw it, running out the door to another speaker and another lunch. She ain't spend that day with us, or any day with us in Chicago, turns out.

Still, Daddy made a plan. We picked up food from our favorite Chicago place, with chicken wings you could choose in different flavors, then took it to her at work. I remember asking Daddy why he wanted to bother taking Momma food, when she had been breaking promises and letting us down all weekend. **Sometimes you gotta give up something you want to get something you need.** I'm still not sure exactly what Daddy lost or gained that day, but it seemed really important to him. And like he thought it would be important to me one day, too.

I skip back cross the street with my new rock collection in my pocket and a giant grin on my face, happy cause I made new friends, and cause I thought of Daddy without crying. And, most of all, cause Granddaddy was wrong bout them white kids.

I make it back to my spot in my tree without Granddaddy or Nia even noticing I was gone. At least, don't seem like nobody noticed. Everything is quiet and boring as usual. The empty bag I was using to find bottles has started to blow away and is stuck in the branches of the bush by Granddaddy's front porch. I run to grab it, then pull the list back out my pocket. Looking for bottles ain't quite work out, but there's gotta be another way I can find money and get back to Momma. As soon as I think the word **Momma**, I see her face in my mind. She bout the only person that might actually be happy bout me making friends with Bobby and Charlotte.

When I started fifth grade, I had a hard time making friends. Seemed like all the other kids were doin' stuff together after school and on the weekends, so they were all really good friends with inside jokes and funny stories they only told to each other. But not me. Momma and Daddy never let us do none of that extra stuff, so on the first day of school when everyone was hugging and laughing, I was eating lunch alone in the cafeteria. I came home from school that day tryna hide my sadness, but Momma noticed anyway. She told me a story bout when she was a little girl, growing up with all brothers, and how she ain't ever feel like she had a real friend. "Til I found you and your sister," she had said, pinching my nose and smiling. I refold the list and put it back in my pocket, then grab my book and the empty bag and head inside Granddaddy's house. This time, I'm gon' get him to let me call Momma.

Just like I figured, Granddaddy is on the couch, pretending to watch the TV. I come in just as the music sounds and the host yells, "Come on down! You are the next contestant on **The Price Is Right!**" I always love this part, but I ain't got time to stop and watch. I nudge Granddaddy softly on the shoulder as I sit down next to him. He blinks awake and looks my way, but I pretend the contact was accidental, tuning in to the screen.

"Bid one dollar," I yell, cause that's what I hear Granddaddy say a lot.

"One dollar!" Granddaddy yells in agreement, sittin' up now. We both watch as the actual retail price is announced, and the guy who bid the lowest amount wins. "Hmph," Granddaddy mumbles in satisfaction.

"Hmph," I mumble back, folding my arms cross my chest and sittin' back, just like Granddaddy. We watch for another few minutes before I finally get the nerve to ask. "Granddaddy," I begin, "would it be okay if I call Momma?" I ain't sure why it feels so scary to ask, cept that Momma left us here unexpectedly, and the whole thing feels like a big secret.

Granddaddy sighs. "Well, I don't know—"

"Please, Granddaddy," I interrupt. "I got something really important to talk to her bout and it will be really, really fast, I promise!"

"It's just that—" Granddaddy pauses like he's thinking real hard. "Kenyatta, your momma is getting some rest. I don't know if we should interrupt her."

Rest? I thought Momma left so she could make money, not rest. And why she need rest anyway? She ain't sick or nothin', far as I know . . .

"Just for a minute, okay?" Granddaddy looks at me with the same kind of sad eyes people looked at me with after Daddy died. I nod, not sure why he's being so dramatic, but happy he's gon' let me call Momma.

"Don't worry, I already know the number," I announce triumphantly. Momma made us memorize the number to the motel as soon as we got there. I thought we were only gon' be there a little while, but she made us learn the number anyway. Five-five-five-seven-three-five-five. The digits make a song like a nursery rhyme that made it easy to memorize.

"Nah, she ain't . . . she ain't there." Granddaddy shifts in his seat and rubs his hands together. He waits a few seconds before speaking again. "I'll dial the number, then you talk. Just for a minute."

I nod, even though Granddaddy is already on his way to the kitchen, where the phone hangs on the wall beside the fridge. I wonder why Momma ain't at the motel. Where else would she be? I wanna ask Granddaddy, but before I can, he hands me the phone.

Three rings, then Momma picks up.

"Hello?" She sounds out of breath. For the first time, I wonder bout what Momma's been doin' this whole time, without us. She probably still gotta go to work at Chrysler, and maybe she's even working extra since we need money for our new house. I don't know exactly what Momma does at work all day, but I know she has a lot of important meetings and stuff. Once, I asked her if she was the boss at work, cause it seemed like she was always in charge. She answered, **I'm a boss, but not the boss.** I still don't know what she meant. But one thing I do know: Momma don't love her job at Chrysler like she loves writing.

A few years back, before Daddy spent so much time on them stairs, Momma got it in her head that she was gon' go back to school.

"What for?" Daddy asked, when she told him bout her plan to apply to the local college down the road, where she could take journalism classes at night.

"So that I can get a job." Momma didn't look up from the dishes she was washing.

"You already got a job." Daddy laughed, coming up behind Momma for a hug she ain't return.

"So that I can get a job doing what I love."

"Writing?" Daddy said with a smirk. By this time, Momma's lips was a straight line, and she was washing dishes so hard that they bounced and clattered against the sides of the sink.

Daddy ain't say nothin' else that night, and Momma ain't stop frowning. That was the last time I heard Momma talk bout school around Daddy.

Still, not too long after that, Momma started goin' to school. It made her always tired and grumpy, probably cause she had to work all day then go to school at night, plus do homework that kept her up all night drinking coffee and yawning. But that ain't stop Momma. She woke up early and stayed up late and got good grades, only quitting school when Daddy stopped coming home, cause somebody had to make sure me and Nia was gettin' to school, too.

I swallow hard. Not much has ever stopped Momma. So why would she let anything keep her away from us now?

"Hello?" Momma says again, this time louder.

"Momma, it's me! Kenyatta." I ain't sure why I put my name on the end, like she forgot bout me after just a week apart.

"Hey, KB." Her words don't sound quite happy, but not exactly sad. There's something strange in her voice that I don't recognize. For a second, the thought creeps into my mind that maybe Nia was right, maybe Momma ain't coming back, and maybe she don't even wanna talk to me now. But I know that can't be true. Maybe she was just watching her stories and one of her favorite characters died again, or something like that. Probably something like that.

"Whatcha doin'?" I ask, tryna sound casual.

"Just . . ." Her voice trails off. "Missing my girls."

"I miss you, too," I say, twisting the phone cord around my finger.

"How have you girls been doing?" Momma asks, then: "How's Nia?" I think bout telling Momma the truth. That Nia is barely talking to me, and when she does, she's being mean. That Granddaddy is mean, too, and don't even want me to play with the only friends I got here. But something bout Momma's voice sounds like she needs to hear that everything is okay.

"We're having fun, Momma. Nia even watched me catch fireflies." Not exactly a lie.

"Really?" Momma seems surprised. "I'm happy to hear that. I'm so, so happy." But her voice don't sound happy at all.

"What have you been doin', Momma?" I think bout what I heard Charlie and Granddaddy talking bout earlier, bout some kind of treatment. Could they have been talking bout Momma? But what would she need treatment for? I mean, I don't think she's sick . . .

"I've been . . . relaxing," Momma says, but her voice sounds more worried than relaxed. It's like at church when people used to ask Momma how she was doin' and she'd respond, **Too blessed to be stressed**, even though she was definitely stressed.

"You been at the motel?" I whisper, turning away from Granddaddy. He already told me she wasn't there, but I wanna hear what Momma gon' say.

Momma is quiet for a few seconds, then says, "Yes, I'm at the motel."

I blink hard as I try to think of what to say. Momma is lying, and Momma hates when people lie. She's always telling me and Nia that the worst thing to be in the world is a liar. So why she lying to me now, and bout something so silly?

"Oh," I finally respond, cause I can't think of nothin' else. We sit in silence for what feels like forever. Then I hear a voice in the background.

"Well, I gotta go—" Momma says, suddenly talking louder.

"Who was that?" I ask, even though I figure she don't want me to ask.

"Oh!" Momma responds quickly. "I think that was, umm, I don't know. Maybe a housekeeper or something. I should go check it out. Bye!" Momma practically yells, then hangs up before I can respond.

I stand there with the phone still up to my ear, even after the dial tone sounds. I can't believe Momma lied to me, and then hung up on me. That ain't nothin' like the Momma I knew.

"You all done?" Granddaddy taps my shoulder lightly. I circle to face him and slowly nod, placing the receiver back on the hook softly.

"You all right?"

I guess Granddaddy sees the hurt in my eyes or the confusion on my face. I shrug.

"What happened?" Granddaddy asks, following me to the couch. I sit down and shrug again.

"Kenyatta, tell me—" Granddaddy begins, but by then I got my own questions.

"Where is Momma at?" I ask, voice steady.

Granddaddy sighs and lowers his head. "Your momma is a grown woman. Ain't none of mine or your business where she at, Kenyatta."

"I'm her daughter," I reply, heart beginning to beat faster. "Don't I get to know where my own momma at? Especially since my daddy just died and I ain't got nobody else?"

Now when Granddaddy looks at me, his eyes are wet. But he still don't budge. "I know you miss your momma, but we just gotta wait for her to get—" He cuts himself off quickly, then finishes. "We gotta wait until she comes back. That's all."

My head is spinning with all kinds of questions. First, Momma left us here with no warning. Then Charlie was asking bout her all weird, and now Granddaddy being weird, too. And Momma ain't at the motel, like she s'posed to be. Who knows where she's even at, since nobody won't tell me nothin'. I feel tears starting to form, but not cause I'm sad. "Why you won't answer me, Granddaddy?" I yell. "Why everybody keepin' secrets from me?"

I think Granddaddy gon' try to give me another kiddie answer, but then he looks me straight in the eye, his wrinkled face settling into a scowl. "Why you ask so many damn questions, Kenyatta?" He spits my name from his mouth. "You betta be careful, askin' all them questions. One day you gon' realize, the truth ain't always somethin' good. And all them secrets—they there for a reason."

As he slowly stands, the words repeat in my head like bullets shot from a gun. **The truth ain't always somethin' good.** I feel the sting of each word long after the smoke clears, long after they pierce my flesh through and through.

For the next few days, Granddaddy don't talk much. I don't mind, cause after the way he yelled at me, I ain't tryna talk to him anyway. The only person I wanna talk to now is Daddy, and he's gone for good. Even still, I talk to him before bed each night, closing my eyes tight til I can see his face behind my eyelids, and there he is again just like he always was. I like to tell him bout the new books I'm reading and bout my new friends and bout Momma and Nia being weird now. Daddy listens without interrupting, rubbing my hair while I talk. Even though that's not what he was like before, that's what I make him like now.

I wonder if Nia still talks to Daddy, too. Truth is, they was always closer than me and him ever were. Sometimes I would even hear them up late after they thought me and Momma was sleep, still talking and playing. But that Nia is gone now. This Nia don't seem to remember Daddy at all.

I step out on the porch and look around for something new to keep me busy. Another day in Lansing with nothin' to do. And since Nia out sittin' on the porch today, I can't even play with Bobby and Charlotte. I walk toward the field in the backyard. I stop and look at a flower, yellow on the outside, but deep purple inside like a ripe plum. I pick the flower and when I take a closer look inside, I notice something is moving. I peel back the yellow petals, slow. Cozy inside the purple center is a fuzzy caterpillar, black on both ends, but bright orange in the middle. I pick the caterpillar up soft, cause I don't wanna smash it in my fingers. Once the caterpillar is safe in the palm of my hand, I run back to the house, nearly tripping up the steps in my excitement. I expect to find Nia on the porch, but she ain't there no more, so I run into the house.

"Granddaddy, guess what," I screech once I'm inside.

"What's that?" he replies, his eyes flickering with something like a smile. This is the first time we really talked since he yelled at me, and look like Granddaddy ready to make things right. I ain't sure I wanna try to get close to him again, but I ain't got nobody else to share my excitement with. Granddaddy gon' have to do.

"I found a caterpillar!" I stretch out my hand to reveal my treasure. But on second look it's an ugly little bug, covered all over with tiny hairs, like the whiskers on Daddy's chin that used to tickle me when he remembered to kiss me good night.

"Good for you," Granddaddy responds. I think he ain't happy bout the caterpillar or maybe he still mad at me, but then, without another word, he rises from his seat and slowly makes his way into the kitchen. I can hear him rumbling around. I hop from toe to toe, wondering what he went to find. Finally, he comes back, carrying an empty mayonnaise jar.

"Here, use this," he says.

"For what?" I ask, reaching out and closing the cool glass between my thumbs.

"More caterpillars," he says with a wink.

"Thank you!" I remember to yell as I race back outside to find Nia, letting the door slam behind me. Granddaddy don't like when I do that, but I ain't got time to stop. Not even when I notice my shoes are untied. Instead, I run in zigzags to avoid tripping over the wild laces. When I finally spot Nia, she is sittin' under the giant oak in the front yard.

"Nia! Nia, guess what?" I yell.

Nia responds with a tiny flick of her wrist, instructing me to leave her alone. I continue in her direction, though. I want Nia to love the

caterpillar just like I do. For a while, I was nothin'
but angry at Nia. But the more I thought bout
that sad look on her face when she was alone in the
room, the more I began to wonder if Nia was
struggling, too, just like me. I ain't ready to try to
be friends with her yet, but it's always hard to stay
mad at Nia for too long. Even when everything
changes around me, Nia is usually the one thing I
know ain't gon' go away.

As I run, I realize just how much I miss Nia.
Miss laughing with Nia til my sides ache. Like
that Christmas when Momma wrapped all our
gifts in newspaper instead of wrapping paper.
Momma swore she could buy wrapping paper if
she wanted to, but really it was a waste of
money—and wasn't the personalized wrapping
more interesting anyway? Turns out, she was right.
Momma wrote little stories for every gift, some
true and some make-believe, but all funny. Me
and Nia laughed at her little notes written in red
pen cross the black-and-white newspaper, rolling
around on the floor and cackling and slapping
each other's thighs whenever the laughing slowed
down. I hope the caterpillars can make us like that
again. At least it's worth one more try.

I run to Nia's side and wave my hands in front
of her eyes. As usual, loud music is blaring from
her Walkman. There is a gentle wind that licks
Nia's hair cross her face, which she tries to pull

and tuck behind her ears. Instead, the stubborn locks drift and dance.

"What do you want?" she asks, finally gettin' rid of her headphones.

"Look at what Granddaddy gave me," I exclaim, holding up my prize possession.

"An empty mayonnaise jar?" Nia rolls her eyes.

"Well, it's empty now, but it won't be soon. Check it out." I open my palm to reveal my caterpillar. It uncurls its little orange body and begins to slink slowly to the edge of my hand. We both watch as the caterpillar lifts its legs, ready to leap to freedom.

"Let me see," Nia replies, hands outstretched. To my surprise, she seems kinda interested. I eagerly pass the caterpillar into her hands. She ain't moving, just watching. The caterpillar crawls cross her palms and she laughs. The first real laugh I heard from Nia since our first night in Lansing.

"It tickles!" Nia screeches.

"I know, ain't it funny?" I giggle.

"Let's get it in the jar before it crawls away!" Nia wriggles her hands around to keep the caterpillar from falling. I open the lid to the jar, and we watch as the caterpillar slithers inside.

"Now what?" I ask.

"Well, he probably needs grass. And air," she replies smartly, "so I'll poke holes in the lid; you look for some nice, green grass."

"Got it!" I yell, already running out back to the field. I smile big as I run. Most of the time when we do stuff together, it's Nia's idea. But this time it's my idea, and seems like Nia's actually excited and not just being mean. I find a patch of grass that is bright green and tall. I grab a handful, hoping that when Nia sees it, she'll think it's perfect.

I run back to Nia with the grass. She don't say **perfect**, but she smiles her best smile at me. We fix the jar up with grass and a little dirt, and Nia uses a small knife from Granddaddy to poke holes in the lid. We put the caterpillar inside and watch him first land on the bottom in a heap, then poke around in the grass, then start to crawl around like he's finally home.

Nia decides he's a boy, and we name him Fuzz. Nia lets me pick the name.

I think back to the last time I spent a whole day doin' something with Nia. Last year, just before Christmas. Daddy is alive, but things ain't good. Momma and Daddy yell a lot, all the time. Grown-up words that I try to drown out with my **Power Rangers** VHS tape. But even with the volume to the top, I know things are bad.

One day is worse than the others. Daddy yells a

lot of things at Momma, then leaves the house with an old suitcase that's got holes by the zipper. And it's the day of the big snowstorm. Momma goes to work like ain't nothin' wrong, but the school calls a snow day for our district. Normally, Daddy stays with us when Momma goes to work, but Daddy don't come back none that day. Nia is just old enough by law to babysit. I know this cause I hear Momma saying it on the phone. I wonder if my sister is nervous cause it's her first real time babysitting. But I feel excited. I imagine we might spend the whole day playing school, like we used to.

But when Momma leaves, Nia barely even looks my way. And she only speaks to me once, to ask what I want for breakfast.

After cereal and burnt toast, Nia pops on the TV. I wanna watch Nickelodeon, but Nia makes me watch Momma's soap operas. I get restless and start to watch the scene outside our window instead. The snow is still coming down, but not as hard now. The giant flakes ain't in no hurry, as they plop lazily onto the tops of trees, making the whole street a frosted doughnut covered in powdered sugar. I watch the snow fall, then watch cars slipping down the street, then watch a man wearing a robe shoveling snow. Then I'm bored.

"Can we go outside?" I ask.

Nia ignores me.

"Nia!" I yell, just as a woman in her underwear slaps a bearded man on the TV screen.

"What!" Nia exclaims.

"Can we go outside?" I whisper.

"No, I'm watching my stories."

"Please, Nia. I'm bored! Puh-leeeease." I give her my very best cute pouty face. I even blink my eyes quick and bat my lashes like I see Nia do to get outta trouble with Momma.

"Fine," she sighs, "just for a minute."

I race to the closet and get my coat and boots on before Nia even stands from her seat on the couch. I pull the door open too hard so that the door sticks wide open and I gotta pull it back in and shut it tight. Then I'm gone. I jump right away into a large mound of icy-cold snow and start making a snow angel with my arms and legs flailing wildly. Flakes of snow spin up into the air, landing on my nose in tiny pools of cold water.

Nia sits on the porch, chipping polish off her fingernails. I grab a pile of snow with my bare hands, packing it into a tight snowball. My only pair of gloves has holes in the fingertips, so I'm better off with nothin'. I look around for a target and decide on our front mailbox, which is old and close to falling off. I aim, then fling the snowball with all my might, hitting the mailbox perfectly in the middle.

"Yes!" I scream, happy, just as the snowball hits. But then I watch as it falls slowly from the mailbox, landing directly on Nia's head with a dripping wet plop. She don't move; I don't breathe. Finally, she looks up, wiping snow away with her red palms. Then she stands and takes one step toward me, and another.

"I'm so sorry, Nia," I start.

But I am interrupted by her playful yell: "This is war!"

To my surprise, Nia grabs two snowballs, one in each hand, and throws them in my direction. I screech and run for cover. We pitch snowballs at each other til our hands are icicles and our mouths are stretched into frozen smiles. We run in the house and collapse on the couch in a fit of giggles.

"That was fun!" I laugh.

"I know!" she replies. "We haven't done that in forever!"

"I know! And I beat you last time, too!" I squeal with delight.

"Uh-uh, no you didn't! I won! Say it!" She tosses me back farther into the couch cushions, pinning my arms beneath my head. I struggle against her weight, but I ain't ever been strong enough to beat Nia.

"Say it!" Nia yells. "Say I won!"

I can barely breathe from laughing so hard. Nia tickles me and won't stop. "No, I won!" I manage to stammer.

"No," she starts, just as the phone rings. She pauses her thought, then crosses to the kitchen to answer the call. Soon I hear her speaking quietly, probably to one of her friends. I sneak a little closer, hoping she ain't gon' be on the phone long, so we can play some more. I ain't ever gon' forget this day. I know it.

"I wish," I hear Nia whisper into the phone. "I'm stuck here with the brat."

I feel the sting of tears before I make it back to my room. As soon as my door is closed, they fall from my eyes like traitors.

But our day with Fuzz ain't like that day, cause Nia ain't being mean this time. I peek over at her, see a smile still shining from her face. I bet now's a good time to try to get her talking. Nia always knows more bout what's going on than me. Maybe I can get her to tell me what she knows, starting with the truth bout where Momma is at.

"You miss Detroit?" I ask. Nia lets Fuzz crawl cross her palm before answering.

"A little." She pauses, then: "I miss Momma." Nia turns away so that I can only see the side of her face. I wonder if she misses Daddy, too, but I'm not sure it's a good idea to ask yet.

"Yeah, me, too," I say, but Nia stays quiet. "Here"—I offer the jar as Fuzz crawls to the edge of her hand—"put him in here." Nia uses her thumb to slide Fuzz into the jar, where he scoots to the grass-filled bottom.

"You know what I miss most?" I ask, determined to try again. Nia looks up at me without speaking. "I miss our old house. With Daddy. You think we gon' get a new house when Momma comes back?" Something flickers cross Nia's face—hope?—but then she smooths her shirt and shrugs before focusing again on the jar.

"We should find more caterpillars," Nia says. "I bet Fuzz needs some friends."

"Yeah," I whisper. I hope Nia ain't mad at me for bringing up Daddy. And I hope Fuzz's new friends ain't gon' get in the way, like Nia's.

When Granddaddy calls to us from the house we run inside for dinner, fast and in crooked lines with bugs buzzing in our ears. I ain't figure out Nia's secrets tonight, but I did get closer to her than we've been in a long time. I look up and spot my favorite star in the sky, the sparkly one right in the middle. I bet it's the same one that used to be Momma's favorite, too, when she was my age. I wink at our star and make a wish that things will be the same tomorrow. Maybe even the start of everything going back to normal.

I wake up early the next morning. The sun is barely peeking through the heavy curtains, but Nia is already dressed. She takes a last look in the mirror and starts to head out the door.

"Where you going?" I ask quietly.

"My friend Brittany is in Lansing for the rest of the summer now!" Nia exclaims. "When I told her we had to stay, she remembered she got an auntie that lives here." Nia straightens her poufy ponytail with both hands. "Granddaddy already left for church, but he said I can go hang out with her and maybe spend the night."

"But what bout Fuzz?"

"Fuzz? Oh, right. Umm, maybe tomorrow." Nia walks away without even looking back. I know she won't think bout Fuzz again.

I lay in the bed awhile, staring at the crack in the ceiling before I finally get up. I ain't excited like before. But I get dressed, and I head outside. I look for caterpillars in the field and by the big tree. I find four caterpillars, then I'm bored. It just don't feel the same without Nia.

I hide the jar under the porch and climb up to my spot in the tree. From here I can see the road, so I watch for Nia to come back. Maybe she gon' come back soon so we can still have time to play. I stay there, watching, til the sun hides behind the hills. Til the field is covered in shadows and it's too late for caterpillars, or sisters.

4

Lansing is like staying up late on a school night, them times when Momma and Daddy would get in a fight. We'd feel happy to stay up late but couldn't really enjoy it cause of all the yelling. Nights that are happy and sad all at once, just like being here.

It's been thirteen days in Lansing, and since I still ain't collected a single bottle or learned the truth bout what's going on, I'm no closer to gettin' back home to Momma. I wish time would slow down, give me enough time to get the money before summer ends and I'm stuck here forever, but it don't. Now it's the end of June and scorching hot. With the sun comes patches of sidewalk that burn my bare feet. But the air is still light in some places, gently blowing the flowers that were already colorful but now look covered by exploded paint cans. And with a smell so rich it soaks my nostrils. Lansing is summer like I never knew summer before. I wanna know it always, but I always wanna leave. This is how I spend each moment: busy loving and hating, having and letting go.

I sit on the sinking porch, watching Bobby and Charlotte cross the street blowing bubbles and playing freeze tag. I don't dare try to play with them today cause Granddaddy been back and forth outside to work on his garden. So I just watch. Then, once they get called inside, I stoop down and pick dandelion stems growing where the cement cracks. Six stems, then I'm bored. Nia's been in the house all day cause she says it's too hot and miserable to be outside. For once I don't disagree with her. My tank top is soaked through; I can see my belly button where I should see fabric. I been inside for four glasses of water already and it ain't quite noon. I watch my sandals sear tan lines in my ankles. I stand the heat for good reason, cause I love it out here. My favorite part of Lansing is the quiet. So much to see and smell and hear, and so much quiet to do it with. Ain't none of that in Detroit. In that city, feels like the only peace you can find is when you leave.

I chew my thumb and remember a day back home even louder than most. A day when police officers showed up to our house with loud knocks and yelling and guns hanging from their hips. They asked for Daddy and found him on them stairs. Momma screamed at them, but they took Daddy anyway. I wanted to ask why the police came, why he went to jail. But any time I asked those kinds of questions bout Daddy, I either got yelled at to stay outta grown folks' business or laughed away like nothin' was wrong and I was just being silly. So, instead of wasting my time asking, I quietly thought he was gone for good, cept bout a week or two later, by the time of the big book fair at school, he was back. I remember cause I asked him for some change to buy a book that I circled in red pen. He looked at the paper, at my crooked red circle, and cried.

"KB!" Nia's voice yells from inside.

"What?" I know I ain't allowed to answer that way. When somebody calls my name, I gotta say **yes** or at least **huh**, but never **what**, not even to Nia, or Momma will yell. She says it's disrespectful. But Momma ain't here and Nia ain't the boss of me. "What?" I say again, louder this time. Nia is on the porch now and smiling like I ain't seen in weeks.

"Granddaddy says we can go to the swimming pool today!" Nia thinks she's telling me the best news in the world, but I only pretend to be excited. I ain't ever liked swimming pools, mostly cause I can't swim. Nobody ever taught me and when

I tried to teach myself, I nearly drowned when Momma and Nia weren't paying attention.

"Really," I answer with an exaggerated smile. But then I think bout my list and my empty paper bag. I bet it might be easier to find bottles at the pool than around Granddaddy's too-clean neighborhood. This might not be so bad after all.

"Let's go find our bathing suits!" Nia runs into the house with steps that are more like hops, so I do, too. But my excitement is for a different reason than hers.

"Okay!" I follow Nia to our room and grab my paper bag—still folded on the end table where I left it—on the way.

I search through the old backpack that holds all my clothes, looking for something to wear. I know it won't be a bathing suit, cause I ain't got one. At home, we usually just swim in long T-shirts and undies, or shorts if we go to the neighborhood pool, even if we get funny looks for dressing that way. I find a pair of Nia's old gymnastics shorts and a too-small tank top I can tie on one side. From far away, it might even look like a bathing suit.

I get dressed and wait for Nia to change in the bathroom. She used to get dressed in front of me, but lately she's always screaming for privacy and covering her body with her hands if I look her way. I'm surprised when she comes out in a real bathing suit. Red and blue with tiny white stripes, too saggy up top and pinched underneath, but it's a bathing suit. I don't know where she got it from, but for once she ain't complaining bout how she looks, so I don't ask.

"Ready?" I ask, interrupting her hair ritual. She looks at me through the mirror and smiles. Not quite an ice cream cone smile, but close.

The neighborhood swimming pool is packed. Maybe cause it's so hot, or maybe cause it ain't nowhere else to go around here on a Saturday. Kids fight for space on the pool steps. Mommas lay on lounge chairs or talk together in small circles. Big kids play pool games in the deep end, while little kids hang on the blue-and-white safety rope in the middle of the pool. Everybody is screaming and playing, yelling and fighting. I love the quiet at Granddaddy's house, but this feels more like home.

Granddaddy stayed in the car when we got here, so it's just me and Nia. We walk around the pool area twice looking for seats but can't find none. Even with sandals on, the cement burns our feet as we search. Finally, we pick a small piece of wet ground by the gate. We take off our shoes, holding the gate for balance. I got my paper bag hid inside my towel, cause I ain't want Nia asking me no questions. As she lays down her towel, I sneak the bag out, quickly sit down on my towel, and hide the bag underneath.

I look around the pool area. Just like Granddaddy's neighborhood, don't seem to be no bottles around here, cept the ones people are still drinking from. I watch, hoping somebody might finish soon. There's a family with a white momma but a Black daddy, and a baby girl who's a strange mix of the two. The daddy—who drinks from a short bottle of Coca-Cola—is missing a tooth right in the front and has tattoos all over his neck and arms. The momma—who ain't drinking right now but has a bottle of juice peeking out from her bag—has rolls of skin falling from the sides of her swimsuit, and pale skin that don't match with the bright red hair falling down her back. She holds the baby, who got rolls of skin like her momma and no teeth like her daddy, but in a way that's cute cause she's a baby. I watch and watch, but after a while I get bored cause it don't seem like they gon' finish with them bottles anytime soon.

There's a group of kids in the pool, three boys and two girls, all with skin like Daddy's and lips kinda like Momma's. Two of the boys look like almost teenagers, one maybe older than the other, but the third boy is the baby of the group. He sits on the pool steps splashing water while they play. The girls look like they bout my age. They take turns dipping their heads beneath the water as one of the older boys counts. Ringlets of hair fall straight beneath the water, then coil like a spring soon as the girls come back to the surface. I smile cause my hair coils up like that, too.

Nia is beside me, but not watching like I do. She lays on her back with her eyes closed, knees slightly bent, face offered up to the sky. Even though them other girls are pretty, Nia is still the prettiest girl I've ever seen. I wonder if I ask Nia can we go play with those kids, would she say yes? But before I can ask, a voice yells from cross the pool. "Nia!"

I look for the voice, but not faster than Nia. She pops up and yells back. "Brittany!"

A yellow-skinned girl with thick lips and knobby knees hurries over from the other side of the pool. Her bathing suit looks just like Nia's, but with stars where Nia's got stripes. I bet that's not a coincidence. Brittany stands in front of me and wrings her thick, black hair in her hands, letting it cascade down her back. "I'm so glad you came!" she exclaims and rushes into Nia's arms for a hug.

"Of course, I couldn't wait to get out of that boring house!" Nia and Brittany giggle and I realize what happened: Nia ain't ever wanna come to the pool with me. She wanted to come to the pool with Brittany. I stand up and walk away, thinking maybe Nia gon' be sad to see me go and come after me. But when I turn and look back, she ain't even noticed I'm gone.

I walk around the pool twice before I find a spot. Right next to the Black kids I been watching. I sit on the edge and poke my foot in the water. I think it's gon' be cold, but the water is lukewarm and wraps around my toes like wet dog kisses. I pretend not to listen as the smallest boy whines. The two big boys toss a football back and forth. The little boy stretches his arms like baby bird wings but can't reach the ball. The girls go under, touch the bottom, and then kick their legs to the top. I think they're tryna make a handstand, but ain't neither of their legs staying in the air long enough.

"Dang, Dominique," yells the biggest boy suddenly, "you splashin' us!" The tallest of the two girls—Dominique, I guess—shakes her hair to make water spray the boys' faces. Then she laughs and the other girl laughs, too. But the boys ain't laughing.

"That ain't funny!" squeaks the smallest boy. He got a half grin on his face that makes me think he likes the splashing. But the big boys mad, so he gotta be mad, too.

"My bad." Dominique smiles, diving underwater for another half handstand. The boys watch and so do I. She gets her legs just barely out the water, then kicks real hard and real fast. Water splashes on the boys and splashes on me.

"**Dominique!**" the big boys scream all at once, while the other girl and the little boy laugh and laugh. I wanna laugh, too, but I think they gon' notice me watching if I do.

Nia's still in our spot with Brittany, laying close together on Nia's towel, whispering and pointing at a group of boys on the other side of the pool. The boys got small hoops in their ears and when they jump in the pool, they yell, "Cannonball!" loud so everybody can hear. To me, them boys are making too much noise. But Nia keeps smiling and whispering and pointing their way. I roll my eyes, then go back to making circles with my big toe in the water. I wonder if Granddaddy is still in the parking lot, cause I'm ready to leave.

"Wanna play with us?"

I ain't notice the girls coming over, Dominique and the other one. They stand in front of me in the water but don't smile. The girl whose name I don't know got tiny braids all over her head, and tugs on them while they wait for my answer.

"My name is Dominique, and this is Porsha."

I smile and finally they smile, too. Porsha's smile is wide with teeth too close together in the front. Dominique's smile is gone before I can figure out what it's like, so it don't make me feel as good as Porsha's smile.

"I'm Kenyatta," I say. "But everybody calls me KB." Porsha nods then lowers her head quick. I think she feels nervous just like me. But Dominique ain't nervous. She starts flapping her arms and legs in the water as we talk. Like it ain't no big deal to ask a strange new girl to play. Most times, at school, I stay by myself. But I wanna play with these girls today. Maybe cause Nia laughing so loud from cross the pool that I can hear the cackles ringing in my ears.

"Sure, I'll play," I say. Porsha smiles but Dominique don't seem to care. She would be happy either way, I think.

I lower my body into the water, making sure not to get too close to the deep end. Dominique can swim and paddles over to the rope, bobbing her head up and down as she goes. When she dips under the water, she takes a deep breath first, then blows it out loud when she comes back to the top. Porsha follows her close, but it looks like she can't swim, either, just hops up and down on one foot, jerking a choppy path through the water.

"Let's play Marco Polo," announces Dominique. She knows Porsha and me will do what she says. "I'm Marco," she tells us, then suddenly yells, "Marco!" with her eyes closed tight.

Porsha hops away quick, yelling, "Polo!" so I do the same. I yell fast and try to swim, throwing my body forward with arms and legs flailing. I sink right to the bottom instead, swallowing two cheeks full of water as I go. I push off the bottom and explode up from the water fast, coughing and coughing and watching for Dominique.

"Marco," she screams, right beside me now.

"Polo," responds Porsha, but I don't. I make a move to escape, but Dominique catches the edge of my shorts in her hands. "Gotcha!" Dominique pops her eyes open with a smirk. Porsha hops back over to us. Now I think I am Marco, and I don't wanna play no more.

"You gotta close your eyes and count to ten," explains Porsha. She seems almost as nervous as me. Dominique swims off toward the deep end. I'm gon' drown if I close my eyes in the water, I just know it. I look around for Nia and finally find her, standing with the group of boys. Brittany is talking, and all the boys listen, cept one, who's too busy looking at Nia wringing water from her curls.

"Come on, close your eyes!" Dominique yells from cross the pool. Porsha ain't too far away yet and smiles at me from her spot by the pool wall.

I sigh and close my eyes, prepared to die. "Marco," I barely whisper.

"Polo!" Their voices come from nowhere. I leave a small slit open at the bottom of my eyes but still am lost. I take one tiny step forward, float my arms out around me.

"Marco." A bit louder this time, but still no more than a murmur.

"Polo!" Through my secret peeking hole, I see brown feet in the water. I lunge forward and wrap my arms around a solid bulk.

"Gotcha!" I squeal, proud. I open my eyes and see the grip I have around the sturdy, tanned neck of the second-biggest boy. He grins big so that all his teeth show. I throw my arms down too fast, spraying water cross both our faces.

"Sorry," I whisper. If I was white, I bet my skin would be lit red like flames. But luckily my yellow skin don't give me away. I keep my head and eyes low, hoping I might disappear.

"Eww, you wanna kiss my cousin!" Dominique screeches, swimming our way with puckered lips and batting eyes. I think the boy is blushing, but his skin is too dark to tell. I look up and find him looking at me. His eyes are coals, cept right near the middle where they melt into dark chocolate. All his full features make him look like a cartoon. Wide nose, thick lips, and coarse hair on his head that he wears in two fat braids.

"It's okay," he says finally. I don't know if I should leave or stay. I wanna stay, but I ain't ever had a boy looking at me like this one. "My name is Rondell. What's yours?"

By now Dominique has swum over and Porsha has half hopped, half swum over, and them and all the boys are together in front of me. I stare down at my wavy feet in the blue water. "Kenyatta," I whisper to all of 'em, but Rondell smiles like my answer is only his. I feel like they are all staring at me and I want it to stop. I look at Rondell and have an idea.

"You're it," I shout in his direction, then run-walk through the water before anyone can stop me. My plan works. I hear everybody splashing as they swim away from Rondell. He closes his eyes and counts. I am free.

We laugh and play til my fingertips wrinkle. Marco Polo, then tag, then volleyball with an old beach ball someone left behind. Once they figure out that I can't swim, everybody takes turns tryna teach me how. I don't wanna leave when Nia finds me and tells me it's time to go. I notice that boy is still looking at her as we walk away. And Rondell is still looking at me.

Granddaddy is waiting in the car when we reach the parking lot. I can't tell if he's been there the whole time or just pulled up. We climb in the back seat, hair dripping puddles on the cold leather. In the locker room, we changed into dresses. Nia's is long, to her ankles, the color of ripe watermelon. When she walks, the dress pools at her feet like she's walking on water. My dress is just an ugly blue-jean thing I got from the secondhand store. It stops just above my knees, ashy now since I ain't put no lotion on after the pool. I lick my thumb and rub a smear of spit through the chalky white, wishing my dress hid my knees, like Nia's.

"You girls like shopping?" Granddaddy speaks his first words since we got in the car, as he slows to a stop at a yellow light. I reach my hand down under the seat, where I hid my book when we left the house this morning.

"Yes!" Nia screams. I quickly sit back up. I think Granddaddy's chuckling, but the quiet rumble is gone before I can tell.

"Good," he replies. "We gon' go see the new mall. I gotta find a new pair of pants for church tomorrow, and maybe a little something extra." Granddaddy winks at me through the rearview mirror. I hope this means he finally ain't mad at me no more for asking bout Momma.

We drive for a while to get to the mall. The digital clock on Granddaddy's dashboard ain't moved since 5:45 a.m. some morning, so I can't tell how long we been driving. But I count thirty-three traffic lights and read fifteen pages of my book, so I know it's far.

The mall is a squat, gray building. I don't think it's too big til we drive around. Then the building stretches cross enough space to fill bout three of our malls back in Detroit. The parking lot is filled from end to end with cars. Granddaddy circles around to find a space to park. People walk past us with arms full of bags, stuffed to the top with clothes and shoes and who knows what else. I ain't ever seen this many people out shopping. For one, Momma never takes us to the mall. Seems like people in Detroit would rather spend their money on cigarettes and beer and lotto tickets than new clothes and shoes.

We finally find a spot, all the way at the end of the parking lot. Granddaddy parks, slow. We wait for him to turn off the car and open his door before we get out, just like Momma taught us. I start to bring my book into the mall with me, but Granddaddy gives me a quick look that says, **Put it back**. Then he opens the trunk and pulls out a long wooden stick.

"What's that?" I ask.

"My cane," Granddaddy says, placing the stick in the grip of his right hand. He leans his weight on the cane, then closes the trunk.

"What's it for?" I ask. I've seen a cane before, but never in the hands of someone I know.

"Well, how you think I'm gon' walk around that place without it?" Granddaddy jokes, pointing the tip of his cane toward the sprawling mall. Now that I think of it, Granddaddy always walks slow, kinda hobbling from one leg to the other. Not as bad as his friend Charlie, but still slow.

"Okay," is my quiet reply. I don't wanna make Granddaddy feel bad for his limp, so I don't say anything else.

We walk slow through the parking lot, Granddaddy huffing and hobbling as we go. When we finally make it to the door, Granddaddy is breathing so hard I think we should just go back. But he labors on and Nia don't even notice nothin' wrong, so I follow.

"I'm gonna go look for some pants," announces Granddaddy once we're inside. "You girls go on, buy whatever you like." He hands Nia a wad of cash, big like we ain't ever seen. Nia's eyes light up as she takes the money from Granddaddy's out-stretched hands. And I bet my eyes light up, too, cause I ain't know Granddaddy had so much money. I been running around Lansing looking for bottles all this time and turns out Granddaddy got all the money I need.

"Whatever we like?" Nia asks cautiously. I can almost see the ideas circling around in her head. All I can think bout is how quick we could get back home with that much money.

"Yeah," says Granddaddy, "just make sure to get a dress to wear to church tomorrow. And meet

me right here, right inside these doors in"—
Granddaddy looks at his watch, then points at the
giant clock in the center of the food court cross
from us—"let's say forty-five minutes." With that,
Granddaddy hobbles off, and me and Nia are left
standing there with more money than we know
how to spend.

"Where you wanna go first?" I ask Nia, after
we've been standing in one place for too long.
People might start to wonder why two little girls
are standing in the middle of the mall with a lot of
money and no grown-up. While I wait for Nia to
respond, I watch a group of teenagers stroll past,
the boys in baggy pants and the girls in short
shorts. Nia watches them, too, keeping her eyes
trained on them as she stuffs the money in her
pocket. She keeps two bills in her hands, though,
which she hands to me: a twenty and a ten.

"Go wherever you want, okay?" Nia smiles at
me, but the smile don't even reach her eyes before
she turns and walks away in the direction of the
loud teenagers, leaving me alone in the middle of
the mall. I stand there for a minute wondering why
I even feel surprised. This the new Nia now, no
matter how hard I try to make it different. I spot a
bench up ahead and go sit down. I need a plan.

While I think, I look around at the people
walking by. Most of them are in groups—friends,
boyfriends and girlfriends, husbands and wives,

parents and their kids. Everybody is laughing and talking and shopping, no other cares in the world. I ain't ever seen people be so happy and so free. A family of white people with a momma and a daddy and a son and a daughter walks past. The kids hold leaning ice cream cones that they lick as they walk. The momma and daddy hold hands. I ain't ever seen my momma and daddy hold hands in all my life. The little boy skips ahead too far, and I hear the daddy call out to him. He runs back and hops on his daddy's back, passing his ice cream to his momma as he climbs. The momma smiles and the sister laughs and the son rides on the daddy's back.

I feel silly to be watching these strangers so long. The lump is back in my throat. We can't ever be happy like them kids. Not with a dead daddy and no home of our own. I stand up quick, force myself to stop thinking bout Daddy and start thinking bout where I can find books. I know I still need money for gettin' home, and for a minute, I wrestle with the idea of using the money to try to buy a bus ticket home to Detroit. I could pop up on Momma and surprise her at the motel. Well, that is, if she's even at the motel. She would be mad at first, if I just showed up, but I bet after a while, she would just be glad to see me. I think bout it hard, but as I'm thinking I also remember all the stuff that's happened. Daddy dying,

Momma leaving. And all the stuff in between. I run my fingers over the lump of cash in my pocket and decide that right now, I just wanna buy something that's gon' make me feel better.

I walk over to a big board in the middle of the mall that's got a map of all the stores. I find words at the bottom with categories of all the stuff you can find. Clothes, shoes, music, restaurants. I keep looking til finally I spot the word **books** at the end. There's only one store in this whole big mall that has books. I find a little sticker that says, YOU ARE HERE, all the way cross the mall from the bookstore. I start walking.

I count seven shoe stores, two jewelry stores, twelve clothing stores, and one small candle shop; then I am finally at the bookstore. I walk inside quick, but then I'm stuck frozen right away. I ain't ever seen so many new books in one place. Usually, all my books come from the secondhand store. We don't even get books from the library no more, cause Momma says we owe some money.

These books ain't nothin' like the books in the secondhand store. I run my fingertips along spines that smell like fresh trees and feel sturdy in my hands. I look around at the sections of books to choose from and find two sections that might be for me: kids and young adult. I can't decide where I fit between the two. I look over at the kids' section, where there's a Black girl with braided hair, bout my age, reading a book with her momma. Then I peek at the young adults' section, where there's a teenager bout Nia's age, quietly thumbing through a book on her own. I take one last look at the little girl and her momma, then wander over to young adult.

The first book I pick up is called **The Secret Garden**. On the cover, there is a little girl dressed in all white—white dress, white shoes, white hat—to match her pale skin. She stands in front of a strange door, looks like it's hiding beneath a bunch of vines and trees. I turn to the back cover to read more. After some words I can't understand but some I can, I think it's a story bout a girl, bout my age, who loses her parents but finds a secret garden. Even though the garden is old and dying, she tries to bring it back to life again.

I don't look at another book. I head straight to the cashier with **The Secret Garden** hugged close to my chest. I can't be sure, but I bet this will be my new best book.

"That will be nine dollars and fifty cents." The cashier gives me a look like he knows I ain't old enough to be here in this store, buying books by myself. But I reach casually in my pocket for the money wadded at the bottom. Like I been having money and buying stuff by myself for years. The last time I had money to buy something, besides lotto tickets, was five dollars that I got from Daddy for gettin' all A's on my report card. But then he came back the next day after giving it to me and wanted the money back. Cept I had already spent it on a pack of pencils, two quarter bags of Hot Cheetos, and a two-liter of peach Faygo that I split with Nia.

I take the two bills from my pocket, slide the twenty-dollar bill cross the counter. "Here you go," I whisper, hearing Momma's voice in my head telling me it costs too much. It's too much to spend on one thing, and especially cause it's one thing I want, and not one thing I need.

"You can just give me the ten if you want," says the boy, nodding in the direction of my other crumpled bill.

"Nah, I need this one for something else," I say, embarrassed to let him know that I wanna spend the twenty just to get all the change. He fake smiles, like he knows I'm a liar but gotta be nice anyway.

"Here's your change. Have a nice day." He looks away as he passes me a handful of bills and coins that I stuff in my pocket before running out the door with my book and receipt.

As soon as I am far enough away, I reach my hand in my pocket and shake the fabric so that the coins move around. They clink in my pocket like tiny bells. I take out a five-dollar bill, hold it to my nose, and sniff in, deep. The smell is new again every time I smell it, like my uniform shirts on the days Momma brings them back from the laundromat, crisp and folded. I shove the bill back into my pocket and think I might add this money to my getting-home fund, since I ain't found any bottles. But then I remember Granddaddy said we need to buy a dress for church, so I look for another store.

I walk and walk til I spot a store up ahead with a mannequin in the window wearing a pretty dress with pink flowers and dancing green stems. I'm nervous cause I never shopped alone, but I stroll inside and begin to look around. The store is big, with clothes for kids and for grown-ups. I wanna touch everything on the racks. I imagine what it would be like to run my fingers cross fabric soft like cotton candy or smooth like butter. But I don't touch, cause whenever we're in stores, Momma always tells me don't touch nothin' and don't ask for nothin'.

I walk around the store two times before I finally find the dress from the window. It looks even better up close. It's all white, with little flowers that are decorated pink and green and yellow, like fresh-watered blossoms in a garden. The dress ain't too long or too short. It's perfect.

"Can I help you?" A woman with a red tag on her shirt and red lipstick clinging to her teeth approaches, looking down at me over the top of too-big glasses.

"No," I whisper, looking down at the ground. The woman stays there for a minute, watching me, but since I stay frozen, she eventually walks away. I let go of the breath I been holding.

I stare at the rack, filled with that same dress over and over, search for my size. This past winter I grew outta my 8/10 clothes and had to move up to the next size, with my very first 10/12 hand-me-down dress, burgundy and stiff, a gift for my daddy's funeral. I find the last dress in my size and check the price tag: $89.99. I put it back on the rack and leave the store, rushing past the saleslady, who's still watching me with mean eyes. No point even looking around more, when I already found the perfect dress that I can't have.

"Kenyatta," speaks a voice behind me just as I leave the store. It's Granddaddy, slowly shuffling my way. I look past him at that giant food court clock and it's only been thirty-six minutes, so I guess Granddaddy got back over here early. But right on time.

"Granddaddy." I plan to smile, but instead my eyes fill with tears as soon as I speak.

"What's wrong?" Granddaddy asks, now standing in front of me. I want him to reach out and touch my shoulder, or maybe even give me a hug.

But he just stands there. Cane in one hand, shopping bag in the other.

"I found a dress for church," I sniffle, "but I ain't got enough money to buy it." We're still standing outside the store with the mannequin in front, wearing my dress proud like a flag. I look at the faceless figure and frown.

"Well, how much is it?" Granddaddy uses his cane to nudge me out the way of a group of boys who are making a bunch of noise and bumping into a bunch of people.

"Eighty-nine ninety-nine." I avoid looking at Granddaddy when I tell him the price. I bet he'll laugh. If Momma was here, she'd tell me that's too much money to spend on one dress. We could go to the secondhand store and get ten dresses for that same amount. "This is all I have left." I hand Granddaddy the change from the bookstore.

"Come on," Granddaddy says, pocketing the change and hobbling into the store. Toward my dress. He finds it on the rack in the back, right where I left it. I grab the 10/12 and hold it up for Granddaddy to see.

"Like it?" With the dress pressed against me, I twirl around once, tiny. I think I see Granddaddy smile, just a little bit, as I spin. It reminds me of a moment I once pretended to have with Daddy, cept this one is real.

"Beautiful," is Granddaddy's simple reply. Without another word, he leads me to the cash register, where he pays $89.99 for the dress that makes me twirl.

Two hours later—cause it took us almost an hour just to find Nia, who I guess ain't pay much attention to the whole meeting time and place—we pull into Granddaddy's driveway. He pops the trunk, where Nia's bags fill the whole thing from end to end. I think Granddaddy gon' be mad that she spent so much money, but he don't say nothin'. And seems like Nia's happy for it, cause she's been smiling at him all sweet since we left the mall.

As I search through the pile for my one bag, I think bout Granddaddy buying me that dress. Not only does he have a lot of money, but seems like he is also ready to give it to people, if that's what's gon' make them people happy. It makes me feel special, knowing that Granddaddy cares bout making me happy. I'm not really used to anybody spending a lot of money on me. There was this one guy at church who used to buy me and Nia candy and give it to us after service, but Momma found out and yelled at him, so he never did it again.

Other than that, the only time people ever really bought me stuff was sometimes on my birthday, most of the time on Christmas, and every once in a while, when I got all A's on my report card—like I always did—somebody would give me a quarter or a dollar for the accomplishment. Even Daddy gave me that five dollars, once. But never Momma. Momma bought us food and clothes and took care of us and stuff, but she was not the type to just be giving us money all willy-nilly.

"KB," Nia's yelling, grabbing her bags, "don't forget about our clothes."

It feels like days ago that we went to the swimming pool, but my wet clothes on the floor of the car remind me of wrinkled fingers and Marco Polo. And Rondell. I grab my dripping clothes, my new best book, and the bag that holds my new best dress and head to the porch without waiting for Nia.

Granddaddy unlocks the front door and I head inside. I wanna try on my dress, twirl and twirl around the room til I can't stand up straight. But as soon as I walk in the bedroom, Nia comes in behind me.

"I like your dress," I whisper as I watch her take it out the bag.

Nia shrugs. "It's okay, I guess." She lays it out on the bed before rummaging through her other bags. From what I can tell, she bought jewelry, shoes, and makeup, too.

"You gon' try it on?" I ask, pointing at the dress. Nia shrugs again. I can't believe she's acting like all this ain't no big deal, when we ain't never went shopping at the mall and bought so much new stuff like this.

"Remember that time Momma told us she was gon' take us shopping for school, and we got all excited and circled stuff in that store ad from the newspaper?" I can't tell if Nia's listening, but she stops digging through her bags, so I keep going. "But then we found out that shopping just meant Momma taking us to a bunch of different garage sales, all in a row?" The memory fills my mind and I start to laugh. To my surprise, Nia laughs, too. Back then, it was more sad than funny, but for right now, it's got me and Nia laughing together.

"The hilarious thing," Nia says between chuckles, "is how we took the ads with us to the garage sales, thinking we might still find the same stuff there."

"Momma was so mad when you asked that old lady if she could show you the brand-name section."

"Oh my gosh, I forgot about that!" Nia buries her face in her hands. "She was fussing at us the whole way home."

"Yeah," I say, but then my voice trails off as I remember what happened after that. After a long, tense car ride, we got home and found Daddy passed out on the kitchen floor. I can still see the terror on Nia's face as she ran through the front door, yelling Daddy's name. Momma screamed at me to call 911 while she and Nia slapped Daddy and poured water on his face. Before I could dial the final 1, he was awake, and I knew to hang up, quick, before someone showed up.

Looks like Nia's remembering that bad part, too, cause she goes back to digging through her bags with a faraway look in her eyes, her laughter a distant memory.

I turn to the closet and pull my new dress out the bag. Just a minute ago, I wanted to try it on and twirl. Seems like every time I get my hopes up bout something, another thing happens to remind me that even the good stuff is always tainted with bad. I hang my dress in the back of the empty closet. As I reach the door, I turn back to take one last look, but the flowers are already invisible in the shadows.

Night arrives the same way each time. A chill in the air I can't quite call cold, even though it makes the little hairs on my arms stand straight.

Fireflies lighting patterns I sometimes chase, but other times I simply watch. Different dinners cooking, blending together into one big smell that blankets the block. Then, the quiet. A gentle stillness that weaves its way through, til there's nothin' left but peace. Despite the dark, night is my favorite time of day.

I sit on the front porch with my new book in my lap, but tonight, I can't read. I'm thinking bout how these days, seems like everybody I know is keeping secrets from me. I know Momma keeps secrets to protect me and Nia from bad stuff. That's why she never told us why Daddy would leave the house in the middle of the night, even though I'd hear the squeaking screen door when he returned, and Momma's shouted whispers soon after. I know Granddaddy is keeping secrets cause he ain't sure how much stuff Momma wants us to know. Seems like all grown-ups lie to kids, just cause they can.

But Nia ain't always used to hide stuff from me. Back when we used to be best friends, before she started trying so hard to act like a grown-up, all her secrets were mine. She'd whisper them in my ear at the dinner table, and we'd hide laughs between bites. I don't know when exactly Nia started to act different, or why.

I chew my thumb and watch a baby caterpillar crawl cross the porch, then onto my ankle. One time, I tried to talk to Momma bout it, bout how Nia was acting different and not playing with me no more. But Momma kept sweeping without even looking up at me, only patting my head like I was a dog and saying, "She's growing up, KB. It's gon' happen to you, too, one day." The thing I ain't understand then or now was why growing up had to mean Nia couldn't be my friend no more.

"Kenyatta." Granddaddy's voice booms from inside. I pinch the caterpillar carefully and set it down on the porch before heading inside, where Granddaddy's sittin' in his usual place, in front of the TV. But the screen is blank and the house is quiet, cept the muffled sounds from outside. Crickets, flowing water, and a train in the distance. And even more distant, the drip-drip-drip of Nia taking a shower.

"Yes?" I tentatively open the door and step into the warm room. I hope he ain't bout to make me explain wanting a dress that cost so much money. Or why me and Nia was split up when he found us. Granddaddy surprises me by tapping the space on the couch beside him with his calloused hand.

I join Granddaddy on the couch, but he don't speak for a while. I wonder if he just called me over to keep him company, not to say anything. But then he starts to speak, not looking right at me but past me, like he's worried bout what he's gon' say.

"The other day, you asked me bout your momma." The sentence hangs in the air between us, with neither of us willing to go up and grab it, pull it back down. I ain't think we would talk bout this again. Seems like Granddaddy ain't really think it through, cause now he sits with nothin' more to say. I peel dirt out from beneath my fingernails while I wait for him to say something else. I can't think of nothin' to count, so I just peel and peel. Finally, after seven fingernails, Granddaddy coughs and shifts his seat on the couch.

"I was mad when you asked bout where your momma was at," he continues calmly, like all them fingernails wasn't between his last sentence and this one. "But I shouldn't be mad. Cause you got every right to know."

"Know what?" I fidget in my spot, crossing and uncrossing my ankles.

Granddaddy looks at me now. "When your momma left you and your sister here in Lansing, it was cause she needed some time on her own. To figure some stuff out."

"What stuff?" I ask quick, before he can say more.

"Well." Granddaddy clears his throat. "Your daddy dying, it really took a toll on your momma. She's a strong woman, bout the strongest person I know. But right now, she just needs a little extra help."

"Cause she been so sad?" I think back on all of

Momma's smiles since Daddy died. Seemed like she was tryna make 'em look the same, but they wasn't quite right.

Granddaddy nods. "Exactly," he says. "Your momma is real sad. And she needs a little extra help to feel better right now. So that's what she's doing, getting help." Granddaddy clears his throat, like he tryna decide what to say next. "I'm gon' tell you the whole truth, Kenyatta, cause it seems like you old enough to know what's going on. Okay?"

I nod so fast I make myself dizzy.

"Your momma is in something called an in-patient facility, where she sees a psychotherapist to help her deal with her depression. That's what it's called, the type of sadness your momma is dealing with. Depression. It's not just like regular sadness. Depression can make you angry as much as it can make you sad. And it was making your momma feel so tired and anxious that she felt scared bout what would happen, so she knew she needed some help. She needed some time away, to focus on nothing but getting better."

I sit there awhile, tryna sort through all the big words and big ideas. "How you know all that?" I ask. "You been depressed before, too?"

Granddaddy laughs. "Well, I'm sure I have, but we ain't used to have a name for it back then. Black folks always say that ain't nothin' we goin through that God can't fix. Your momma the one that taught me that even with God, we still might need help in other ways, too."

I sit there not saying anything. After a while, Granddaddy reaches over and takes my hand. I look at my hand in his and it looks tiny. But in his big, warm hands, my hands also look comfortable. Safe.

"Kenyatta, you know that your momma would rather be with you girls than anywhere else in the world, right?"

I nod. I start to feel the tickle in my throat that lets me know I might cry, but I try to hold it back. "You think she gon' get better?" I finally ask. To my surprise, Granddaddy laughs.

"I know she gon' get better," he says, "cause your momma always does whatever she puts her mind to."

I can't help but smile, cause I know it's true.

"She was just like you when she was little," Granddaddy says with a sigh. "Always with a book in her hands and a million thoughts in her head."

"She was like me?" I ask. I always figured Momma was just like Nia as a kid, since they both seem so alike now. Quiet and moody.

Granddaddy don't answer with words, just stands, slow, and walks to the bookshelf. He reaches down and picks up the large brown book that I noticed before and figured was a photo album. It takes him a while to stand back up, but finally Granddaddy carries the book back to the couch and sits beside me. Turns out, it is a photo album, and when he opens it, dust rises and falls from the cover. I wonder how long it's been closed, and how many days and weeks and years are stuffed inside. I always secretly wished for a photo album filled with pictures of me, like maybe Momma had been collecting photos and macaroni art and birthday cards since I was born, and all of it was stuffed between the pages of some old, dusty book that I'd find one day, and remember it all. But if Momma was keeping a book like that, she was hiding it real good, cause I ain't ever even seen a picture of myself as a baby.

Granddaddy balances the album on his knees and opens to the first page, which has two pictures, black-and-white, of a woman I don't know. She has hair like dark, coiled yarn, and skin that melts one feature smooth into the next. In the first picture, she is sittin' in a wicker chair. Even though it's not the same room in the picture, it looks like the same wicker chair in Granddaddy's living room. I take a quick peek to be sure. I wanna count the strands on each chair to see if they match, but Granddaddy might turn the page. In the second picture, the woman stands in front of a small house. She is holding something in her arms, a blanket wrapped tight.

"Who is she?" I ask, pointing at that second picture, where her smile stretches cross her black-and-white face.

"That's your granny," is his quiet reply. I stare at the picture in silence. Momma never talked bout no granny, but here she is, smiling like Momma.

"This is the day we had your momma," he finally continues, pointing at the wrapped-up blanket. Turns out the blanket is Momma, so small I can't even see her in the faded image. I knew Momma had her own momma, cause I know for having babies you need a daddy and a momma and some eggs, but I ain't sure how many or exactly for what. But I do know that Granddaddy was the daddy and this granny who Momma never mentioned was her momma.

I wonder how Momma could forget to tell me bout her, cause in just one minute of staring at her picture, I think she might have the best face I've ever seen. Her hair is straighter than mine and longer than Nia's, with soft bows clipped by her ears. Since I can't see the colors, I imagine the bows are bright red like ripe cherries. She is wearing a short dress that dances on one side, like the wind was blowing that day, and she has to pull and tug to keep the blanket wrapped around her baby.

Granddaddy turns to the next page, which has just one photo. The woman again—Granny—and a dark-skinned man with a soft face and big smile. He holds her hand and she has flowers in her braided hair.

"Is that you?"

"Yes. On the day I married your granny," Granddaddy says, and for the first time I wonder if Granddaddy's quiet ain't from being mean, but from being sad. I study the picture. Granny and Granddaddy are outside, but it don't look much like a wedding, cept for the flowers. Blooming buds are everywhere—in Granny's hair, on the ground, pinned to Granddaddy's jacket—and I bet they are all different colors like the flowers in the field. I bet Granddaddy picked them all and when he gave them to her, she smiled. I ain't ever seen Daddy give Momma flowers. And that's not the only way I notice they are different. Daddy ain't ever have this much time to spend, just talking and remembering and being with me. Granddaddy don't seem to mind the time at all.

We look at pictures for what feels like days, probably cause so many days go by in the pictures. Granddaddy tells me stories bout all of 'em. And not like before, when I had to make him talk to me. Now the words pour out of Granddaddy as quickly as we can turn the pages. First, Momma as a baby. Then the wedding. Christmas and New Year's and Easter, then Christmas again. Some are inside a small house bout big as our motel room and dark like a cave, some outside, the sun so bright all the faces look like they're glowing.

My favorite is one of Momma. Looks like she's bout my age now, with glasses big as her face and the same smile lighting her cheeks. I like all the special holiday pictures, but my favorite is this regular ol' day, Momma on the floor of a room with carpet thick as uncut grass, holding a doll in her hands. She ain't looking at the camera, only at that doll. In the background, Granny's watching Momma watch the doll. I guess it's Granddaddy taking the picture, so close I can see a glimmer of light reflected in Granny's dark eyes. Momma looks at that doll like she looks at me and Nia, smiles her best ice cream cone smile. I trace the worn edges of the photo with my fingertips, Momma's smile on my face.

But then I swallow hard. That giant lump in my throat is back, like when Daddy died. Or even before that, like the time he yelled at Momma and slammed the door so hard the house shook. I tried, for Momma, not to cry them times. And I try not to cry now, for me.

Granddaddy turns the page. I thought I would be sad to stop looking at the perfect picture, but now I feel relieved it's over. I watch as Granddaddy flips, more quickly now, through photos of Momma. Over and over, I watch Momma live and breathe in the yellowed snapshots. I see why Granddaddy said she was like me, cause in almost every picture, Momma got a book. Soon, Momma is older. I also see why people say Nia looks like her, cause in some of the pictures I think it's Nia, not Momma, laughing on the porch or singing in the choir. They even parade the same pose in pictures: hand on hip, turn to the side—but not the other side—half smile to show off a perfectly round dimple, then snap! I think bout goin' to get Nia to show her the pictures, showing her how much Momma looks like her; how much she looks like Momma.

Before I can, Granddaddy hands me the photo album so that it's laying in my lap, and I keep flipping through the pages while he goes to sit in the wicker chair from the photos. I smile at another picture of Momma and Granny, this time sittin' on the porch with Momma between Granny's knees and Granny braiding two braids in Momma's hair. Just like Momma braids mine. "What happened to Granny?" I ask, as I realize that the more I keep turning pages, the less she's in the pictures. In fact, after a while, she ain't in none of the pictures at all. Granddaddy don't answer right away, so I set down the album and creep closer, leaning on the arm of the couch.

"She died," is his eventual reply. I wait for more, but it don't come.

"When?" I finally ask. I know he don't wanna talk bout it, but I do.

"When your momma was ten."

I finally have the answer, and I don't know what to say. When Momma was ten? I think bout losing Momma now, when I'm ten, and suddenly the throat lump is even bigger. Losing Daddy wasn't no easy thing, but losing Momma? No wonder Momma never talks bout Granny. I bet the lump in her throat is so big by now that she couldn't even squeeze out the words if she tried. I open the photo album again and flip to my favorite picture, with Momma and the doll. It looks so different now, even though I'm looking through the same eyes. But different, somehow.

"That's the last picture of the two of them together." Granddaddy sits beside me again, resting his weight into mine so that we push each other straight. I look up from the photo album and into his dark eyes. Ain't no tears, but they're the saddest eyes I've ever seen.

"I bet you and Momma really had to be there for each other, once she was gone." I offer Granddaddy a smile, but he lowers his eyes like he just remembered something he ain't mean to remember. Then he takes a deep breath and reaches over to grab his Bible from the table.

"Your momma wanted to be on TV, did she

ever tell you that?" I shake my head, just as Granddaddy pulls a picture out from between the pages of his Bible. The picture looks old, with crumbling edges and yellowed sides. Just like the old photos from the album, but for some reason, kept separate.

I take the picture from his trembling hand. Momma ain't ever said nothin' bout being on TV. She acts like she don't like TV at all, since she never wants us to watch too much.

I look at the picture, and just like that, Momma is young again. Probably older than Nia, but still not quite a grown-up. She got makeup all on her face that makes her look like a life-sized doll. Her hair is curled tight on top of her head, with spiral ringlets falling into her frozen expression. I can't tell where she's at in the photo, cause it's so close that only her face shows. Her eyes are soft and her smile is true. I think it's the prettiest I've ever seen Momma, cept when she's sleeping. I love watching Momma when she's sleeping, and wild hair covers her calm face.

"That there was her headshot," Granddaddy interrupts my thoughts. "She begged and begged for one, but I always said no."

"What's a headshot?" I ask quick, before he can go on.

"It's a kind of picture that shows only your face. Just like this one." He strokes the image gently, like he's afraid it'll crumble in his hands. "You need one to get jobs like a model or an actress." I think he sees the confusion in my eyes, cause then he adds, "To be on TV."

"Oh." I look at the picture closer. "I bet Momma got a good job with this one." In my mind, I see Momma on TV, smiling her ice cream cone smile at the cameras. A grin stretches cross my face as I think bout Momma this way, but Granddaddy frowns.

"No, she ain't get no job at all." Granddaddy rubs one hand with the thumb from his other, first in slow circles but then faster. "Like I said, she was begging for a headshot for a while. But I kept saying no, mostly cause I ain't know nothing bout letting my little girl be on TV. And with her momma gone . . ." His voice trails off like he got lost in his thoughts.

I sit up straighter, try to look right in his eyes, but he keeps looking away. "So, if you kept saying no," I ask, "how did she get this picture?"

Granddaddy snaps out of it and, much to my surprise, laughs. "Well, have you ever tried to tell your momma no? It's not an easy thing to do." Now I laugh, too, cause I know what he means. Momma is always smiling and usually nice, cept when you try to tell her no.

Granddaddy continues. "I came home from work one day and found your momma sittin' on the couch, holding this picture in her hands. I could tell she was upset bout something before I could even tell what she was holding. She stood up, told me that she disobeyed my rules and got the headshot from some man she met at the mall." Here, Granddaddy pauses. I bet the memory hurts, cause Granddaddy slams his eyes shut.

"I looked at the photo"—Granddaddy takes it from my hands and looks at it like it's his first time—"and it was the most beautiful thing I had ever seen." I see tears forming puddles in his deep eyes. "She looks just like her momma, always has." I think he's gon' cry, but his tears are tiny soldiers, perfectly balanced on the edge of a steep hill. I need to learn his secret for keeping 'em up on that hill.

"So, what happened?" I wanna hear the rest of the story. Granddaddy silently folds his hands cross his lap and scoots over just a little bit, so we're no longer touching. His face is still sad, maybe too sad to talk, like he got a lump blocking his voice, just like mine.

"I made a mistake," is his quiet response.

"What did you do, Granddaddy?" I can't imagine what could be so bad that they would stop hugging when they see each other.

"I . . ." He stops, stares at the back of his cracked hands. "I told her I ain't even wanna hear nothing bout it." He swallows, hard. "Then I threw the picture down on the ground and"—Granddaddy pauses—"I left. She was the most excited I had ever seen her. And I acted like I ain't even care."

Listening to his story reminds me of the ways Daddy tried to keep Momma from doin' what she loved, too. Seems like her whole life has been bout doin' stuff for other people, but not doin' the stuff she actually wanted to do herself. Realizing this makes me sad for Momma, but I also can't help but feel bad for Granddaddy, who is still staring at his hands. I don't know how to respond without making Granddaddy feel worse. "Why?" I finally ask. Looking at him now I can see he does care, seems like a lot, so I can't understand why he would pretend like he don't.

"Sometimes, Kenyatta, parents make mistakes. I was afraid of so much back then. Having a daughter, not having a wife." Granddaddy shakes his head. "I ain't wanna lose my little girl, too." Grown-ups don't usually tell me this much, especially not quiet Granddaddy, so I consume each of his thoughtful words greedily.

"So, what did Momma say?"

Granddaddy chuckles. "She said, 'Just tell your friends I'm a star,' and stormed out the room before I could. We ain't talk for a whole week after, then when we did, it was never quite the same again. She thought I ain't believe in her. I thought she wanted to leave me. We couldn't find our way no more, after that." Granddaddy folds his hands cross his lap, pulling each fingertip with another as he talks.

I consider everything he said, tryna make sense of it all. "But why did she say to tell your friends she was a star, if you told her she couldn't even try?"

"Well, she knew that, and I knew that. But that was just her way of saying she ain't need me no more. I stopped her that time, but I ain't ever stop her again." Granddaddy takes one last look at the photo, so wonderful and heartbreaking, then sticks it back between the pages of his Bible. I wonder how long he's gon' keep it there, before he puts it back in the photo album. Or maybe it was never in the album to begin with. Maybe it always lives in his Bible, where he can look at it and regret.

"I bet Momma ain't mad no more," is all I can eventually say. But even I know that what happened to Momma and Granddaddy can't be changed. Just like two Christmases ago, when Momma finally saved enough money to buy us the TV we'd been begging for, but then Daddy took it away. I don't know what he did with it, but I know it was him, cause I heard Momma yelling at him bout it the next day. That was the first time I heard her use that word, **fiend**, but not the last. And I

can't be sure, but I think this is something like
that. A girl and her daddy, and something that
seems small but is too big to ever get through. It
can be that way, with daddies.

Me and Granddaddy don't say no more words. I
try to think of something to count, but truth is,
I just wanna leave. I think bout Granddaddy making Momma feel like he ain't care, and it makes me
feel sad more than anything else. Momma is
grown-up and probably don't care no more bout
headshots or being on TV. But I can't be sure, and
the thought of Momma alone in Detroit and sad
fills my head.

"Can I call Momma again?" I ask, quiet. I don't
want Granddaddy to think I'm taking sides.
Especially since he ain't been looking in my eyes
this whole conversation. But I need to talk to
Momma. It don't make much sense, but for
some reason, I feel like I can still fix it. I can help
Momma and Granddaddy be happy again. Take
pictures together and hug each other tight. I
already lost my daddy; I can't stand the thought of
Momma losing hers, too.

"I promise I won't say nothin' bout what you
told me, bout her treatment and everything."

Granddaddy chuckles. "Treatment?" He shakes
his head. "I see you more like your momma was as
a girl than I realized."

I ain't sure what Granddaddy means, til I

remember that the word **treatment** came from his conversation with Charlie, which I wasn't s'posed to be listening to. Oops.

"Oh," I start quickly, "I, umm—"

"It's okay," Granddaddy interrupts. "You can call her." He says it with a sigh, like he wants to say no but can't think of a good reason. I smile to show him I ain't mad. Just cause I wanna talk to Momma don't mean I can't smile at Granddaddy. I think.

Just like last time, Granddaddy dials the numbers and I wait for Momma to answer. Granddaddy heads back to the living room, leaving me alone with Momma. This time she answers on the second ring. I speed through all the **I miss you**s and **how you doing**s so I can get to the real reason for my call.

"Momma, I wanted to ask you something," I say, after listening to Momma pretend to be watching TV at the motel. I wait for Momma to respond, but the line is silent. "You still mad at Granddaddy bout that face picture?" I try to think of the right word, cause I know that's not right. "Headshot, I mean. You still mad at Granddaddy bout that headshot? Cause he's really sorry and I think y'all should hug again and be happy." I spit it all out, too fast. Momma don't respond. "Hello? Momma?"

"I'm here," she finally responds, but she don't say nothin' more.

"Did you hear what I—"

"KB, how many times I gotta tell you to stay out of grown folks' business?" I've heard that line a million times, mostly from Momma, but I ain't expect it now.

"But, Momma, it ain't like that! Granddaddy showed me the picture on his own, he wanted me to know—"

"He wanted you to know what?" Momma cuts me off, almost yelling now. "That he ain't want me to be happy? That when my momma died, I lost the only parent I had that loved me? That instead of protecting me, he hurt me?"

"Hurt you? Momma, what you mean? Granddaddy loves you. And they was just words. He ain't mean it."

"It was not just words!" Momma screams. "He—" I hear quiet sniffles coming through the phone, but no words. I ain't ever heard Momma yell like that. I don't know what to do, so I just hold the phone to my ear, frozen.

"I'm sorry," Momma finally cry-whispers. "I shouldn't have said all that to a little girl."

I wanna tell her she's wrong, that I love for her to tell me grown-up things. That I need to know more grown-up things so I can understand all that's happened. But before I can, she talks again.

"Gon' and wash up for dinner, now. I'll talk to you soon."

"But, Momma—" I try to stop her, but she's already gone from the line. I hang up the receiver and stand in the kitchen awhile. I could go to Nia, but I bet she won't want me there. I could go to Granddaddy, but I bet he's still sad. So I stand in the kitchen. Count all the things in my head that don't make no sense. Forty-two, then I lose count.

We wake early the next morning for church. Granddaddy plays loud music from the tiny stereo in the bathroom. Church music with booming organs and bouncy singing. I hum along to the songs I know, from when I was in the church choir in Detroit. We ain't been to church since we moved to the motel, so I've forgotten most of the words. I wonder why we don't go to church no more. Maybe cause it's so far away now. Or maybe cause the last time we did go to church, all the women in the big hats kept asking bout Daddy, and Momma kept lying.

I go to the closet in our small bedroom, where my church dress hangs next to Nia's. The two couldn't be more different. My flower dress looks immature beside Nia's ankle-length masterpiece. Her dress is rose colored, and when I sneak a feel, my fingertips melt into the cloth. I remove my dull garment from its hanger, where suddenly it hangs limp. I sigh. Time to get dressed.

But Nia ain't gettin' dressed yet. In fact, I don't know where she's at, cause she woke up early and left the room while I was still laying down, dreaming bout a firefly that learned to talk and lived in my pocket. Once I get dressed and force my hair into a fuzzy ponytail, I go to the kitchen to see if she's there. Granddaddy is at the table drinking his coffee and reading the paper, like always. But no Nia.

"Have you seen Nia?" I ask Granddaddy. It's the first we've talked since last night and I ain't so sure he wants to talk now, cause he barely looks my way.

"No," is his only reply, then he goes back to his paper.

I run out the front door, being careful not to let the ruffles on my dress get caught in the screen as it slams shut. I don't see Nia on the porch. She's not up in my tree, or out by the pond. I don't even stop to collect all the caterpillars I pass on the way, just look and look but I can't find Nia nowhere. I start a race against a bee back to the porch, when I hear a tiny noise that sounds like it's coming from under the house.

"Nia?" I tiptoe toward the noise, slow. I ain't sure if I'm gon' find Nia or a wild animal. Either way, I worry I won't be welcome.

"Hello?" The strange noise is louder now, like a mix between a laugh and a whimper. I stoop down low, put my head where the noise is at. I'm either bout to find my sister or get my nose bit off by a wild possum.

"What are you doing here?" Nia screams. It's dark in the small crawl space underneath the house where she hides. I can barely see her, but she must see me cause now she's yelling.

"I was looking for you," is all I can think to say. A wild possum don't sound so bad no more, as I look away from Nia's angry face.

"Leave me alone." Nia wants the words to be mean, but really, they just sound sad.

"Time to get ready for church." I back out of her little, hidden place and head back to the house. Even though I know she won't, I hope in my head that she'll cry. Sometimes Momma cries, sometimes I cry. Nia is the only one who don't cry. Seems like once all the secrets started, the laughing and playing stopped. Nia changed, then Daddy died. And I can't tell if she's happy or sad with him gone.

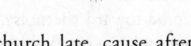

We get to church late, cause after Nia finally came back to the house, she took forever to get ready. She arranged her hair into four different styles before settling on the fifth, then frowned at her dress a full seven minutes before putting it on with slow fingers. She even smeared makeup onto her unblemished face—pink lipstick and blue powder on her eyes—even though I know she ain't s'posed to.

We drive to the church with none of us talking. Usually I'm the one that makes us all talk, but today I don't feel like saying nothin'. Instead, I stare out the window and try to fill my head with Lansing, to push out all the memories from Detroit.

The church's parking lot is packed full of cars, but the church is tiny situated on the corner of a small street that feels busy cause it's crowded. I wonder how so many people will be able to fit inside. Eventually Granddaddy parks in front of somebody's house on a side street behind the church. My church shoes are too tight and pinch my toes as we walk in the direction of music and shouting. One hundred fourteen painful steps, then we are there.

The church is overflowing with people. I pat my hair; it's already turned poufy in the steamy sanctuary. I hope we will stay in the back, but Granddaddy parades us all the way to the front, where we sit in a row so full that even with squeez-ing in sideways, we still bump knees with everybody. The women around us wear big, fancy hats that stand up off their heads with pearls and ribbons and feathers. The men stand close to their women, dressed simply, waiting for directions. When somebody's in need, the men are the first ones there with water or tissues or a shoulder where someone can lean. The kids try hard to pay attention, to avoid the strict look of a momma or a granny. They sneak peppermints from a purse, draw doodles on Kleenex, beg for a way out that ain't gon' come.

Up in the pulpit, the choir finishes a long, loud song, and then a woman wearing a peacock dress—covered in feathers and too many colors— reads the announcements. I listen to two, one bout an upcoming church retreat and the other bout Vacation Bible School, then I'm bored. The church nurses, dressed in all white and moving silently through the crowd, pass out fans and tissues. A nurse goes by, her hair falling from her modest white hat in black waves. Tiny bits of red lipstick show on her teeth when she smiles. She has glossy skin and hands that look soft like velvet. I accept one of the paper fans that she offers.

"You know, your momma used to be a church nurse," Granddaddy whispers in my ear.

"Really?" I whisper back. Granddaddy nods, then goes back to watching the pulpit.

I sneak another look at the nurse and imagine

Momma with the fans, hair in long braids beneath a plain white hat. Ice cream cone smile. Glowing skin and trembling hands.

The fans at church are always the same, with a happy smiling picture on the front and a bunch of words on the back bout funeral homes. Once I learned what a funeral home was, I asked Momma why church fans would always talk bout 'em. All Momma said was, "KB, everybody gon' die." I still ain't sure what that's got to do with fans.

The lackluster peacock lady with the announcements finally finishes and takes her seat in the first row. She is followed by a man who reads a scripture from the Bible, then another man who asks all the deacons to come to the front for prayer. I am surprised to find Charlie's aged face in the crowd, as he stands and proceeds to the altar. Then I'm even more surprised to see Granddaddy stand and head to the front, too.

"Granddaddy's a deacon?" I whisper to Nia, but she ain't paying attention. Her focus is on a group of teenagers by the door who seem to be sneaking outside, one by one. I shake my head and turn my gaze back on Granddaddy. Deacon Granddaddy, I guess.

"Do you need prayer today?" The man in the pulpit, with his money-green suit and hair parted right down the middle, reaches his arms out to the congregation. The organ swells and falls in rhythm with his speech. All around the sanctuary people begin to stand. Mommas leave children back in the pews, I bet with warnings to stay put and keep quiet. Men quietly shake hands as they pass one another. Even a few children head to the front. I wonder what they need to pray for. I hardly ever pray on my own, cept when I pray over my food before I eat. I wouldn't know what to say to God, unless somebody gave me the words.

The altar is full of people lined up to pray. Only two deacons ain't got nobody to pray with yet: the only woman deacon, on the end in a deep violet suit dress, and Granddaddy. From here it looks like his eyes are closed, so I can't tell if he knows he's alone or not. But I know he's alone. Before I can stop myself, I stand up and go to him.

"Deacons," continues the man in the pulpit, "take the hands of the person standing across from you." Granddaddy, eyes still closed, covers my tiny hands in his. Then he opens his eyes and smiles. I wonder if he smiles at everybody who comes to pray with him, or just me.

"Let us bow our heads." I do as I am told, pushing my chin down into the soft folds of my dress. I try to peek out from the bottom at Granddaddy, but even with the bend in his back and my eyes rolled all the way to the top, he's too tall for me to see.

The man in the pulpit prays in a booming

voice. Tiny murmurs from the crowd add a chorus underneath. Once the coast is clear, I peek my eyes open and lift my head to look around. Mostly, I look at Granddaddy. Watch the top of his head as it bobs along with the prayer. Study the cracks and bends of his rough hands on top of mine. Inspect the movement of his mouth as quick words depart his lips. It looks like he's been praying all his life. Daddy always said praying was something people only did when they needed something or did something wrong.

"Kenyatta," Granddaddy whispers. It catches me by surprise, cause he's s'posed to be praying and I'm s'posed to be listening. I hope he ain't catch me watching. But his eyes are still closed tight as he continues. "What do you want to pray for?"

Even though I came up here to pray, I ain't expect that question. I only came to be close to Granddaddy. But now I gotta act like I wanna pray. I think and I think.

"Can we pray for Momma?" I eventually respond. It's all I can think of, especially cause of the headshot and the talk with Granddaddy and the talk with Momma on the phone. I wait for Granddaddy to say yes or no, but he don't. Just nods real small so I can barely see it, then starts to pray. The man still prays loud up front, but Granddaddy prays soft beneath him, like an echo.

"Lord, we thank You for Your grace and Your mercy," he begins. Seems like praying always begins that way. "We thank You for Your Son, Jesus Christ. We come to You now asking for protection and strength for . . ." He stops, I wait. "My daughter. We ask for protection and strength for my daughter, as she raises two beautiful daughters according to Your divine will."

The prayer goes on and on like that. I count the times he says **Jesus**, twelve. I count the times he says **mercy**, six. I count the times he pauses before mentioning Momma, nineteen. By the end of the prayer I'm bored and he's crying.

After church, we make dinner. It's the first time we've made dinner all together since arriving in Lansing. Granddaddy makes fried chicken legs and corn bread. Nia makes macaroni and cheese, just like Momma. Granddaddy lets me help him mash the potatoes in a big, heavy bowl. I even get to pull the corn bread out from the oven when it's done. For dessert, we have an apple pie that none of us made. It came from one of the ladies at church, the one with the biggest hat and the dripping, fake smile.

We eat at the table together but don't talk. For

once, I don't watch Granddaddy and Nia. Instead, I stare at the Bible sittin' cross the room on the little ledge by the door, where Granddaddy left it after church. I think bout Granddaddy's prayer and bout Momma and secrets, then I think bout Bible study with Charlie and that verse that got me searching for bottles that I never found. I twirl my fork in my hand as I think and think.

"Can I get more?" Nia asks, pointing at the pan of corn bread. Granddaddy nods and says, "Of course, anything for my girls," and it reminds me of goin' to the mall and Granddaddy giving us all that money and buying me my favorite dress. All these different thoughts swirl around in my head, til all of a sudden, they fit together into one clear plan. The last plan I'm gon' need here in Lansing, to get us back home to Momma.

"You like your dinner?" Granddaddy asks, and I realize I been sittin' here not eating. I take a bite, quick, and nod.

"It's perfect," I reply, and it is. Instead of tryna find money, I'm gon' get Granddaddy to give us the money we need to be together again. Even with Momma at the treatment facility, I bet we still gon' need money for a new house. So, while Momma focuses on gettin' better, I'm gon' focus on fixin' Momma and Granddaddy. Once I do that, he's gon' give her anything she needs to get her girls back.

I smile and chew, satisfied with my perfect plan. Granddaddy and Nia smile, too. Maybe they smiling just cause I smiled first, or maybe it's cause they got a feeling already that I'm gon' be the one to fix us all.

PART II

July 1995

5

On Granddaddy's block of N. Rutherford St., there are only five houses. Two on Granddaddy's side, three on the other. The other house on this side is at the end of the road, with rotting boards in the window instead of glass. Two of the houses cross the street are flat and small, with fields of green grass out front and porches that wrap around the house. Kinda like Granddaddy's house, but not so old. That just leaves one more house cross the street. It's the only tall house on the block, with a sloping roof and two stories that tower over the short, squat houses, directly between them like a giant conductor. The house is brown everywhere but red on the roof and door, with greener grass and cleaner windows than all the other houses. And a chimney that looks like it makes real smoke. This is the house where the white kids live.

Since that first time we played together—bout two weeks ago now—I ain't had no chance to play with Bobby and Charlotte again. Either they momma be outside whenever they are, watching over 'em like they some babies, or Granddaddy and Nia be outside doin' the same to me. But not today.

I watch, excited, as Granddaddy grabs his cane and his hat with the feather sticking straight up from the side. Hops in his Cadillac. And drives off after telling us he's heading to the grocery store. This is the first time I've seen Granddaddy go to the grocery store in the three weeks since we've been in Lansing, so I don't know how long it will take. But I bet it's gon' take a while, since Granddaddy's so slow. Plus, the fridge is bout empty and only one frostbitten pack of meat is left in the very back of the freezer. And I heard Granddaddy say he gotta buy some extra special stuff for Fourth of July. I don't know exactly what that means, cept tomorrow is a holiday and we need more food.

As soon as Granddaddy disappears around the corner, I run inside to check on Nia. I find her sittin' in Granddaddy's spot on the couch, watching Momma's stories. The opening credits are still rolling, so that gives me at least an hour before Nia would come looking for me. Perfect.

I skip back to the room tryna look casual, then come back out holding my book in one hand and the little bag where I been keeping my rocks in the other. "I'm going outside to play!" I announce loudly, making sure Nia sees my book and rocks when she looks up, which I hope is gon' make her think I'm bout to play alone.

"Okay," Nia says, eyes still mostly glued to the TV screen. Before, it would've made me sad that Nia ain't pay attention to me, or offer to come outside and play, too. But now I got my own friends. I don't need Nia when I got Bobby and Charlotte.

I step out on the porch and look cross the street. The red front door is open, which usually means that Bobby and Charlotte are outside playing. I look around for they momma but don't see her nowhere. Excited, I run closer to get a better look. I still don't see Bobby or Charlotte, but then I hear Charlotte's laugh. It sounds far away, but like it's gettin' closer and closer. Sure enough, Charlotte turns the corner and comes riding down the street in her wagon, with Bobby pulling her while riding roller skates. Looks like he might be new to the skates, cause he's teetering and tottering, pulling Charlotte in wild zigzags down the sidewalk.

Once they get closer, I start to wave. Charlotte's eyes light up bright when she sees me.

"KB!" Charlotte yells, causing Bobby to lose his balance. He falls down, landing flat on his butt. Then looks over at me and waves. I giggle and wave back, then stash the decoy book and rock collection behind a bush before crossing the street.

"Can you guys play?" I ask, once I'm standing on the sidewalk in front of them. Bobby grips the edge of the wagon to support his weight as he tries to stand up, but the wheels start moving again and he lands back on the sidewalk.

"Here," I say, offering my hand, "you look like you need some help." I try not to laugh, but as Bobby struggles to his feet, a small snort escapes from my nose. Charlotte hears it and starts laughing, too. Soon, all three of us are laughing so hard that we end up in a heap beside Bobby.

"Like my new skates?" Bobby finally asks once all the laughing stops, but that makes us laugh again.

"Yeah," I manage to answer, "too bad they ain't come with lessons!" We all laugh some more, then Bobby unties his laces and begins taking off the skates.

"Yeah, yeah," Bobby replies, rolling his eyes. "Y'all are laughing, but I bet you couldn't do any better!"

I stay quiet, cause I know he's right. At least bout me. I ain't ever tried to skate, and I bet if I tried now, it would be an even bigger disaster than Bobby's.

"I bet I can!" Charlotte responds, always eager for a fight with her brother. Before they can get into it too far, I jump in.

"Hey, where did you guys just come from? Around the corner?" I point to the end of the street, where there ain't nothin' but green as far as I can see.

"Yep, we went around the corner," Charlotte answers proudly. "There's some more houses over there and even a little playground!"

"Really?"

"Yep," Bobby takes over, "it has swings and two slides, and even a giant tire swing."

"I ain't ever rode no tire swing!" I exclaim. "Can we go?"

Bobby and Charlotte look at each other, then Charlotte lowers her eyes. "Well, we're not really allowed to play with you."

"Play with me," I repeat. "Why not?"

"Well, our mom said—"

"Sure, we can go!" Bobby interrupts, loud. "Mom is having her book club, remember?" Bobby says this part to Charlotte, and she nods. "She said we can play at the playground until time for dinner. Let's go!"

"But, Bobby!" Charlotte yells, as Bobby picks up his skates.

"It's fine." Bobby gives Charlotte a look that stops her from talking. She gets in the wagon and once Bobby has his skates back on, he grabs the handle. "Ready?" This time, he's talking to me.

I nod, even though I ain't quite sure what's going on with Charlotte. Or Bobby, for that matter. But I ain't seen the playground yet and this might be my only chance to go. "Ready," I say, and follow Bobby as he alternates between pulling Charlotte and trying not to fall.

We don't talk on our way to the playground, which is fine with me cause it gives me time to look around. The farther we get from Granddaddy's house, the more spread out everything is, and empty. In between houses there are whole fields filled with nothin' but grass. In the city, the only time it gets real quiet is in the middle of the night. But here, it's the middle of the day and the only thing I can hear is the squeak of the wagon wheel as Bobby pulls and pulls.

As we walk, I recite in my head the little melody bout stepping on a crack and breaking your momma's back. Usually, I avoid all the cracks. But today, I step on every last one with a strange satisfaction. I count twenty-six cracks—and only wonder once if it might actually break Momma's back—then we get to the playground. It ain't too big, but it's got swings and slides just like they promised, and even a giant seesaw right in the middle.

Charlotte jumps outta the wagon before Bobby even stops pulling. "KB, do you want to swing with me?" I bob my head up and down but she's already halfway to the swings. I take off after her and make it to the swings just as she starts pumping her legs back and forth to get the swing going. Bobby takes off his skates and then his socks before running barefoot to the big slide.

"So, how come you live across the street from us now?" Charlotte asks, once we're both swinging back and forth, high, on the same rhythm. Her hair today is in one big ponytail, gathered up at the top of her head and falling to her neck as she dips her head against the wind. Some of her curls refuse to stay within the tight grip of her pink ponytail holder, and those wispy strands of yellow hair fall into her pink-cheeked face.

"Well, I don't live here," I yell back. "We just here for the summer." I pump my legs faster to keep up with Charlotte. Once we're back on the same level, I add, "Momma gon' come back for us soon."

"Oh," Charlotte says, then she is quiet for a while. She starts to swing slower, so I start to swing slower. "Then, where do you live?"

I pump my legs five times, back and forth,

before I answer. "Well, we used to have this house on a dead-end street. I ain't like it so much."

"You don't live there anymore?"

I shake my head. "After my daddy died, we moved." I pump my legs faster again, to avoid looking at Charlotte.

"Oh," she finally says.

"But it's okay," I jump in quickly, "cause we gon' find a better house, just me and Momma and Nia."

"You want to go on the slide?" Charlotte suddenly shrieks, like she ain't hear my response.

"Okay," I whisper, even though I ain't done swinging. Ain't done talking, either. But Charlotte starts to count—

"One, two, three!" She waits til she's close to the top, then jumps off the swing, sailing in the air for three full seconds before landing in a heap on the grass. I drag my foot on the ground—once, twice, three times—til I slow down enough to take a tiny jump off the swing. Then I run after Charlotte, who is already halfway up the ladder to the slide.

"Wait for me!" I yell, but Charlotte is at the top now, standing next to Bobby and saying something I can't hear. When I make it up to the top, Charlotte is blushing, and Bobby is staring straight at me.

"So, how do you like it here in Lansing?"

Bobby asks, and now I know they was talking bout me.

"It's all right," I say, then try to change the subject. "You guys wanna go on the tire swing? I ain't ever rode one!"

Charlotte peeks at Bobby, then shrugs.

"How come you say 'ain't' all the time?" Bobby asks. Now I shrug. I keep my eyes focused on my shoes, so I ain't gotta look at Bobby as he presses me for answers, or Charlotte as she pretends not to hear.

"Just asking," Bobby says, like I was the one who offended him. Then he takes off down the slide yelling, "Last one down's a rotten egg!" Charlotte rushes down after him, leaving me standing there, rotten. Bobby runs to the seesaw and Charlotte joins him, each taking turns up in the air and then down, down on the ground. I slide down the slide, slow, then take my time on my way over to the seesaw. I still wanna play with Bobby and Charlotte, but seems like maybe something changed, and I ain't even sure what.

"You want a turn?" Charlotte asks, offering me her best smile. I smile back and nod. Guess ain't nothin' wrong after all.

I take my time climbing onto my side of the seesaw, cause I ain't sure if Bobby gon' take it easy or go too high. Back when I used to play on the seesaw at school, the boys would always trick the girls into riding with them, then kick off too hard and fast so that the girl spends the whole time yelling and falling. Bobby don't seem like one of them kind of boys, but I can't be sure.

"It's okay," Bobby says with a smile. Now I got two smiles, one from Charlotte and one from Bobby, so I feel better. I climb onto the seesaw and begin to ride back and forth, up and down, with Bobby leading the way.

"Do you like it here?" Bobby asks after a while.

"Mm-hmm," I respond between jumps, "this is a fun playground."

"No, I meant Lansing." Bobby's jumps are smaller now, slower. "You're living here now, right?"

I look around for Charlotte to see if this is what she told Bobby, but she's on the swings again and too far away to glare at. I turn back to Bobby and repeat what I said earlier. "We just here for the summer, til our momma comes back."

"Oh." Bobby is silent, like he's tryna decide if my answer is right or wrong. Then his face perks up. "You want to go to the tire swing now?"

I smile, even though I don't really feel like smiling.

"I can't believe you haven't ridden a tire swing before!" Bobby continues, like I ain't even there. "We have one in our backyard. You don't have a tire swing at home?"

I shake my head back and forth cause I can't get no words out. It don't seem to matter to Bobby, though, cause he hops off the seesaw, still smiling, and races over to the tire swing. Just like the one he has at home.

"Everybody ain't got a home," I whisper, even though he's already gone. I sit at the bottom of the seesaw, butt to the dirt. Hear the roar of a lawn mower somewhere, and the **ding-ding-ding** of a fire alarm or bell or kitchen oven timer saying, **Dinner's done.** Bury the hum of voices calling out to me beneath the buzz of a bee and the tiny whistle the wind makes when the swing pushes back and forth. Untie and tie my shoes. Once. Twice, then three times; still, I feel the weight of their questions pressing down on my chest.

That night, me and Nia stay up late to help Granddaddy shuck corn and clean greens. I ain't ever done either before, but Granddaddy shows me how. I'm happy cause it helps me take my mind off what happened with Bobby and Charlotte earlier. I ain't sure if they gon' still wanna be my friend, now that they know I ain't got a perfect family like they do.

"Here," Granddaddy says, handing me an ear

of corn. The corn Momma buys always comes in a can, but Granddaddy's looks fresh from the ground, wrapped in a rough, green cover that Granddaddy calls the husk. I peel the husk and tug away the little leftover strings, then hand the corn to Nia. She breaks the cob in two, rinses it in the sink, then puts it in a glass bowl with a plastic lid.

"Do we need this?" I ask Granddaddy, pulling a big pot and lid from beneath the sink.

"No," Granddaddy starts, "we gon' cook that corn tomorrow, on the grill. We just gettin' everything ready tonight."

The greens take longer than the corn and look like giant leaves with a stem right in the middle. We start by cleaning the greens, which takes more work than I expect. First, Nia pulls the stems from the leaves. Then rips the leaves til they're scraps of dead plant. Granddaddy fills the big kitchen sink with water and Nia dumps all the greens inside.

"Come here, Kenyatta." Granddaddy stands right in front of the sink with Nia already on one side, so I stand on the other. "The first time I cleaned some greens, I was bout your age," Granddaddy tells me. "My momma taught me how once, then I had to do it on my own every time after that. We ate greens every Sunday growing up, just like most of the Black folks in the South." He begins moving his hands in the sink as he talks, making tiny chunks of greens dance and swim in the murky water.

"What do you have to do?" I ask curiously. Nia seems curious, too, as we both watch Granddaddy without blinking.

"Well, do you know where greens come from?" he asks.

"The dirt," Nia surprises me by responding. She leans in close.

"You're right," Granddaddy replies, "greens grow up from the dirt just like a lot of vegetables. But greens are even different than those, cause they keep a lot of that dirt in their leaves and stems. See?" Granddaddy holds up one of the leaves that we ain't cleaned yet. I get real close and notice patches of brown mixed in with all the green.

"Eww, it's dirty!" I screech.

"Exactly, and that's why we gotta clean 'em real good. Otherwise, you get you a big ol' bowl of collard greens and it's gon' be nasty. Don't matter how well you cook greens, if you don't clean 'em well, they won't taste right."

Nia nods to show she understands, so I nod, too. But then I ask, "So how do we get 'em clean?"

"Well, first we fill the sink with cold water. I already did that part." We nod. "Then we rinse and tear the greens. You girls already did that part." We nod and smile. "Now we got all our greens in the water, so we gon' dip 'em and dip 'em, just like this." As Granddaddy talks, he uses both hands to plunge the floating greens underwater. Up and down over and over so that all the greens go under, then rise back to the top.

"Can I try?" I ask, hopeful.

"Sure," says Granddaddy, shifting away from the sink to make space for me.

I dip my hands in the icy water, much colder than I expected. The greens feel firm, but sometimes tiny bits of leaves get loose and attach to my fingers like wet tissue. I grab as many greens as I can into my small hands and dip them beneath the water. All the way to the bottom so I can feel the cold metal of the sink. Then I drag them back to the top, again and again.

"How we gon' know when it's done?" Nia asks. I'm surprised she's still just watching. Not asking to do it herself or running off to the room to be alone. I sneak a small smile to myself, being sure she don't see.

"Good question." Granddaddy smiles. "Kenyatta, grab up as many of the greens as you can and hold 'em up against the sink."

I do just as I'm told, gathering all the greens so that most of 'em are held tight against the sink in my clammy hands.

"Now, look at the water." We all look and

see that the water is dark like mud. "What do you see?"

"Dirt?" I ask, thinking I must be missing something.

"Dirt," confirms Granddaddy. "We gon' know our greens clean when ain't no more dirt in the water. Let's start again." He removes the plug and drains the gloomy water from the sink. Then refills it with clean, cold water. I let the greens fall back into the water and start the process from the beginning, dipping and sinking and floating the greens. Once I'm done, we check the water again. Less brown now, but still some. We do it all again and again. That makes four sinks of clean water til we get clean greens.

We simmer the greens in a big pot of water overnight. Granddaddy says he gon' come check on 'em while we sleep. We leave the corn wrapped tight in the fridge, cause it's gon' go on the grill tomorrow. Then we gotta clean up our mess. Momma always tells us that we can never leave the kitchen messy when we go to bed. Looks like she learned that lesson from Granddaddy. We wipe counters and wash dishes and empty the trash. Finally, we are done. Granddaddy turns off the lights and I follow Nia down the hall.

"Good night," Granddaddy calls to us just as we make it to the bedroom door.

"Good night," we say at the same exact time. Then both yell, "Jinx!" I ain't played jinx with Nia in a while. We used to drive Momma crazy with all our loud games, but now the house is mostly quiet, with Nia doin' her own thing and me tryna figure out mine.

"Owe me a soda," Nia says with a smile. I don't even fight to prove we said it at the same time. I want Nia to win.

In our little room, we get ready for bed. Nia wraps her hair; I braid mine. Tomorrow will be a good day, I think. Granddaddy says we gon' go to a big barbecue with family and fireworks and lots of food. I'm happy not just cause we get to meet family, but cause it might get me closer to fixing Momma and Granddaddy. And even if it don't, I bet it's gon' be fun to have a big, happy family like the kind I always see on TV. Maybe not perfect, but close.

I crawl into the covers, feel Nia's knee against mine. Yeah, I bet tomorrow's gon' be a real good day. Maybe Nia will even play with me the whole time.

6

Granddaddy wakes us up early the next morning. So early that the little bit of sun I can see through the window still looks orange and pink, instead of its usual yellow. So early that I fall back asleep for another ten minutes, before I finally yawn and stretch, rubbing my eyes. It took me a while to fall asleep last night—for once, even counting didn't help—cause I was too excited thinking bout today. I rub my eyes some more, then when I finally struggle to open 'em, Nia is right in front of me, already up and humming to herself as she gets dressed. I watch her for a while since she can't notice me looking. If she saw me watching her, she would probably complain. She's always telling Momma that I don't respect her privacy.

Nia looks in the mirror, so I squeeze my eyes

closed before she finds me in her reflection. Then I yawn and stretch again, pretending to wake up for the first time.

"Good morning," I chirp.

"Get on up," is Nia's reply, "Granddaddy said we gon' be leaving soon." I get out of bed and find clothes to wear. I decide on a pair of jean shorts with white frilly lace at the bottom and a plain red T-shirt. Nia is wearing a flowing pink-and-purple sundress, but I don't like to wear dresses unless I have to for church. Nia fixes her hair in a ponytail, then fixes my hair in a ponytail, just like I like. Once we're all ready, she pulls me beside her so that both of us are in the mirror. One tall, one short. One in a dress, one in shorts. Both smiling Momma's smile.

"Perfect," Nia says, and it is.

I find Granddaddy in the kitchen, at the table with his mug of coffee, like always.

"Good morning," I sing as I begin making myself a bowl of cereal.

"Good morning," he responds without looking up. Soon, Nia joins us and gets her own bowl of cereal. We sit at the table in silence and eat and drink, like always.

But this morning is different, cause I'm too excited to stay quiet. "You think we gon' meet a lot of family?" I ask Granddaddy.

He nods. "Oh yeah! Let's see, it's gon' be a

bunch of folks from the church, but also some of my cousins and they kids, then I bet—"

"Kids." I perk up. "There's gon' be other kids there?"

"Oh yeah, plenty of 'em. Hope yawl girls ready to have some fun." He winks and it makes both me and Nia smile.

I sit there quiet again, thinking bout all the fun we bout to have. But more important than having fun is finding out the truth bout Momma and Granddaddy. Seems like Granddaddy told me one story, but Momma might have a different one. And since neither one of 'em seemed ready to say more bout it, I know I gotta find some other people to fill in the gaps. Hopefully, my new family that I'm gon' meet today will have the answers I'm looking for.

Soon as we done with our breakfast, Granddaddy stands and clears his dishes, then says, "Time to go!" Me and Nia clean the table and take the dishes to the sink. While Nia washes 'em, I tiptoe over to the stove and creep open the lid of the greens to sneak a glimpse inside the pot. All the leaves that were once floating up at the top, green and crunchy-looking, are now soft and dark. Nothin' like the greens last night. Nia grabs the corn from the fridge while Granddaddy grabs the pot of greens and the keys that hang by the front door. We are ready to go.

At home with Momma and Daddy, we ain't ever really celebrate the Fourth of July. The last time I can remember, I must've been bout six or seven. Daddy came home from work that day with an armload of groceries. He ain't usually work much but had just started a new job at the Wiggly Pig Market down the street from our house. Momma was so happy when he started that job that she laughed and laughed while Daddy played music from the stereo and spin't her around.

They probably gave Daddy a discount on the food, cause he came home with more bags than I had ever seen from the market. And when I looked inside, there were four different kinds of meat— chicken, ribs, sausages, burgers—enough for a feast. In the other bags, we had bread, buns, ketchup, mustard, corn (the kind in a can), baked beans with brown sugar, and two packs of Kool-Aid (grape, my favorite, and tropical punch for Nia). I hugged Daddy so hard around his neck when I saw all the food. Mostly cause I could tell he had made Momma happy.

Me and Nia put all the food away in the cup-boards, while Momma cleaned the kitchen and Daddy started the grill. I joined him in our tiny backyard to watch. The slab of cement where our grill rested was too small and sloping downward, so Daddy had to keep a brick under one leg of the grill's rusted frame. I sat still, watching as he assembled the black coals, then turned them into fire. I started to ask Daddy how he made it happen, but not knowing made it feel like magic.

Once the fire was burning, we all sat in the living room together. Daddy pulled out our old deck of cards, still with jokers standing in for the missing two of clubs and jack of diamonds. Usually, cards was just our thing, me and Daddy. But this day, we all took turns playing go fish and tunk. Then me and Daddy showed Nia how to play speed. When it was time for me and Nia to play against each other, I remembered what Daddy taught me: **Sometimes, when you wanna speed up, you gotta slow down first.** I stacked the cards in my hand each time I pulled, and by the end, I had one card left and Nia had almost a full deck. When the card I needed showed up, I threw down the card in my hand and yelled, **Speed!** Nia ain't look so happy to lose, but when I found Daddy watching me from cross the room, the smile on his face was the biggest I ever seen. Later, I got to sit in Momma's lap while Nia and Daddy played. Momma even let me play with her hair, twisting it into tiny braids and then letting it go. When I looked around our cramped but comfortable living room, we finally looked like one of them families on TV.

That day was one of the best we had. Usually, our good days would turn bad at some point. But not that day. Daddy kept grilling, Momma kept dancing, Nia kept playing, and I kept a smile on my face that lasted a whole day long. We ate enormous plates of grilled food for breakfast, lunch, and dinner. We played cards and listened to music. At the hottest part of the day, we sat outside on the porch and Daddy surprised us all by grabbing the water hose and spraying us with icy-cold water. When Momma ran in the house to get away from him, he ran in after her, water hose and all. Me and Nia watched, surprised, as our momma and daddy ran around the house yelling and making a big mess like kids. Like they wasn't worried bout nothin'.

That night, we sat on the porch with plastic cups of sugary Kool-Aid. The air was still thick but finally gettin' cooler with a breeze. Up and down the street, families that looked like ours did the same things; talking and laughing and living. For once, it was a real neighborhood. Nobody was shooting guns or fighting or running from loud police sirens. It was peace.

At some point, Daddy snuck inside the house

and came back with a brown paper bag. Inside, we found fireworks! Not a whole lot, but more than I'd ever seen in my life. He pulled out two sparklers, which he lit and handed to me and Nia. We ran around in circles through the uncut grass, scribbling words in the air that disappeared after a second. Then there were all kind of fireworks. Some that scattered around on the ground like bugs sprayed with Raid, some that flew into the air and made a loud whistle, some that popped so loud like gunshots. But gunshots with glowing lights and smoke that sizzled patterns into the clear night sky.

I remember wanting to live in that day forever. I was only six or seven, but I already knew by then bout a lot of bad days. Days when Daddy just wasn't himself, no matter how hard we all tried to make him be. Days when Momma and Daddy would fight, and I would hide under the covers with a book. Memories I tried my hardest to forget, even now. But that night I tried to memorize every smell, every feeling, every moment.

We ain't ever celebrate the Fourth of July again after that one. Sometimes I wonder if it was even real, or if I made it up in my mind. Already, the sound of the fireworks is quiet, less vibrant. The whole scene, when I replay it in my mind, is blurry. Like a bad recording. A forged memory. Or maybe it did happen, cause God needed me to know happy just one time, so I would really feel it when He took it away.

Me and Granddaddy and Nia arrive at a big park after a long time of slow driving. Momma drives slow to keep me from gettin' carsick, which I like, but Granddaddy's slow is more like riding on a turtle. Plus, in all the excitement I forgot to grab my book, so I ain't have nothin' to do the whole way cept count songs on the radio. Seventeen. I jump out the car and stretch my arms and legs. We grab the food from the trunk and a large, striped blanket. Then we walk toward a crowd of people playing loud music that makes me wanna clap and stomp.

There are five long picnic tables underneath a dome-shaped shelter. Lopsided barbecue grills poke up from the grass circling the cement mound. All four of those grills are filled end to end with smoking meat. All the people in the shelter are loud and happy and Black. Women stand in groups talking and laughing. Kids run around in circles, with some parents chasing. Other parents just let 'em run. Men hold cans of beer and play games that make 'em shout. The music is the beat that they all talk over and dance to, all in rhythm. Seeing everybody here like this reminds me of the barbecues we used to have on our old block, when all the daddies would argue over who could grill the best, and the mommas would sit on their porches, braiding hair and sipping lemonade. This is just like those times, cept better, cause this is my family.

Granddaddy walks to the table on the end, so we follow. He sets the pot of greens down beside a bunch of other pots and pans. Nia hands him the corn, which he takes to the man flipping meat on the first grill, who's wearing an apron and smoking a cigarette. I set the blanket on the table beside the greens. But it looks funny up on the table like that, so I take it down and set it, still folded, on the grass.

"Granddad!" A dark-skinned boy with ashy knees and ankles runs toward Granddaddy with a huge, white-toothed grin on his face that clashes with his dark skin. He looks happy to see Granddaddy, but when I turn and look at Granddaddy, I don't see the same. Instead of the smile I expect to see, he got an expression on his face that looks more like a frown, cept not quite.

"Stop all that yelling, boy," says Granddaddy, evenly. The boy stops running all at once, like he was smacked head-on by a train. A train with crossed arms and, now, a full frown.

"Sorry," mumbles the boy, head down. His hair

is like little black balls of cotton, longer on the top than on the edges. He got scars all over his arms and legs, and one big one right cross the back of his neck. The most interesting thing bout him, though, is his nose, which is wide with nostrils that flare so I can almost see straight up his nose when he talks.

"Gon' and say hi to your cousins, boy!" Granddaddy's voice is louder and meaner than I've heard before, and I ain't sure why. Nia lowers her eyes and bites her nails, so I lower my eyes and bite my nails. But then I look up to smile nicely when the boy begins to introduce himself, even though Nia don't.

"Hi, I'm Javon"—he speaks quietly—"what are your names?"

"Nia," short and sweet, then I follow with, "I'm KB," and an even bigger smile. I ain't ever had a cousin before. I think bout them kids in the pool, the cousins, and wonder if that's what it's gon' be like.

"Where's your brother?" Granddaddy interrupts, voice still booming.

"Over there." Javon points to a group of boys playing basketball on a court cross from the pavilion. Neither of the basketball rims still got the net attached, and there's giant cracks all cross the cement, but none of the boys seem to notice as they yell and dribble and laugh. "I'll go get him."

Javon runs off and I wonder excitedly which one is my other cousin.

"Come on, girls, let me introduce you to every-body." Granddaddy's voice is suddenly nice and soft again. I wonder if he is nicer to us cause we're girls. Or maybe since he made Momma mad so long ago, now he feels like he gotta be nice to us to make up for it.

We follow Granddaddy around the picnic area. He shows us off to a whole bunch of grown-ups whose names I don't remember. They all say things like, "Are these Jacquee's daughters?" and "Look how big you are!" and "Do you remember me? I ain't seen you since you was this high!" Even though it's nice to be fussed over, I'm impatient to get to my cousins. I tune out the adult voices and think bout how I'm gon' get my new cousins to tell me bout Momma and Granddaddy.

"And this here," Granddaddy interrupts my thoughts, "is your uncle Willie." I stay quiet while Granddaddy explains that Willie is Momma's brother. Momma never talked much bout having brothers, even when we asked, but I know she got four of 'em, all older than her. Seemed like Momma didn't wanna talk bout them, cause she never even mentioned them having any kids. They were already grown-ups by the time she was born, which I guess is why they wasn't in none of the pictures in Granddaddy's book. Willie is the oldest. He is tall and skinny with a bald head and skin bout a half shade lighter than Granddaddy's. I look and look but can't find no way he looks like Momma.

"I can't believe I'm just now meeting my beautiful nieces," says Willie—**should I call him Uncle Willie?**—as he stares at Nia and then me. "You look just like your momma," he tells Nia. I wish somebody would look at me for once when they say that. Sometimes, if I look in the mirror long and hard enough, I think I do look like Momma. But it's hard to see cause our skin's so different. If I was brown like Momma, I bet people would say I look like her, too.

"How old are you girls now?" Willie continues. I wait for Nia to answer. She always talks for us when grown-ups start asking questions.

"I'm fourteen and she's ten," is Nia's quick response. I wonder if she's gon' mention that my eleventh birthday is just ten days away now, but she don't.

"Wow, fourteen and ten," responds Willie, scratching his head. "I can't believe it's been that long." He looks down at the ground for a second, like he's sad or worried bout something, but then looks up again, quick. "Well, my boys ain't much older than you, KB. I got Javon, who's twelve, and Jesse, who's bout to be fourteen. Almost your age," he finishes, looking at Nia in the end.

"We already met Javon," I whisper, scared to talk but excited that I finally got something to say. I hop from one foot to the other while I wait for his response.

"Oh yeah?" Willie answers. "That boy is a rock head. Don't let him get you in no trouble." I ain't sure what he means by that, but I nod.

"Willie! You up at the spades table!" a woman calls from the picnic table farthest away, where she sits with two other men. She is wearing a long dress that brushes the ground, and giant hoop earrings almost the size of her head. Her voice is powerful and the men at the table sit up straighter when she speaks. They got a deck of cards right in the middle of the table. One of the men shuffles, and then the other man cuts the deck into two halves, putting one on top of the other.

"Gotta go," says Willie. "I been waiting all day to beat my cousins at spades." He smiles at me and Nia, then walks away. When he smiles, I can finally see how he looks like Momma.

"That boy Willie," says Granddaddy once he's gone, "always been the one I had to watch." Again, I ain't quite sure what he means by that, but again I nod.

"Are Momma's other brothers gon' be here?" I ask.

"Just Willie and Leroy," Granddaddy responds. "Calvin left Michigan for California awhile back, and Tony joined the army as soon as he turned eighteen. He's stationed at Patch Barracks in Germany now. Stuttgart." I can't tell if Granddaddy seems sad or mad bout this last part, but I don't get much time to wonder. "You girls hungry?" Granddaddy asks, and we both nod enthusiastically. As we walk, I'm stuck thinking bout Momma having brothers; brothers who are all around the world now, living their own lives apart from one another and apart from Granddaddy. We might be far apart now, but I can't imagine a future where me, Momma, and Nia ain't close.

Granddaddy hobbles over to the big table with all the food, and me and Nia follow close behind. There are aluminum pans filled with ribs, some covered in barbecue sauce and some plain. There are at least three different kinds of chicken: chicken wings in barbecue sauce, grilled drumsticks with black marks stamped into the skin, chicken thighs smoking from the grill. Our greens are still covered in pans beside the meat. There are also four pans of bubbling macaroni and cheese, two big bowls of potatoes—one mashed and one cut into little squares, three kinds of green beans, and a whole table filled with nothin' but dessert. I ain't ever seen so much food in my life. Back at the motel, felt like we were eating less and less every day. Now my stomach growls at the sight of so much delicious food just waiting on me to eat.

"Gon' and get you a plate," says Granddaddy. I wonder if he notices how hungry I look. I don't waste no time, though. I find a stack of paper plates and take one from the top, which I fill quickly with two ribs, a chicken drumstick, heaps of greens, macaroni and cheese, mashed potatoes, and green beans. I wanna ask for a cob of corn, but the apron man with the cigarette looks kinda scary. I take my plate and sit down next to Nia, who made a much smaller plate than mine. She only picked two chicken wings, a small pile of macaroni and cheese, and a bigger pile of greens. I wonder if she put all them greens on her plate to make Granddaddy happy.

We eat quiet, cept for all the chewing. Momma always tells me to stop smacking when I chew with my mouth open, but today she ain't here to stop me. I chew nice and loud, rolling all the food over and over in my mouth to let the flavors seep into my tongue. Everything is delicious, but I like the greens best of all. Mostly cause me and Nia and Granddaddy made 'em.

Nia finishes her plate first, but even with twice as much food, I ain't far behind. I wanna ask for seconds, but Nia jumps up and throws her plate in the trash, so I do the same.

"Granddaddy, can we go play?" Nia asks sweetly. I smile cause she said we. That means she wants me to come, too.

"Yeah, gon' 'head," says Granddaddy with his mouth full of half-chewed ribs. He has barbecue sauce on all his fingers and a little bit on his face, but for some reason he don't use the clean napkin beside his plate.

"Let's go," Nia says to me. I quickly obey, running behind her long stride. Just then, I remember that Javon never came back with his brother, like he said he would. I guess Nia thinking the same, cause we head that way.

"Not too far," Granddaddy remembers to yell after us. Just like Momma.

"Okay!" I bet Granddaddy can barely hear Nia's response, cause we almost to the basketball court now.

I count four, five, six, seven boys on the court playing basketball. And a crowd more watching from the sidelines. Javon is in the group of boys that ain't playing. He sits on the bench yelling at anybody that touches the ball.

"Come on, defense! Let's go! Get it, Jesse!" I can't tell who he's cheering for, cause Javon is yelling at 'em all. I scan the court and wonder which boy is Jesse. My cousin.

"Foul!" A boy even lighter-skinned than me with reddish freckles sprinkled on his cheeks yells from his spot on the ground. Looks like another boy pushed him down. "Dammit, Jesse!" I can't believe this little boy, probably bout my age, said a bad word. I turn my head back and forth, but ain't no grown-ups around, and don't none of the other kids seem to care. Not even Nia, and I bet she one of the oldest here, cept for some of the tall boys on the court.

The boys stop playing to help freckle-face still laying on the ground. Well, some of the boys help him. The others just laugh and walk off the court.

"Damn, Skeeter. Always messing up a good game!" Looks like Javon be cussin', too. He stands to help the boy on the court, who act like he don't want no help at first, but reaches his hand out toward Javon anyway. Javon slaps his hand and laughs.

"That was a foul," whines Skeeter, still on the ground. I wonder if he might be hurt for real, but then he gets up and limps over to the bench. Javon notices me and Nia standing on the sidelines and heads over. My hands are suddenly wet and sweaty, so I wipe 'em on my shorts.

"Hey, Skeeter! Come meet my cousins!" Javon smiles from ear to ear as he walks over. His smile is kinda like his daddy's smile, which is kinda like my momma's smile. I'm just meeting him, but that smile makes him feel like home.

Javon introduces me and Nia to Skeeter. Nia

smiles a fake smile; she's watching the game on the court. I smile a real smile, quick, then put my head down.

"Nice to meet you," says Skeeter. He reaches out to shake my hand, which is still kinda wet, but his palms are sweaty, too.

"You all right?" I ask him, shyly.

"Oh, you saw that foul? Yeah, I'm cool." He still seems upset, but Javon chuckles a little bit. "What's funny?" retorts Skeeter.

"Nothing." Javon laughs. "Just you always crying foul!" The more Javon laughs, the redder Skeeter's cheeks turn. I ain't ever seen Black people whose skin could turn red like white people's, but then again, Skeeter is also the lightest Black person I ever seen.

"Which one is your brother?" I ask Javon. He looks around for a few seconds, then points at the water fountain, where a tall boy splashes his head in the water.

"There he is," Javon answers, then yells, "Jesse!" The boy looks around and Javon waves him over our way. Jesse is much taller than Javon and lighter-skinned, but they got the same face and hair. Cept Jesse is starting to grow a tiny mustache that pokes out from his upper lip like a fuzzy slug. I can't believe he ain't quite fourteen yet, cause he looks much older than Nia.

"Hey," he says casually, in a voice almost deep

like a man's, but not quite. He's so tall I gotta turn my neck up to look him in the eyes. When I do, his eyes surprise me. They are a light brown that's almost golden, with little flecks of green scattered here and there. I ain't ever seen nobody with eyes so pretty, especially not a boy.

"Hey," responds Nia, just as casually. I wonder if she noticed his eyes, too, cause now she's picking at her nails to avoid looking at his face.

"Hi, I'm KB." I smile at Jesse while he smiles at Nia.

"I'm Jesse," he finally responds, but I ain't sure if he's talking to me or her.

"Nia," my sister finally says. This conversation's gettin' too slow and weird for me. I shift my weight from one foot to the other and see that Javon's doin' bout the same.

"We met your daddy," I say. "We ain't ever known none of our uncles before, or our cousins."

"Oh, we cousins?" Jesse asks. Nia nods. "Well, more like step-cousins. I got a different daddy." He avoids looking at Javon when he says this part.

I look at Nia for an explanation, but she just lowers her head and plays with the end of her ponytail. "Cool," she finally says, so I repeat, "Cool."

It's always been just me and Nia, even though I secretly wanted a brother. Having a brother just seemed like it would be more fun than having a sister. I look at Javon, imagine us playing stuff together like racing and football. Then I imagine Jesse carrying me around on his shoulders. These cousins might be one of the best things that's happened since we've been in Lansing.

"Hey, wanna play hide-and-seek?" Javon asks. He jumps up and down, so I jump up and down. I think bout all the secrets, but I'd rather play with my cousins now than talk. The secrets gon' have to wait. Nia and Jesse look at each other, like they need to know each other's answer before they can decide.

"Sure!" I respond, then look to Nia. I hope she gon' play, too.

"Okay," Nia says, at the same time Jesse says, "Sure."

"All right, I'll be it!" Javon presses his face against a tree and starts counting, loud and slow. I guess they're done playing basketball, even though the game is back in full swing. I peek over as red-faced Skeeter runs back and forth up the court with boys twice his size.

"Seven, eight, nine . . ." Javon continues to count. I gotta find a place to hide. While I was busy watching Skeeter, Nia and Jesse disappeared off somewhere. I run past the basketball courts, gettin' farther away from the picnic tables, which are now the size of twigs. I spot a plain-looking building, maybe a bathroom, and run in that direction.

Turns out it is a bathroom but looks like it's closed for cleaning. There's yellow tape all around it to block people from going inside. I think bout ducking under the tape, but I'm too scared, so I crouch down by the back door instead.

"Ready or not, here I come!" I can hear Javon's yell from cross the park, and it sounds like he's heading in my direction. Sure enough, it ain't long before I hear quiet footsteps, then giggles. "Found you!" Javon yells, wrapping his arms around my waist from behind.

"Dang!" I yell, laughing. I thought bout saying that bad word at first, the one that starts with **D**, but I guess I still care bout making Momma mad at me. Soon as I think bout Momma, I remember that I'm s'posed to be doin' more than just playing.

"You ever met my momma?" I say to Javon, right before he takes off.

"Nah." He turns around. "But my daddy talks bout her all the time."

"Really?" I lean up against the tree, so Javon leans up against the tree.

"Yeah, he's always talking bout his super-beautiful little sister who could read whole books by the time she was four." Javon chuckles and I do, too. Sounds like Momma.

"So how come you never met her, then?"

"Well, you know, all the drama and stuff."

"Drama?" I peel a piece of bark off the tree and try to act casual.

"You know," Javon says, "all the stuff with her and Granddaddy."

"Oh, you mean the headshot?"

Javon nods.

"But ain't that a silly little reason to never see your family again?"

"You think what Granddaddy did to her after that was **little**?" Judging by the way Javon tilts his head to the side and squints his eyes, seems like he knows something I don't know.

"What you mean?" I whisper, afraid to ask.

Javon sighs. "Come on, KB, we gotta go play. Nia and Javon prolly lookin' everywhere for us by now!"

"But—"

"You're it!" Javon tags me and takes off running. Just when I was so close to figuring out what happened between Momma and Granddaddy. Which, according to Javon, was a lot more than a silly argument. **What really happened?** I sigh, then lean against the building and count.

"One, two, three." As I speak the numbers out loud, I count all the things that might've happened between Momma and Granddaddy, to match. "Seven, eight, nine." **He kicked her out the**

house. He grounded her in the basement for weeks. He . . . abandoned her? "Eighteen, nineteen, twenty." I finish counting before I come up with anything that makes sense.

"Ready or not, here I come!" I run off in the direction where Javon went, then remember that Nia and Jesse are somewhere hiding, too. I ain't seen them since Javon was it. I scan the park quickly—basketball court, picnic tables, parking lot, water fountain—but don't see none of 'em nowhere. I decide to run back to the picnic tables to see if they might be over there.

I get there and look at all the faces I don't recognize, to try to find the few I do. I look under tables and behind trash cans. No Nia, no Jesse, no Javon. I do see Granddaddy, though, standing at the grill with the cigarette man. I run over.

"Granddaddy, you seen Nia?" I ask, tryna act the same instead of thinking bout the new mystery stirring in my mind.

"You done lost your sister?" Granddaddy asks, turning his head around to look.

"Nah, not like that," I quickly reply, before he gets mad, "we playing hide-and-seek with the boys." I pull my fingers, anxious to get back to looking.

"Oh, well then. In that case, I ain't seen her." Granddaddy winks. I can't tell if he knows where she's at or not, but either way, don't look like he gon' help me.

"Thanks, Granddaddy!" I take off running, even though I ain't sure which way to go. Then I hear a noise that makes me run back the way I came. Sounds like somebody's laughing, maybe Javon. I peek behind a group of three tall climbing trees. No Nia, no Jesse, no Javon. I check back by the basketball courts, in the parking lot under the cars, under the benches. No Nia, no Jesse, no Javon. Hide-and-seek ain't that fun when you can't find nobody. I think bout giving up, but then remember the yellow tape by the bathrooms where I hid before.

I look around the building, but ain't nobody outside. Maybe they crossed the yellow tape and went inside. All three of 'em must be in there together, probably laughing at me. I look around to make sure ain't nobody watching. Then lift the middle of the tape just enough so I can duck under.

The building has three wooden steps, then a flat level platform. On one side is a door that says MEN'S and on the other a sign that says WOMEN'S. Now that I'm closer I can see that this ain't no regular building. It's more like a porta potty, but a little bit nicer. I study both doors and try to pick. Jesse and Javon are both boys, so it makes more sense that they went in the men's room. But I bet Nia still made them go in the women's room, even though it was just one girl and two boys. I tiptoe over to the door of the women's room and swing it open, quiet.

The inside is even more tiny than I thought it might be from the outside. Ain't nothin' in there but a single toilet, an empty roll of toilet paper, and a small sink in the corner that drips and drips. No Nia, no Jesse, no Javon.

I head back out to the platform and creep toward the other stall. I wanna sneak up on them, maybe even scare them. I reach the door, wrap my hand around the tiny silver handle, then slowly pull it open. A sliver of light comes in the room with me. The wider I open the door, the bigger the sliver grows. It starts in the corner of the room, then touches the sink, the toilet, then the other corner of the room, closest to the door.

Where I can see Nia and Jesse. No Javon. Just Nia and Jesse, with the straps of Nia's dress pulling down so I can see the soft blue of the grown-up bra she begged Momma for.

Nia and Jesse, with Jesse's hands on Nia's waist and Nia's hands on Jesse's shoulders. Nia and Jesse, kissing like I've only seen in movies.

The first tongue kiss I'm gon' ever see up close is this one, between my sister and our cousin. With too much spit and not enough light. Maybe with more light, they might see me. But they just keep kissing, like they forgot bout hide-and-seek and forgot bout me.

Jesse's hand leaves Nia's waist. Finds the top of her dress, pulls it down. Finds the bottom of her dress, pulls it up. Tiny sounds like squeaks escape from Nia's kissing mouth. I don't know what happens next, not even in the movies. This is the part where Momma always covers my eyes.

I run out from the bathroom, hot tears blurring my path. I trip down the steps and land in the soft grass. I wanna stay there forever. Beg my eyes and mind to forget what I saw. But it's stuck there now. I see it again and again, even with my eyes clenched tight.

"KB!" Javon runs towards me and I remember where I am. Hide-and-seek, Fourth of July, Lansing. I feel so different, but ain't nothin' changed. "You ain't find me!" Javon is still smiling and still innocent. He don't know all that I know, so he can still play and laugh. My whole mind is nothin' but kissing, touching cousins in bathroom stalls.

"You're it." I tag Javon and run away, before anyone can stop me.

7

We been in Lansing for a month now. Four and a half weeks. Thirty-two days. Granddaddy talks more, mostly to me. He tells me stories bout growing up in the South, bout playing sports and marching in protests and falling in love with Granny. My favorite stories are when he tells me bout Momma as a little girl. Nia don't listen to Granddaddy's stories. Instead, she gets to leave the house whenever she wants, to hang out with Brittany, and even some of her new friends from the pool. I play with Bobby and Charlotte sometimes, when Granddaddy ain't watching. Me and Bobby like to play catch with his Frisbee and search for rocks near the curb. Me and Charlotte like to play hopscotch that we draw on the sidewalk and read together in the shaded path beside her house. We took turns reading **The Secret**

Garden chapter by chapter til we finished the whole book in a week and a half. Luckily, I ain't seen they momma again since that first time, which I think is less bout luck and more bout them making sure I ain't ever around when she's around. Luckily, too, we ain't ever talked no more bout none of that stuff that happened on the playground. Which is just fine by me.

Missing Momma don't hurt so bad no more. I go some days without even thinking bout our life in Detroit. I try to forget the special soup Momma would cook when any of us was sick, or the way Momma would rub my hair when I woke up from a bad dream. It's not that I don't miss that stuff, but I got new stuff to think bout now, too, and a new life in Lansing. I've read six books from Granddaddy's bookshelf, found seventeen caterpillars and seven rocks, and climbed my tree enough times to know the way by heart.

Most days, Lansing feels like home. Cept tomorrow, I bet. Tomorrow is my eleventh birthday and I ain't ever spent my birthday without Momma.

All my birthdays that I can remember went bad, one way or another. The first one I remember is when I turned seven. I ain't get no presents that year, or no party. I cried and cried cause I ain't understand, especially since when Nia's birthday came the next week, she got a sleepover with her friends from school and lip gloss. I don't much remember my eighth birthday, but when I turned nine, Momma and Daddy got in a big fight and he left the house without telling me happy birthday. And when I turned ten, Nia forgot it was my birthday.

The only good thing I've ever had on my birthday was Momma. Even with no presents and no parties, even with Daddy and Nia forgetting, Momma always made sure I felt special. Ever since I can remember, she been singing me a special birthday song—the same words as regular "Happy Birthday" but with her own rhythms and notes— which she would sing to me first thing in the morning. Then she would bake me a cake from scratch and let me eat from the whole thing with a fork. I don't know what a birthday is like for other people, but for me, a birthday is a sad day that only Momma can make just a little better. Cept this year, Momma ain't here.

"KB, you in there?" Nia's on the other side of the bathroom door. I been sittin' on the seat of the toilet for a while now, doin' nothin' besides thinking. I ain't sure if I wanna confront Nia or stay away from her for good after what I saw at the Fourth of July picnic. We was s'posed to be playing together, but as usual, Nia had other plans that I ain't know nothin' bout. Plans that involved kissing a boy. But not just any boy. Nia kissed a boy in our family, the new family I was so excited to meet. Even if Jesse got a different daddy, he's still family to me. But I guess not to Nia. Lately, Nia care more bout friends and boys than family, and it makes me wonder if I even matter to her anymore.

I unravel a wad of toilet paper and pretend to wipe, then flush. I was already mad at Nia for being mean to me all the time, but now I feel more than mad. Like a mix between wanting to scream at Nia and wanting to hold on to her so tight she can't never get away, can't never do nothin' like what she did that day, again.

"Gimme a minute," I finally say. Nia ain't even mentioned my birthday tomorrow, so I bet she forgot again. And I bet Granddaddy don't even know bout it. My birthday gon' probably go by with nothin' from nobody. I wonder if Momma gon' even call.

"Hurry up!" Nia's knocks on the door are gettin' louder and closer together. I laugh, quiet so she can't hear. Then make noise with the toilet paper roll and flush the toilet again, pretending to hurry but really going as slow as possible. I wash my hands one, two, three, four times. Then, finally, when I've heard Nia suck her teeth six times straight, I open the door and come out.

"Oh, were you waiting?" I fake smile. Nia

pushes past me and slams the bathroom door behind her.

Just before I get to our room, Granddaddy calls, "KB?" His voice is coming from the living room, so I trudge down the hall and past the kitchen with the little square table.

"Yes?"

"Come sit down with me." Granddaddy pats the seat beside him on the couch. I sit, hoping I ain't in trouble for pretending to use the bathroom when Nia had to go.

"I been thinking," starts Granddaddy, "bout what you might wanna do tomorrow."

"Tomorrow?" I ask, cautious.

"Tomorrow," says Granddaddy, "for your birthday."

I smile. I bet Momma told him, but I wonder when. I ain't heard Granddaddy talk to Momma since we been here, even though I figure they gotta be talking sometimes. How else would Momma be checking on us?

"I ain't thought bout it," I answer, cause that's the truth. Nobody ain't ever asked me what I wanna do for my birthday.

"Well, gon' and think bout it now. We can do whatever you like." He smiles and pats my knee, then turns back to watching TV.

If somebody had asked me this question back

in Detroit, I bet I woulda had a bunch of ideas. Like beg Momma to take us to the Detroit Zoo. Or invite my only friends from school, Chantelle and Rhonda, over for a sleepover. Maybe even visit my favorite library to check out some books. But I ain't really got no friends here in Lansing, cept the white kids that I'm keeping secret from Granddaddy, and the Black kids I met at the pool but don't even know how to get in touch with again. Don't seem like either of those gon' be an option.

I tap my finger against my chin and think bout stuff I like to do in Lansing. I ain't really like the mall as much as Nia, and the pool was fun, but I don't wanna pick nothin' that's gon' let Nia be with her friends all day. This birthday gon' be bout me. Suddenly, I get an idea.

"Granddaddy, do Lansing got a Pizza Land?" I pick it cause it's a place I know Nia hates. She says it's for babies. We only been to Pizza Land twice in Detroit. Once was a birthday party for a girl in my class I ain't even know, and once was a day when Momma took me and Nia there right after school, and we stayed straight through lunch and dinner instead of going home to Daddy. It's got pizza and slides and games. Perfect for a birthday.

"That big place with the cartoon cat on the door?" Granddaddy asks.

I nod, enthusiastic. "Cheesin' Chuck!" Last

time we went, a stuffed-suit Cheesin' Chuck walked around giving kids high fives and free tokens. I chased him and got more tokens than any of them kids, while Nia sat with Momma and frowned.

"Okay, I know that place. It's not too far from the new bookstore. Maybe we can stop by there after?" Granddaddy winks and my smile grows even bigger.

"That sounds like a great idea," I say, tryna be cool like this ain't gon' be the best birthday I ever had. Only thing might make it better is if Momma would come. But I know she can't, so instead, I can't help myself but hope that Nia gon' remember my birthday this time.

I wake up early the next morning, even though I barely slept all night. I can't remember ever being this excited bout anything. I look around for Nia, but she's already got out the bed and left the room. I bet she's planning a surprise birthday breakfast for me. I hurry and get dressed, then run to the bathroom to brush my teeth and wash my face. I can take a shower later, but for now, I can't wait to get my birthday started.

When I skip into the kitchen it's with a huge

smile on my washed face. Granddaddy is sittin' at the table with his coffee, like always.

"Good morning," I sing.

"Well, good morning to you, birthday girl!" Granddaddy pats a chair and I sit down beside him.

"Where's Nia?" I ask. She ain't in the kitchen, and I don't see or smell no breakfast cooking, neither.

"That friend of hers came by this morning to see if she could go out for a bit," says Granddaddy. When he sees the frown growing on my face, he adds, "She's gon' be back in time for your birthday celebration, she promised."

I nod with my lips pressed tight. Figures that Nia would leave today, before I could even wake up.

I open the pantry, where I find one last packet of oatmeal in the box. I microwave it and take it, plain, back to the table. Each spoonful is thick and bland on my tongue. I eat slow to make myself consider each rotten bite. Just like each rotten birthday. I don't know why I thought this one was gon' be any different.

Just then, the phone rings. I look over at Granddaddy, expect him to answer it, but he don't move. Just sips his coffee, slow.

"I'll get it," I half say, half ask. I ain't ever answered Granddaddy's phone before, but he don't object. I pick up the beige receiver from its cradle on the wall and put it up to my ear.

"Hello?" I wonder what I should do if I don't know the person on the other end. Sometimes Momma makes me screen her calls—which later I learned is just a fancy way of saying tell her who is on the phone before she decides if she wanna talk. I don't like doin' that cause I ain't good at thinking so fast on the spot. It might be easier if she just told me the whole list of people she don't wanna talk to before I pick up the phone, so I could know.

But I do know the voice on the other end.

"Happy birthday to you, happy birthday to you, happy birthday, sweet Kenyatta, happy birthday to you." Momma's voice, when she sings my special birthday song, is light and sweet and floats in the air like a helium-filled balloon. A smile stretches the whole way cross my face.

"Thanks, Momma." I try to seem casual, when truly that one little verse meant so much. Most days here I get through without missing Momma too much. But I'm happy she knows today ain't one of them days.

"Birthday plans, big eleven-year-old girl?" Momma asks. I wonder if she already knows but is pretending not to know so I can say. Either way, I play along enthusiastically.

"Granddaddy's taking me to Pizza Land and the bookstore," I reply, then add, "And Nia, too." Momma's always fighting Nia to make her be nice to me, which I think makes it worse. So, I don't mention to Momma that Nia ain't here now. I don't want her to start that same fight.

"That sounds like fun," Momma says. I can hear her smile through the receiver, clinking bells being rung in a row. One of my favorites, of all her smiles.

"Yeah." My voice drops cause I hope it don't make her too sad that this is the first time she's missed either of our birthdays.

"Well, you have fun." Momma's voice trails and I think it's already too late to keep her from being sad. "Eat an extra slice of pizza for me." The smile is back, but the one that hangs on her face limp like a too-big dress. I twist the phone cord between my fingers and listen to Momma's breathing on the other end.

"I will, Momma." I try to think of something else to say, something good to make her happy. But all I can think of is Nia and Jesse and the little sounds I heard coming from her mouth when he lifted her dress.

"Oh, where's Nia?" Momma asks, like she can read my thoughts.

"She's . . . in the bathroom," I whisper. Granddaddy pauses his place in the newspaper, but then he keeps on reading.

"Okay, well, can you please tell her I said hi?"

Momma asks. I nod, then remember she can't see me through the phone.

"Yes, ma'am," I respond.

"Ma'am?" Momma laughs. "Looks like you're learning some new manners in Lansing, huh?" Her laugh gets even louder. I can't tell if it's the word that's so funny, or me saying it.

"Granddaddy taught me **sir** and **ma'am**. To say to grown-ups." I wanna tell her bout the picnic and meeting cousins, too, but I can't talk bout that without hide-and-seek.

"Well, I'm glad you're having fun in Lansing." Momma's voice is quiet now. "And I know you will have so much fun tonight."

"Thanks, Momma." I wish I could hug her or see her smile. I think bout the last smile I ever got from Daddy, on the morning before he died. I was outside playing, and he came onto the porch. Looked like he was bout to go somewhere, but he seemed confused like he had lost something. Then he saw me. His face stretched into a giant smile that touched his eyes til they were wet with tears. If I'd known that would be the last smile, I woulda smiled a bigger and better one back. I don't want the last smile I got from Momma to be the last. I ain't sure how much more I can lose.

"KB?" Momma says. In this one call, her voice done gone from super happy to super sad, and now sounds back to happy again. I can barely keep up anymore.

"Yeah, Momma?"

"I just want to say," Momma starts, then pauses like she's changed her mind. "Happy birthday," she finishes with a sigh.

"Bye, Momma." Without waiting for her to say it back, I unwrap the cord from my fingers and tuck the phone back into its cradle; humming to the rhythm of my sad birthday song.

We get to Pizza Land right before dinnertime. My stomach rumbled the whole way. Just like Granddaddy said, Nia made it in time to come with us. But she's got her ugly friend Brittany with her, too. I don't want Brittany at my birthday, but here she is anyway, wearing too much lip gloss and a pair of jeans so tight they look like dark blue paint.

"What kind of pizza you want to order?" Granddaddy is finally smiling so big for once that I can't help but to smile back, just a little.

"Cheese," I answer, making sure Nia don't see my smiling face.

The booth where we sit is between another girl with a birthday, and a family with a loud, crying baby. Granddaddy uses three napkins to wipe the table clean before we can sit down. The seats are ripped in the middle and I scratch my legs when I slide into my spot. Granddaddy lets me put the little plastic number in the middle of our table, so they know where to bring our pizza.

"Want some tokens?" Granddaddy asks me. He don't bother asking Nia, cause she complained the whole way here that Pizza Land was for babies.

"Sure." I don't wanna play none of these games by myself, though. I look at the girl at the next table, wearing a birthday hat on her head and a giant pin with the words **Birthday Girl** in pink cursive. She got her momma and daddy with her, plus three little girls that must be her friends, all wearing pink party hats and all wearing dresses that twirl when they spin. All perfect. The four of them jump up and down as the daddy pours gold tokens into tiny paper cups, one for each of them. They take off running toward the games as I stare up at the ceiling, pretending not to care.

Granddaddy hands me a five-dollar bill and points in the direction of the machine that makes tokens. "Gon' 'head and get you some."

I smile in a way that I hope says to Granddaddy, **Tokens will make this all better.** All the other kids are running and yelling. I'm the only one walking to the token machine like I ain't in no hurry. When it's my turn, I smooth out the crumpled bill against the edge of the machine, then feed it to the hungry monster. It chews and chews, then spits out a wad of shiny coins.

Back at the table Nia and Brittany are giggling and whispering like Granddaddy ain't even there. My face suddenly feels like it's boiling. I bet Nia thinks she's something, now that she's kissed a boy. I bet that's what she's whispering bout. She don't even look up when I get to the booth. I slam my handful of tokens down on the table, hard, so they bounce and flip and dance all over. Two of 'em even fall in her lap.

"KB!" Nia's mad now, but I don't care. "Watch what you're doing!" Nia looks to Granddaddy for support, but he don't say a word. I remind myself to give him an extra-special hug later.

"My bad," I whisper, even though I did it on purpose. I gather up all my tokens and place them one by one into one of those paper cups with loud clinks, and once Nia's good and mad, I walk away.

My first stop is the basketball game, cause it's one I know I can play. You just gotta shoot the balls in the hoop, even when the hoop moves back and forth. Nia taught me that during that last long day at Pizza Land, and it's one of my best games.

Five boys are already waiting when I get there. No girls. I stand behind two boys who argue bout whether football players or basketball players make more money. It's funny, though, cause the boy

arguing for football is shaped kinda like a basketball, and the boy arguing for basketball more like a
football. In front of them is a boy that's tall like
a grown-up, with a face full of pimples. He's got
tiny whiskers above his upper lip and below his
chin, and he smells like wet clothes that's set out in
the sun all day. I take a couple steps back, so I ain't
smelling that stink.

Just then, another boy comes and squeezes
between me and the arguing boys.

"Hey, I'm in line!" I start to yell, then stop
quick, cause I recognize the face that turns around
and smiles at me. I ain't think I would see him
again after the pool, but here he is.

"Kenyatta," Rondell yells, even though we so
close I would hear it if he whispered. "What you
doin' here?"

"It's my birthday," I say, still surprised to see him.

"Happy birthday! How old you turn?" Rondell
asks, smiling even bigger. His hair ain't in braids
no more. Now it's in a big Afro on top of his head.

"Eleven." The new age sounds funny when I
hear it out loud for the first time. "How old are
you?" I ask after a few seconds, to be polite.

"I'm eleven, too." He stammers it slightly, then
looks down at the carpet. The pimple-face boy
starts playing a new game of basketball, so me and
Rondell move forward. He don't stop watching me
when we move.

"So, what you doin' here?" I ask, tryna think of the right things to say. I ain't used to talking to boys, and especially not all alone.

"Me and my cousins get to come here when we do good stuff," he answers, proud. "And my football team won our first game today, so my momma brought all of us to celebrate." When he mentions his momma, his eyes wander to find her in the room. I look, too. He lands on a tall, brown-skinned woman with twisted hair piled on top of her head. She sees Rondell and waves, so he waves back. Her smile is nice, but not as nice as Momma's.

"How long you been playing football?" I ask, pulling one of my arms with the other behind my back. Seems like I ain't got nowhere to put my hands all of a sudden.

"Since I was seven," Rondell answers. "My pops played football, so I wanna play just like him. He was even good enough for the NFL."

"Does he play with you?" I ask, following Rondell's gaze down to his unlaced shoes.

"Naw, he dead." He says it quick, so I gotta repeat it in my head two times just to hear it. Once I understand, I stay quiet a few seconds more.

"Oh," I finally say, even though I wanna say more. Maybe tell him that my daddy's dead, too. Maybe then we can talk bout it, or maybe then he won't be so sad.

"Yeah," he whispers, before I can say anything else.

The two arguing boys move up in the line, so it's our turn next. Rondell and me ain't talking no more, just waiting, quiet, for our turn. Nia's still giggling with Brittany, looking cross the room, then ducking they heads back low. I follow Nia's eyes to see what they keep staring at, and it's the tall, pimple-face boy that was in front of the arguing boys in line. Figures.

"You got any brothers or sisters?" I ask Rondell. He's got his hands tucked into his pockets.

"Just one brother, but he's older than me."

"How old?" I ask.

"Seventeen. He's bout to graduate from high school next year."

"Y'all get along?" I ask, looking back at Nia, batting her eyes at the boy. I think I wanna punch her.

"Yeah, most of the time. Cept when his girlfriend come over, then he don't talk to me." Rondell laughs so I laugh, too, even though I don't really think it's funny.

"Our turn!" Rondell yells suddenly. The arguing boys finished their game: the short one scored forty-four points and the tall one thirty-two. They walk away, now arguing bout whether or not the short one cheated.

I take a token from my cup but Rondell beats

me to it, putting his tokens, one for each of us, into the game. Then he stands back and smiles at me real nice. I smile, too, grab a worn basketball, and get ready. The starting buzzer sounds, so I aim and shoot without looking over at Rondell. All I can hear is the ding of the bell when I make a shot. I count along in my head, two points, then twelve, then seventeen.

Buzz! The final bell sounds and the game is over. I look up at my score: twenty-eight. Then I look at Rondell's: six. I think he's gon' be frowning cause his score so bad, but he's laughing and laughing.

"What's so funny?" I ask. "What happened?" Rondell don't answer for a minute, cause he's laughing too hard. Finally, he calms his laugh down to a chuckle.

"I hate this game," he finally manages to say.

"What you mean? Then why you come play?" I look at him, confused, as he grabs my arm and pulls me away. Two more boys are waiting for a turn, so we gotta move. Rondell pulls me over to a corner where there ain't no games and no people.

"Cause I saw you," Rondell says once we get there. He waits, I think, for me to say something, but I don't, so he continues. "I hate basketball. Tried out for the JV team and didn't get picked. My cousins been tryna get me to play that game all day. But I ain't play. Not til I saw you over here." Rondell's looking at me all funny, kinda like he gotta use the bathroom.

"JV team?" I ask, just realizing what he said. "Don't you gotta be in high school to play JV?" I only heard the term once before, when Nia was on the phone with one of her new high school friends bout a cute boy on the JV team. "Ain't you just bout to start middle school, since you eleven, too?" I ask. His face goes blank and he looks down at his shoes.

"Yeah, I just meant I was gon' try out later, when I'm older." Rondell still stares at his dusty shoes and I don't know what to look at.

"I love basketball," I say, sticking to the safe part of the conversation. "I been playing this game for years and watching even longer than that." I pause, twisting my hair in my fingers. "My daddy taught me, but he's dead now, too." I think Rondell gon' look at me all sad, like everybody else do when I tell 'em Daddy died. But he don't, just watches my face real close, staring straight into my eyes.

"Maybe you can teach me," he says, smiling sweet. It feels good to have somebody to talk to bout Daddy. Nia don't care to talk bout him, Momma's too sad or mad to talk bout him, and nobody else seems to understand. Cept Rondell now.

"I can do that." My answer makes Rondell happy; I can tell cause his smile gets so big that it covers his whole face. I wonder if this is why Nia likes boys.

"Wanna play something else?" Rondell asks, and I nod. We take off in the same direction, like we already had a plan where to go. I glance over at our booth, but Nia's gone. Brittany's sittin' there alone with Granddaddy. I can't tell if they're talking, but I bet they not.

While me and Rondell wait to play Skee-Ball, I look around for Nia, but I don't see her by the games, or in line for more food. I watch the bathroom door and count four girls that go in and six that come out, but ain't none of 'em Nia. I start looking for that tall boy with the pimples, but I can't find him nowhere, neither. My stomach gets to hurting.

"You okay?" Rondell asks, and I nod.

"Our turn," he eventually says, and I pretend to be excited, lunging forward too fast and almost spilling the coins from my paper cup. I take out two tokens and start both our games. The screens light up to say we're playing head-to-head. I grab one of the balls, rock colored but not as heavy, and roll it down the aisle to try to hit a target. I land right under the center, which earns me a loud **ding!** And a quiet whistle from Rondell, so I laugh and tilt my head to one side like I seen Nia do before.

That's when I see her. Just behind Rondell, by the game where you hit the big weasel with the hammer. Laughing too loud and batting her eyes like she got dirt in 'em. Just like I thought, Pimple Boy's there, too, whacking the furry animal when it pokes its little head through the holes.

"Did you see that?" yells Rondell. "I got it in the middle!" The game dings and dings and Rondell yells and yells.

"I saw it!" I lie. "How many points you get for that?" We both watch as his score climbs up and up.

"Two hundred!" Rondell is so excited, almost makes me forget bout Nia. Almost. "Your turn," Rondell tells me. Farther on, Pimple Boy finishes his game and whispers something to Nia that makes her laugh and playfully swat his shoulder. My skin starts to feel prickly all over.

I pick up a ball that feels more like a bowling ball now. Nia and Pimple Boy disappear. Just like Nia and Jesse. I heave the ball down the sloped lane.

"Kenyatta!" I hear Rondell yell at the same time I see my ball crash into the screen. It hits so hard that a long crack appears in the plastic.

"My bad," I whisper. But as the crack spreads bigger and bigger, I feel good for some reason. My fists are clenched tight, and I try to relax, but I can't.

"You okay?" Rondell asks again.

But I can't answer, cause my tongue feels glued

to the bottom of my mouth. Everything feels like it's moving too fast. I wanna tell Rondell that no, I ain't okay, but I'm tired of feeling outta control. So I open my mouth and say instead, "Wanna see something?" Rondell seems confused and says something, but I can't hear nothin' now, cept Nia making them little sounds over and over in my head. I gotta make 'em stop. "Come on." I walk away from the Skee-Ball machine, still dinging cause we ain't finish our game.

"Where we going?" Rondell comes up behind me quick, and I don't respond cause I don't know. But I keep walking like I do know. If Nia can disappear with boys, so can I. I turn the corner and stop in front of the back door, at the end of a long hallway. Rondell stands in front of me, back to the door.

"What's this?" Rondell asks, looking around. Ain't nothin' to see back here, though, cept old cardboard boxes that used to hold tickets and tokens and pizzas.

"I just wanted someplace quiet." The noises in my head get louder and louder and the world's spinning around me. I try not to wonder where Nia went with Pimple Boy, but the question repeats in my head like a scratched CD. I feel like my eyes are filled with red, like the cartoon animals on TV when they get so mad their heads boil over with hot lava. I imagine angry whistle noises shooting from my ears, like I'm the old teakettle Momma kept hidden behind the pots and pans at the old house, then refused to leave behind when we moved to the motel.

"Okay," Rondell whispers. He shuffles his feet, so he's moving but ain't got nowhere to go. In my head, Nia kisses Jesse with her wet mouth, letting him lift the skirt of her dress til her panties show. Tiny purple patterns the only thing left to cover that "thing" Momma always tells us we gotta protect. Don't look like Nia wanna protect hers, though, cause in my mind, the boy's starting to blur the patterns with his greedy fingers.

The patterns fill my eyes til I'm blind, and when I say to Rondell, "You ever seen a girl's panties?" the noises are so loud I can't hear my own voice. My throat's dry like I been screaming for hours. Up til now, I been tryna hold it all in. But standing here on my birthday with a stranger who wanna give me more attention than my own sister, I feel like the world is on fire and I'm somewhere lost in it. I try to find Rondell, standing in front of me.

"Uh, not really," he says, but he's changed, Rondell, I've changed him somehow. He looks like he's thirsty, licking his lips over and over. The brick wall behind him seems like it gets closer and closer. I'm facing the door; Rondell's facing me. All I know is I gotta do something to stop the noise.

And I don't know why this would stop it, but it's what I do: while Rondell watches, I unbutton my pants. I ain't ever undressed in front of anybody before, cept Momma and Nia. I don't know why I'm gon' do it now, I just do. Rondell stares as my zipper goes down, down. Just enough so he can see a triangle of pink-patterned flowers. I wish I wore some better panties today, but now it's too late. Rondell licks his wet lips.

We stay there like that, without moving. I'm waiting til the noise stops, but Rondell's staring like he's tryna memorize all the patterns. My fists don't clench no more and I ain't frowning no more. Rondell looks at me hungry, like Jesse when he was touching Nia. I count five long seconds in my head, then start to pull the zipper up again.

"Wait," says Rondell quick, "don't do that yet." He reaches his hands toward mine, and I clench my fists again.

"Why?" I ask, hands guarding my zipper.

"Cause I still wanna see," Rondell whines. I ignore him and zip my pants as fast as I can. I think maybe I made a mistake, copying Nia when she did something so bad. I button my pants just as I hear a voice behind me.

"Kenyatta?" I freeze at the sound of Granddaddy's rumble. Then lower my hands to my sides, slow, so he can't see what I was doin'.

Rondell stands in front of me frozen, with big eyes looking straight past me.

"Hey, Granddaddy." I turn and smile like ain't nothin' wrong.

"What you doin' back here, girl?" Granddaddy hobbles at me, faster than I've ever seen. "Come on back here nah!" I start walking before he can reach me and Rondell, scared what might happen if I don't. I ain't ever seen Granddaddy so angry. I don't know if he's the type to smack my face or swipe my bottom, or just talk to me real long and hard.

"Yes, sir." I lower my head and walk away from Rondell without saying bye. Granddaddy don't say nothin', either. We just leave him standing there invisible. My heart is racing and I'm more scared than I been in a while, but the Nia noise is gone from my head. What I hear now is Rondell's longing whine.

We get back to the empty booth and sit down. I look around and find Nia and Brittany together, sittin' on top of a game meant for playing. Laughing with Pimple Boy and his friends. And I stop watching, cause now I just don't care. I chip wood from the table with my fingernails to avoid looking up at Granddaddy.

"Kenyatta," he says in a way that forces me to look up at him. "Who was that boy?"

"Just my friend from the pool. Rondell." I keep it simple, cause I don't know what he gon' say next.

"What was you doing back there with him, all by yourself?" Granddaddy seems nervous to ask his own question. He keeps clearing his throat and rubbing his hands.

"We just went to look for the bathrooms," I lie, tryna think quick. "Then we saw the red alarm on the door, so we was guessing if it would make noise if somebody touched it." Granddaddy's eyebrows dig deeper into his face, so I quickly add, "We ain't touch it, though. We was just talking pretend."

Granddaddy sits there without a word, but he nods. I can't tell if he believes me or not. He's just sittin' there staring at me, like he can read my mind, so I try not to think bout unzipping my pants, or Rondell's eyes once I did.

"Did your daddy talk to you bout boys, before he died?" Granddaddy's question is not what I expected. I shake my head no. "You wanna talk bout boys with me?" I shake my head faster, no. I ain't even sure how I feel bout what just happened with Rondell. But what I am sure of is that I ain't ready to talk to Granddaddy bout none of it.

Granddaddy chuckles. "The one thing you need to know bout boys, Kenyatta, is that they always thinkin' at least one step ahead of you."

I scrunch my face, then say, "What you mean?"

"You said you and that boy was looking for bathrooms and playing with door alarms, right?" I nod, slow. "Well, maybe that's what **you** was doin', but that boy, he was at least one step ahead of that. Believe you me." Granddaddy sits back and folds his arms, like he's all done proving his point.

"But it was my idea," I whisper, leaving out the part where it was me who was two steps ahead of Rondell; me who made the plan to show him my undies when all he wanted to do was play Skee-Ball.

"That's the other thing bout boys," Granddaddy says, leaning forward now. "They **real** good at makin' girls think that somethin' is their own idea, when really, it be that boy's idea all along."

I ain't sure Granddaddy's right bout this, but I don't say nothin'. Instead, I give Granddaddy a small half smile that I hope says, **You are right bout boys.**

"It can be tricky," Granddaddy continues.

"Boys?" I ask.

"Love," he replies, looking right in my eyes now. "Bout your age is when it really starts gettin' tricky. You start gettin' all these new thoughts and feelings, and you just wanna act on all of 'em, all the time. But you gotta remember, don't everybody got your best interest in mind. So before you go sneaking around with any of these

243

nappy-headed boys, you gotta figure out what it is that **you** want. And then you do that, and nothin' more."

I smile again, but this time I mean it. "You got real good advice," I say. Granddaddy smiles. "I bet you was real good at talking to Momma bout boys."

Granddaddy stops smiling all at once and stares down at the table. Then, when he finally says something, it's just a noise. "Hmph." He folds and unfolds his hands, then looks back up at me.

"You know, I hated your daddy when I first met him," Granddaddy finally says, "couldn't stand him." He chuckles, but I don't, just cock my head to one side and scoot in closer. "Your momma was in high school. Think she was bout sixteen at the time. He was older than your momma by a few years. I remember he had a car, some old raggedy thing he used to blast loud music from. Then come tryna pick up my daughter." Granddaddy shakes his head at the thought. I listen without interrupting. I ain't even know Granddaddy knew my daddy.

"So when you start liking him?" I ask, pulling up another bigger strip of wood from the table.

"What makes you think I did?" Granddaddy asks with a serious face. Then he laughs, but I can't tell if he's making a joke or being for real. "Me and your daddy had a real tough time," he says, looking down at the table. "I think mostly cause of your momma, cause she was still mad at me bout everything. But it had something to do with me, too."

A splinter from the wood I been chipping sneaks through the skin of my middle finger. I look down and see it there, a tiny sliver of wood hiding in my skin. I pull it out, quick, then pop my finger in my mouth to quiet the sting.

"It was hard for me to accept your momma growing up," Granddaddy continues, more serious now. "Especially with her momma gone. I had only raised boys before, and all by myself." Granddaddy lowers his head. "The boys ain't have the same momma as your momma did. I raised them on my own, after they momma left." The secret swirls around in my head as Granddaddy continues. Momma never mentioned that her brothers had a different momma than her. Then again, she never mentioned her momma at all, so I guess it was just another one of them secrets.

"The point is, I ain't know what it meant for a girl to change into a woman. So when I started seeing it in your momma, seeing she was changing into a woman, I ain't want her to grow up cause I was afraid I'd lose her forever." I'm watching Nia as Granddaddy talks, laughing and playing with her friends, and I wonder if Granddaddy was afraid of losing Momma like I'm scared bout losing Nia.

"Did you?" I ask, quiet. "Lose her?"

Granddaddy don't answer my question for a while, just stares at his folded hands on the table. Then finally he looks up at me with watery eyes. "Well, I got you here now, don't I? So I must ain't lost her yet." He stares at me long with them watery eyes, but his tears can't seem to fall. They stay perfectly balanced in his eyes, even as he reaches cross the table and squeezes my hand. I smile. Just that little squeeze feels like wrapping up in a warm blanket and drinking hot cocoa. Better yet, hot cocoa with marshmallows.

"Anyway." Granddaddy shifts. "I ain't hate your daddy forever. In fact, just before you were born, me and him had a big talk bout everything. He was a really good cook, had me over for dinner and made smothered meat loaf and mashed potatoes."

I lick my lips remembering Daddy's famous meal, one of my favorite dinners in the world. Then I realize this is the second time tonight I thought bout Daddy without gettin' sad. "Thank you," I whisper to Granddaddy.

"For what?" Granddaddy returns my smile. Truth is, I'm just happy for him talking to me like nobody ever does, like I'm a person with thoughts and feelings, not just a kid or somebody that ain't even there. When Daddy died, Momma was so sad she forgot to notice I was sad, too. Her and Nia got to fighting a lot, and that was how we spent our days leading up to the funeral. Momma crying, Nia fighting, me with nobody to notice either way. It feels good to be noticed now, for once.

But I don't say all that, just, "For a perfect birthday."

"You're welcome," Granddaddy says. He pauses, then continues. "You know, it's good to talk bout the people that's gone, Kenyatta." Now I'm positive he can read my mind. Granddaddy fixes his eyes right on my eyes. I concentrate on the dark spots as he talks, to keep from looking away. "When we lose someone we love, it's easy to just pretend they was never there. To try and make it easier. But it don't work, cause they was there. And now you got a big ol' hole where that person used to be." Granddaddy reaches cross the table and taps his finger against my shirt, right above my heart. Then moves his hand toward mine, like he gon' grab it. But he don't. "You gotta fill that hole with the memories, else you might lose 'em for good."

Granddaddy don't say nothin' else after that, so neither do I. Just enjoy our perfect moment. I feel closer to fixing Momma and Granddaddy, and also closer to something else I ain't even know I was looking for. I sit with Granddaddy at our worn table in the back of Pizza Land—kids yelling and playing and screaming around us—and I don't have a care in the world.

We get back to the house late, after Granddaddy's slow driving and stopping at the bookstore for two new books bout Anne: **Anne of Avonlea** and **Anne of the Island**. I clutch the books to my chest and follow Nia straight to our room to get ready for bed. We ain't talk the whole ride home. And Nia don't seem much in the mood for talking now, either.

Nia takes off her earrings and places them in the little box that she keeps in her purse. Then she removes her necklace and picks up her scarf to wrap her hair. Nia moves so graceful, like a ballerina.

"Nia," I begin, swallowing hard, "I wanna talk to you bout something."

She's sittin' in front of the mirror now and I'm standing behind her. Through the mirror she rolls her eyes, then sighs. "What?" she asks, working her fingers through her feathery hair.

"Well, Granddaddy was talking to me bout Daddy. Did you know they knew each other?" I watch to see if her expression changes, but she still just looks annoyed.

"Duh, of course they knew each other. Momma and Daddy was married. Don't you think Momma would introduce her husband to her dad?"

I consider that question for a while, cause I don't think it's that simple. Then again, Nia don't know bout the headshot and Granny and the fights. I think bout telling her, but then I remember all the secrets Nia been keeping from me and wonder if it's a good idea. "You remember that meat loaf and potatoes Daddy would make?" I ask. Daddy's meat loaf used to be one of her favorites, too. We used to always complain when Momma made dinner instead of Daddy. That would make Daddy laugh and Momma frown, so then we would have to hug her and tickle her til she smiled again.

"I ain't ever like that meat loaf," Nia says, wrapping her hair like she ain't just tell a big fat lie.

I take a deep breath, then start again. "Remember that time on Fourth of July, when Daddy sprayed us with the water hose?" Nia don't say nothin', so I keep going. "Then, when Momma tried to run in the house to get away from him, he followed her and sprayed the whole front room?" I'm starting to giggle as the memory comes: me and Nia laughing and laughing, watching Momma and Daddy running around the house and acting like kids. But Nia ain't laughing now.

"He coulda messed up our whole house with that water hose," Nia says, then adds under her breath, "Stupid." I sit down on the edge of the bed closest to Nia at the mirror, feeling like the wind just got knocked outta me. Nia don't speak again, just goes on wrapping her hair like she ain't just trampled over my best memories.

I sit there for a while without saying nothin'. I don't know if there's anything I can say that's gon' work. This is how it's been since Daddy died, or even before that. Whenever I talk bout him to Nia, she just gets mad. I know we all miss him, but she won't even talk bout the good stuff. Fill the hole with memories, like Granddaddy said. Instead, she wanna act like he was never here at all.

"Why you so mad at Daddy?" I ask, staring at the side of Nia's unmoving face. I wait and wait, but she don't say nothin'. "You mad at him cause he died?" Now Nia finally turns and looks at me.

"I'm not mad he died! I'm mad at how he died! He had a choice and he ain't choose us! And when I tried to stop him, he—" Nia is talking fast, then stops even faster. Her face in the mirror's changing from angry to plain as I watch. "Really, I'm mad at you, cause you getting on my nerves with all these stupid questions." Nia stands and walks to the dresser.

"I just wanted to talk," I whisper, dropping my head low. Nia shuffles through clothes in her drawer, then pulls out a pair of tiny pink shorts and a beige tank top. Looks like she bout to take a shower. "Nia, wait!" I yell, more anxious than I mean to be.

Nia is already at the door but turns around, arms crossed. "What?" Her face is harder to read than ever. On the surface, it's nothin' but anger. But underneath, I feel like there's something else.

"Who was that boy you was talking to today?" As soon as the question leaves my mouth, I know it's the wrong one. Nia don't ever like nobody all up in her business, especially not me.

"What you talking bout?" Nia asks, her voice a little louder than before.

"You know, at Pizza Land. The boy with all the—that tall boy you was talking to."

"What, was you watching me or something?" Nia is in full attitude mode now, as Momma calls it. She got one hand on her hip and her neck moving from left to right with every word. I've seen this dance before, between Momma and Nia, so I know it ain't gon' end well.

"No, not like that. I mean, I did see you, but not cause I was watching." I can feel my face flush as I stumble over my words. "It's just, he was in front of me in line at that basketball game, then I saw you talking to him, so I was just wondering if you knew him." It sounds stupid, even to me, but I ain't got no better excuse in my head right now.

"It's none of your business," Nia snaps, "and don't be telling Granddaddy nothing bout me and that boy, neither." She gets real serious when she says that last part, but I don't know if it's cause she thinks I'm a tattletale, or cause she got something to hide.

"I ain't tell him nothin'," I mutter. Why don't Nia know I would keep her secrets forever, from anybody? I never even told anyone bout that time she lost the special house key Momma gave her on the little plastic ring. We looked for it for days, and when we couldn't find it nowhere, I helped Nia sneak Momma's key so we could make a copy. She should know, I always got her back.

"Good." Nia looks at me a second longer, then turns to leave, but pauses with her hand on the doorknob and a sunnier look on her face. "And KB?"

"Yeah?" I say, hoping she gon' apologize.

Nia takes a couple steps toward me, close enough that I could reach out and grab her. Hug her. "Stay outta my business," she says, then leaves with her fake sunny face turned to storming rain clouds.

Usually when Nia does stuff like that, it makes me cry. But for once, I don't feel sad at all. She turns on the shower and the Nia noises pop in my head again, louder. I stuff my face into a pillow, thinking it's my pillow, but it smells like her shampoo and body wash. I scream into it, long and hard, to drown out all the noise.

But I can't. The noises get louder, Nia and Jesse touching and kissing and giggling in my mind.

Then Nia and Pimple Boy running around like kids, laughing and chasing, and then it's just Nia, teasing and calling me "Crybaby KB," ripping up the memories in my head. Memories I work so hard to keep, but she rips and crumbles like trash. I see Nia making Momma cry and laughing at Granddaddy when he walks slow. Wearing them stupid headphones and them nasty dresses. In my head I just see Nia now. And I don't like what I see.

I lay in the bed and count my fingers, over and over, while I wait for her to come back from the shower. When I hear her footsteps near the door, I pretend to be sleeping. Nia opens the door quiet, like she's sneaking. I peek my eyes open and see that she ain't get dressed in the bathroom. She has a fuzzy purple towel wrapped around her body like a cocoon. Her hair is still wrapped, and her face is scrubbed clean so that her skin glows.

First thing when she comes in the room, Nia looks to see if I'm watching. I squeeze my eyes shut, quick. She shuts the door behind her and starts to dry off with the towel. I wait til she turns her back to me, then I know it's time.

I ain't ever been in a fight before. One time, a group of girls circled around me at recess, tryna make me say a bad word. There was three of us in the middle of the circle, me and Chantelle and Rhonda. We was best friends, mostly cause none of the other girls in the class liked us. They found out we ain't like to cuss. Which made us babies, cause everybody else in fourth grade was cussin'.

They yelled at us to say two bad words—the one with the **D** and the one with the **F**—or they was gon' beat us up. Rhonda and Chantelle said the words right away. But not me. I had already said both them words at home, by myself. But I ain't wanna say 'em then to prove no point to them mean girls. Momma been telling me since I was little that can't nobody make me be a good or bad person, cept me. So I said no. And waited to get jumped, as the girls screamed, "Goody-Two-Shoes!" in my face.

Cept there was a boy in the class named Curtis. He never spoke to me or even looked at me in class. The meanest girl, Tammy, told everybody that Curtis was her boyfriend, and would talk bout him all day long. But that day, he came and stood up to Tammy, for me. That day was the closest I been to a fight, and nobody even hit me and I ain't hit nobody. Once it was all over, I said thank you to Curtis for standing up for me, then never spoke to him again for the rest of fourth grade. Now I gotta stand up for myself, cept this time the mean girl is Nia.

I spring off the bed so fast it don't even make its usual squeak. My feet hit the ground already running. Nia starts to turn around, but I reach her before she can see me. I jump on her back and wrap my hands around her face, cause it's the first thing I reach. She yells and falls to her knees, caught off-balance.

"What are you doing?" Nia screams, tryna pull my hands off her face. But now I got her scarf off and I'm pulling her hair and scratching her neck. She puts her hands up to try to block her face.

"I hate you!" I scream, over and over. Nia tries to stand, but I grab her towel and pull her back. It falls from her body in a heap as she tumbles naked to the floor. She tries to cover her tiny breasts with her hands, like she ain't been showing her body to all them boys. The only person she cares to hide herself from is me.

I dig my nails into her shoulder and see red blood pop up like beads of sweat. Nia's eyes move from confused to startled to angry. She picks me up and slams me on the ground hard. I can't breathe no more. I lay there, gasping for air, with naked Nia pinning me down. She tucks my arms to my sides and closes them in with her knees, then leans into me so I can't lift my head or chest.

"What are you doing?" Nia yells again. I still feel like I can't breathe. I dart my eyes around wildly, since I can't move no other part of my body. "KB! What is wrong with you?" Nia half yells and half begs.

"I saw you!" I finally manage to yell. "I saw you

and Jesse!" The image pastes itself again in my mind, Nia and Jesse and Nia's undies. The image starts to blur in front of my eyes til it's suddenly me instead of Nia, Rondell instead of Jesse; my undies. I start to shake.

"What are you talking bout?" Nia says, but the memory already flashed cross her face before she could hide it.

"You know what I'm talking bout! I saw you and Jesse in that bathroom! I saw everything!" The images blur together faster, over and over. I can't stop seeing what Nia did. What I did. I'm yelling so loud now, I ain't sure how Granddaddy ain't heard yet.

"KB." Nia's noticeably shaken. "I don't know what you think you saw but—"

"No! I know what I saw! Stop treating me like a baby!" I try to jump up, but Nia pins me down again, quick. "I saw you kiss him! And he touched you, in the private places!"

"Shh!" Nia's frantic, looking at the door, like Granddaddy gon' burst in. I don't even care if he does. I want everybody to see Nia like I do now. She's been hiding for too long.

"No, you not gon' shush me!" I yell even louder. "I was gon' keep your secret, like I always been keeping your secrets, but then you gotta be mean to me, too!" I got all of Nia's attention now. "I hate you! You ain't ever cared bout nobody but you!

Not Momma, not Daddy, not me. All you care bout is you! Daddy's dead and you don't even care!" I'm crying now, hot tears sliding down my face and into the carpet.

"Don't say that!" Nia yells. "That stuff ain't true!" Her hands are shaking now and her breath comes faster and faster, but I don't stop.

"It is true, Nia! You ain't even cried since Daddy died! You don't even go to Momma when she cries! All you do is listen to them stupid head-phones and talk to boys!" My words are muddled with sobs and tears now. "When Daddy died, I thought that was gon' be the worst day of my life. Then Momma left us here and I thought that was worse. But the real worst thing is you!" My voice cracks cause I've cried and screamed my throat nearly raw. I wanna wipe my soaking-wet face, but Nia still got my arms pinned. I taste the salt of my tears on my tongue as I cry and cry.

Nia don't say nothin'. She reaches for the purple towel, still in a crumpled heap on the floor, then stands and wraps it around her body. I sit up and wiggle my fingers and toes, which feel like they are being pricked by a bunch of needles. Nia sits down on the edge of the bed and we both stay that way, silent, for a full minute.

"I hate you," I finally whisper. Nia looks up at me and I think I see a tear in the corner of her eye. But then I think I made it up in my head, cause her face stays dry as I talk. "I hate you cause you let our new cousin touch you." Do I hate Nia? Or am I mad at her for tryna act like a grown-up, when all that grown-ups do is hurt me? I shake the thought away. "I hate you cause you won't play with me no more, and cause you laugh at me with your stupid friends. But mostly, I hate you for making Momma cry, and for not crying for Daddy."

Holding on to the edge of the dresser, I get myself up off the floor and walk toward the door. I don't wanna sleep in the same room with Nia no more. I wasted all our time in Lansing tryna make her be nice to me again. But now I see that ain't gon' happen, cause Nia has changed. She ain't the same person she used to be and probably never will be again. Far as I'm concerned, I ain't got a daddy no more and I ain't got a sister no more, either.

"KB?" Nia calls as I turn the doorknob. "There's something you should know."

I pause, but I don't turn back to her. I'm done with secrets, and I'm done with Nia. I walk out the door and shut it behind me, for good.

The hottest part of the summer is ending. The days used to scald like a fresh pot of boiling water, but now they feel like a lukewarm bath that you could soak in all day. Up in my tree, I look around at the neighborhood. Feels like my neighborhood now. The field behind Granddaddy's house has gone from dull to bright and back again, with scattered flowers now leaning and gloomy. Up this high, at the right time of day, I can feel a little breeze through the leaves. Down below, the grass is greener cause it ain't been burned by the scorching sun.

I reach up high to pluck a bright green leaf from above my head, then settle into my favorite spot with folded legs. Most days I read books and look for caterpillars or find rocks. Now I got seven white rocks, four brown, ten gray, two black, and one rock that's so dirty I can't tell what color it was to start. All those plus Bobby's rocks makes twenty-seven. I look for more rocks every day, and whether I find any or not, I always count 'em again. I ain't able to play with Bobby and Charlotte whenever I want, so I count my rocks to remind myself that I still got two friends here I can count on.

I nibble on the end of the leaf's stem, one of my favorite things to do when I'm thinking bout a lot of stuff. I ain't talked to Nia in five days. That's four days longer than we've ever went without talking. Once Nia had some big paper due for English class and from the time she woke up to the time she went to bed, Nia worked on that paper with Momma. More like Momma was working and Nia was complaining. I tried to come in the room with them a couple times, but Momma would shoo me away. Before now, that's the only thing that ever kept me and Nia from talking this long.

This feels different, too, cause now I'm the one that don't wanna talk. Nia has tried to talk to me a bunch of times, but I always walk away. Most of the time I feel so mad at Nia I wanna fight all over again. I thought that first fight was gon' make me feel better, but I only feel worse.

"Kenyatta!" Granddaddy yells from the house, so I drop the leaf from my lips, then climb down from my tree as fast as I can. Inside, I'm breathing hard and bend over to try to catch my breath. When I finally look up, Granddaddy's watching me from his big recliner chair.

"You all right?" Granddaddy asks with a chuckle.

"Yeah," I huff, "just outta breath." In the kitchen I make a glass of water that I drink in one long gulp, then refill my glass and head back to the living room.

"I wanted to talk to you for a minute," Granddaddy says, and I almost roll my eyes, like Nia, but I stop myself.

"I'm gon' be leaving on a fishing trip with Charlie tomorrow, so you gon' be here with Nia overnight." Granddaddy leans back in his chair, crossing his ankles. I sit down on the couch too fast, spilling a couple drops of water that I try to wipe away before Granddaddy can see.

"Nia?" I ask, cause that's the only part I really heard. I still don't know if Granddaddy heard us fighting that day. He ain't ever mention it, but I bet he can tell something's wrong with me and Nia, since we not sleeping in the same room. We don't even talk no more, and sometimes I make mean faces at her cross the dinner table. Either Granddaddy ain't paying us no attention, or he's pretending not to know. Either way, he gotta know leaving us alone together for a fishing trip is a bad idea.

"Yeah, Nia's gon' be in charge when I'm gone. That a problem?" Granddaddy looks at me with eyes that know everything or nothin' at all.

"No, it won't be a problem," I mumble. "Did you already tell Nia?"

"I told her first, to see if she felt comfortable watching you that long. I asked your momma, too, and they both said it was gon' be fine." Granddaddy stares at me like he's waiting for me to tell him different, but I don't say nothin'. "Me and Charlie been goin' on this trip fourteen years. I was gon' cancel it this summer, if I had to. But they said it's gon' be fine." I can't tell if he says it again for me, or for him.

"Okay," I eventually respond. I can't say more than that, cause I know it would be a lie. Granddaddy gets to humming and straightening up the old magazines he keeps under the coffee table. I sit there for five more minutes, five quiet minutes, and pretend like I'm gon' listen to my sister when she's in charge.

※

Granddaddy leaves so early the next morning it's still dark outside. I think the insects even sleep cause I don't hear no crickets chirping and I don't see no fireflies twinkling. I lay on the couch listening to the creak of the screen door as Granddaddy goes in and out. Carrying out his fishing rod, then his cooler, then some stuff I don't recognize that I think is for catching the fish. I wonder if he ever took Momma fishing when she was a girl. I try to imagine them together, him teaching her the names of all the little parts. I bet Momma loved riding on Granddaddy's shoulders. I imagine him carrying her—running—cause this was before he walked so slow. I bet when Momma smiled her ice cream cone smile at Granddaddy, it made him melt.

But now, Momma and Granddaddy barely even talk. When I think bout all Momma done missed with Granddaddy—all **we** done missed with Granddaddy—it makes me wanna grab on to his ankles and beg him not to go.

But I don't, cause I'm s'posed to be too old for stuff like that now. When it's time for Granddaddy to go, Nia comes from the room and they talk by the front door. I try to sneak and listen but can only hear some of it cause the fan in the corner of the room keeps circling back and forth. All I can make out is some stuff bout emergency phone numbers and a first-aid kit. Grown-up stuff, but the boring kind. Cept now, the grown-up is Nia, which don't make no sense. She's still a kid just like me.

"I'm gon' get on outta here," Granddaddy says

louder, looking at me now. "Don't wanna keep the fish waiting." He winks, and I can't help but smile.

"Have fun," I say, and I really mean it. I don't want Granddaddy to have a bad time on his fishing trip just cause I gotta be stuck here with stupid ol' Nia.

"Bye, Granddaddy," Nia says as she shuts the door behind him. Then we both sit there without saying nothin', til finally we hear the crunch of his tires on the gravel as he pulls out the driveway. The curtains in the living room let just a sliver of light in from the climbing sun.

"You hungry?" Nia asks. I wanna ignore her, but I can't ignore the loud grumble my belly just made. So I simply shrug.

Once she's in the kitchen I don't watch, but I listen. I hear the click of the stove as she turns on a burner. Usually she just microwaves oatmeal or pours bowls of cereal, so I ain't sure what she needs the stove for. I hear her rumbling around in the pantry, pulling out a few things, then going back for more. Once, then twice, then three times. Now I'm curious.

I sit up from my spot on the couch and lean forward, just barely so that my neck and head can peek around the corner to the kitchen. I see Nia with her back to me, placing the big cast-iron skillet on the stove. On the counter beside her I see flour, baking powder, salt, sugar, eggs, and oil.

Then she goes back in the pantry one more time and I bet I know what she gon' get. Brown sugar and cinnamon, cause she's making pancakes like Momma.

I wanna get closer to watch, but I don't wanna give Nia that satisfaction. Instead, I watch from right where I am, as Nia takes out a large bowl and starts the mix. I've watched Momma make pancakes more times than I can even count. She's made it the same exact way all my life, never changing a single measurement. I bet I could make 'em just by all that watching, if I tried. But I ain't ever seen Nia watching Momma, so I don't know how she got the recipe.

Either way, she's doin' it just right. Her hands even look like Momma's when she moves. She pours in the flour, then the baking soda, then the salt. Separates the eggs with steady hands. Adds the yolk to the mix, then beats the whites so fast, looks like her arm is one of them electric mixers. She melts butter in the skillet til it sizzles as she finishes the rest. Just like Momma, she saves the brown sugar and cinnamon for last.

I wonder why she's making pancakes now, when it don't matter no more. I hope she don't think it's gon' fix us. The butter finishes melting, and Nia pours half into the mix, filling the kitchen with a sweet, buttery smell that reminds me of Momma.

I lay back on the couch and enjoy the aroma as I stare at the ceiling. I miss sleeping in the room cause ain't no crack in the ceiling out here. Everything is neatly in its place, cept for me with heavy covers that I lug out from the linen closet every night. At some point, I thought I would go back to sleeping in the room, cause the couch is lumpy and it can be scary sleeping in the front all alone. But I don't want Nia to think I came back cause of her, so I drag them big covers out, night after night.

The sweet smells from the kitchen fill my nose and the sweet sound of nothin' fills my ears. I close my eyes for just a second, but it turns out to be more than a second cause then Nia is standing in front of me and shaking my shoulder.

"KB," she whispers, "breakfast is ready." I blink a couple times to wake up, then nod. I figure a nod ain't quite talking. Nia heads back into the kitchen. I can hear the scrape of her chair on the floor as she pulls it out, then sits down at the table. I yawn, stretch, then stand and follow.

The table is full of food that looks too good to eat. A plate of bacon and sausage with a paper towel beneath, soaked through with oil. Fluffy eggs peeking out from one bowl and chunks of fruit in another. Then golden, buttery pancakes right in the middle. I can't help but grin when I see it all. If I ain't know better, I might think Momma been here making breakfast and humming.

"Thanks for breakfast," I whisper as we start loading our plates. If I don't say it, I'm gon' be rude. So I say it, but nothin' else. I pile two pancakes on my plate, two strips of bacon, one sausage link, and a heaping spoonful each of eggs and fruit. I take a quick bite of my bacon and decide to add one more strip to my plate.

"You're welcome," Nia says, and that's the last we talk. We chop our pancakes into little squares, pour syrup on top, then chew and swallow. Nobody makes pancakes better than Momma, but Nia is close.

After we both clear our plates, I wipe down the table and Nia washes the dishes. Then Nia grabs the broom and starts sweeping, so I finish up at the sink. I like washing dishes so I can look out the little window. The sky is filled with clouds today, white and fluffy like colorless cotton candy. I watch a bee fly from one flower to the next, as I think of what I'm gon' do today. Maybe, since Granddaddy's gone, I can see if Bobby and Charlotte wanna play.

Nia's sweeping the last pile of crumbs into the dustpan just as I finish with the dishes. I leave the kitchen happy cause now I can get back to not talking. I pull shorts, a T-shirt, and clean undies from the dresser and take a fast shower, making sure to hit the "hot spots" like Momma taught me. I hurry cause I wanna see my friends and wanna get away from Nia before she thinks we're friends again.

But when I finish in the bathroom, Nia ain't nowhere to be found. I look in the room, but she ain't there. I can tell she got dressed, though, cause she left hair in her brush and a pile of clothes in the middle of the floor. Usually, this is when I would start looking for Nia everywhere. But today I don't care that she's gone. I grab my book and my rock collection and head outside.

First thing I do is look for Charlotte and Bobby, using my hand on my forehead to block the sun, but they ain't outside yet. It's still early, so I guess I gotta play by myself for a while. I march toward the field in the back, hopping over sticks that I count one by one and stopping to look for rocks I sometimes find pressed into the dirt. I've only found one pebble-sized rock when I hear a car pull into the driveway. And it's not actually the car I hear; it's the loud music that feels like it's beating in my chest. I run up front to see who's making the noise, but I think I got an idea before I even get there.

Sure enough, I make it to the front just in time to see Nia climbing into the passenger seat of a raggedy ol' car with rust on its sides and a missing bumper in front. Nia sees me and waves, big and friendly, like she's in a parade. The loud music turns down, but only a little.

"KB!" Nia says in a high-pitched voice. "I'll be back later. Stay inside while I'm gone. Don't answer the door. Or the phone." The car starts to back out the driveway, but not before she yells, "Oh, and I made you a plate of leftovers! It's in the fridge!"

The last thing I hear is her fake laugh, then the loud music gettin' louder as the rusty car pulls out the driveway. I can't see the driver cause the sun is in my eyes, so I climb my tree just in time to see Pimple Boy drive Nia away from Granddaddy's house. The same pimple-faced boy Nia met at Pizza Land, when I made my big mistake with Rondell. I knew Pimple Boy looked older than Nia, but I ain't figure he was old enough to drive. That ain't what matters now, though, cause Granddaddy's gone and Nia's gone and I don't know when she's coming back.

I sit in the tree awhile, cause now I ain't much in the mood for collecting rocks. I ain't much in the mood for anything I can think of, cept maybe screaming so loud that all the people that keep leaving can hear. Granddaddy and Momma and Nia. Maybe even Daddy will hear me from wher- ever he's at. The church folk say he's in heaven, but I don't know if I believe in that; and it don't seem like Momma do, either, since our pastor say that believing in heaven means being happy when someone dies, cause it means they with Jesus. So maybe Daddy ain't in heaven. Maybe he's somewhere that he can hear me, if I get to yelling right now and never stop. Maybe it's better if Daddy ain't in heaven, anyway. People always saying stuff like Daddy up there looking down on me, which I hope ain't true. Cause if it's true, that means he saw me try to get back at Nia by showing Rondell my panties. And he saw that it ain't even work.

Just then, a voice comes from cross the street. Bobby and Charlotte are outside, riding bikes down the narrow sidewalk. I look over my shoulder at the empty house behind me. Then get a crazy idea. Ain't nobody here to care, so I'm gon' ask Bobby and Charlotte to play over on my side of the street today.

"Bobby," I yell from up in my tree, waving and waving. He looks around but can't find me. "Charlotte," I try, but she can't see me, neither. I start climbing down the tree, quick.

"Charlotte! Bobby!" I yell, as I land on the grass with a thud. Now they see me and start to wave. I look both ways, then cross over to their side of the street.

"Can y'all play?" I say once I get there. Charlotte nods; Bobby turns and looks at his sister with a sneer, which I pretend not to notice.

"I want y'all to see something, over there!" I

point cross the street and both Bobby and Charlotte stare at my pointing finger like it's a weapon. "I promise, it's gon' be fun!"

"What is it?" Bobby finally asks, curious. Charlotte don't say nothin', but she's watching me with wide eyes.

"Gotta come see," I say with a smile, pointing again at Granddaddy's house. From over here, it looks small and kinda old, especially when I look back at Bobby and Charlotte's big ol' tall house with new paint and the bright red door.

Bobby looks back at that door now and crosses his arms. I bet he's looking for they momma. "We can't leave our sidewalk."

"Just for a minute?" I ask, then look at Charlotte with begging eyes, cause she's gon' be easier to convince than Bobby. "We can go inside real quick. I have a new book for you." I ain't sure which book I mean, cause I ain't ready to share my new Anne books that I ain't even finished yet. But at least I got Charlotte smiling and thinking.

"Come on, Bobby. Just for a minute?" Charlotte pleads, but Bobby don't budge. "Please? We have time; she's in the shower." She whispers that last part, like I won't hear her or know exactly who she's talking bout. Bobby thinks long and hard, looking back and forth between both our houses. Then, finally, he unfolds his arms.

"Just for a minute," he says. Me and Charlotte

are already halfway cross the street before he can even finish the sentence. He runs behind us and yells, "Wait up!"

Once we get cross the street, I ain't sure what to do. I promised Charlotte a book, but now I'm feeling shy bout them seeing inside Granddaddy's house. I think bout the singing tar-baby statues and the portrait of Black Jesus hanging by the door. "Let's go to the field," I say quickly, hoping they don't ask bout going inside. I wipe sweat from my forehead while I wait for them to agree. In my mind, I think of what I'm gon' say if they do ask to go inside. But, luckily, they follow me without questions. We trudge back to the field—me in front walking slow, Bobby beside me, and Charlotte skipping behind—with the songs of birds ringing in our ears.

"Look at all the flowers!" Charlotte squeals as they pop into view. The wind blows just a little, just enough to make the colors dance. The air is thick with a sweet perfume. Bobby and Charlotte run screeching into the field like they invading a fortress, so I do, too. I press my fingertips against the same flowers I been touching all summer, but they feel different now. Like they just now came alive.

"Wanna play?" Charlotte asks, and I bob my head up and down, quick. I've only been alone back here, chasing butterflies and making up games to play by myself. Now me and Charlotte chase butterflies together, running in circles til we're both dizzy and laughing. Then we play a game with Bobby that we all make up. The sky's bursting with shining light and fat clouds. I been happy before, but this is my new best day in Lansing.

"I'm going to the pond!" Bobby yells, and I'm bout to follow, but Charlotte tugs my hand.

"Wanna look for caterpillars?"

A giant smile stretches cross my face as I nod. Charlotte keeps holding my hand for a few more seconds, and I imagine me and her as Anne and Diana in Green Gables. Real-life bosom buddies.

"Over here," Charlotte yelps. While I was lost in my thoughts, Charlotte was already finding caterpillars.

"Where?" I ask, joining her near a giant rock.

"Here," she says, pointing to the base of the rock, where a whole handful of caterpillars crawl and squirm. We take turns picking them up and passing them to each other. I think bout goin' to get my mayonnaise jar, but seeing how much fun we having, I think it's better to let these caterpillars keep living right where they at.

"Me and my sister found some caterpillars when we first moved here," I say to Charlotte, remembering that day with Nia that feels so far away now.

"Moved here?" Charlotte tilts her head. "I thought you said you were just visiting."

I try to hide my face before Charlotte can tell I'm embarrassed. "Oh," I answer, "well, yeah, we just visiting. Our momma still gon' come back for us. I just don't know when yet."

"Oh," Charlotte replies, and that's all she says. We both go back to looking for caterpillars, but the space between us feels smaller now, like it's packed tight and cramped with all the stuff we ain't gon' say.

"My daddy died, from doin' drugs," I whisper. Just a little bit of the space opens up. "And we came here after, cause we lost our house." I take a deep breath, then let it out. The space stretches with my breath. "I don't know when my momma gon' come back, or even if she's gon' come back at all." The space is as wide open as the field now.

"Oh," Charlotte says again. She chews her hair and looks over at Bobby, looks up at the tree, looks down at the grass. Looks everywhere but at me. I think maybe she don't wanna be my friend anymore, but then she reaches out her hand. I take it and feel a little squeeze.

"Our dad is gone, too," Charlotte says, still looking at the ground.

I wait before I speak. "Did he die?"

Charlotte shakes her head no. "They got a divorce."

I don't know much bout divorce, cept what I hear at church. And lots of my classmates at school had parents who were divorced, and they would talk bout how their parents would fight. Once, after Momma and Daddy had a fight, I asked Daddy if him and Momma would get a divorce. He laughed, then looked me straight in the eye and said, "Do I look like a fool to you?"

The memory makes me smile, but I quickly fix my face, so Charlotte don't think I'm smiling bout her daddy being gone. "I'm sorry," I finally say.

Charlotte squeezes my hand one more time, then lets it go. "You're it!" she suddenly yells, racing off toward Bobby, who's still by the pond. He looks up and sees Charlotte, then they both take off running away from me. As they run, they take turns making silly faces and yelling jokes. Me, I can't stop smiling. Smiling cause I got these new friends, and cause Charlotte's the first person I told the whole truth to, bout us and bout Daddy. It feels good to finally have somebody to talk to, somebody to trust.

"Bobby!" We all hear the scream at the same time. The way she yells is like she's been yelling awhile, but ain't none of us hear til now. Bobby freezes at the shrill sound of his momma's voice, then turns his head quick to Charlotte. She already got tears in her eyes.

"Let's go," says Bobby, pulling Charlotte by the

arm. Neither one of 'em speaks to me, or even looks my way. They just leave, like they was never even there. I sit down, right in the middle of the grass, and taste the salt on my tongue before I even know the tears have left my eyes. I wipe 'em away with the back of my hand, quick. I'm tired of crying and I'm tired of people leaving. I get back up, my shorts wet from the grass, and run frowning back to the house. For once, I'm gon' be the one that leaves.

It's always quiet in Granddaddy's house, but this quiet, now, feels deeper. I pass through the living room and the quiet hangs on all the stuff there—the empty wicker chair, unopened Bible, blank TV screen. I can almost feel the noise begging to enter and fill the spaces with life. But ain't nobody around, cept me. And now I'm gon' leave like everybody else.

I go to the bedroom and exchange my sandals for socks and gym shoes—still muddy from the drive here with Momma. Then grab my old backpack and pack it with clothes, my toothbrush, my two Anne books, and a small blanket. My rock collection's too big to fit, so I decide to take just three rocks—the special ones, from Bobby. I start to leave the room but go back and add my first Anne book to the other two. It's older than the others and more raggedy, plus I already read it, but it's still my best book.

What the Fireflies Knew

In the kitchen I pack crackers, a can of Vienna sausages, cookies, and fruit—two oranges and an apple. I grab a thermos that I fill with water, then I look around and think. It's strange cause I been looking for money all summer and ain't once thought to look here, but most grown-ups hide money around the house; I just don't know where Granddaddy keeps his. I look in jars, drawers, on top of the fridge. I check the bathroom and the living room, but I can't find no money. Granddaddy's bedroom is in the back of the house and I ain't ever been in there cause I ain't ever had no reason. But now I do. I tug the door open and look around.

His bedroom is mostly like the other rooms in the house, filled with creaky old furniture and dusty trinkets. There's a bed in the corner, a long dresser cross the wall, and a rocking chair by the only window. The top of the dresser is completely clear, cept for one framed picture sittin' right in the middle. I recognize the woman right away— not just cause I seen pictures of her before in that photo album, but cause she looks just like Momma. It's the granny I never knew bout, wearing a long dress to her ankles and fancy jewelry that sparkles. But don't nothin' shine as bright as the smile on her face, looks just like Momma's best smile.

I hear a noise outside the bedroom and jump,

almost dropping the picture. Then I realize it's only the sound the toilet makes when it refills with water. I set the picture back on the dresser and get back to looking for money.

Finally, I find some, in a shoebox on the top shelf of Granddaddy's closet. I count two twenties, one ten, one five, and seven ones. Sixty-two dollars. I stuff it all in the pocket of my shorts and whisper a promise into the air to pay Granddaddy back, one day. I return the shoebox to the closet, then close the door to his room again, so it looks like I was never there.

In the living room, I sit on the couch with my clothing-stuffed backpack and my money-stuffed pocket. As I sit there, thinking, a funny memory crosses my mind. It was back in Detroit, when me and Nia was watching some movie where this kid decided to run away from home. Nia was all into it, but I kept complaining bout why the kid would be so stupid, to run away with nowhere to go, and nobody to keep them safe. But now, sittin' here alone with all my little bit of stuff, it just feels like it's what I gotta do. I wish I was in Detroit, though, where I would know where to run. I ain't been many places in Lansing, besides the pool, the church, and the mall. I've rode the bus in Detroit all by myself before, to get to school, but I can't remember even seeing no bus around here. I wish I had a bike, at least. Which makes me think bout

Bobby's and Charlotte's bikes. I look back to be sure I ain't leave no mess around Granddaddy's house, straighten out his rug and wipe dust from his coffee table. Then I leave.

Bobby's bike is laying on the ground where he left it, but I can tell right away that it's too big for me to ride. It even has those gears up top like Nia's old bike. That only leaves Charlotte's bike, which ain't over there no more. I look down the street one way, then the other. No sign of her or her bike, so I guess I gotta walk. I put my arms through the straps of my backpack til its weight falls square on my shoulders.

I look both ways to make sure ain't no cars coming, even though there ain't ever really no cars on this street. As I step onto the sidewalk in front of Granddaddy's house, I have to fight the urge to turn back. Not cause I wanna stay, but cause I got stuff here I care bout. Like my caterpillars and the rest of my rocks. I figure I can get 'em when I come back, but that's the thing bout running away—you don't know if you gon' come back.

"KB!" The shrill whisper comes from behind me. I turn and barely miss gettin' hit by Charlotte on her bike.

"Charlotte! Where'd you go?" I ask loudly, making her shove her finger up to her pressed lips.

"Shh!" Charlotte shrieks. "Or she'll hear you!"

"Who, your momma?" I try to whisper, still a

bit too loud. I look around nervous, like she gon' be watching me from the window. But the house is quiet, with no mommas in no windows.

"Yeah, we were in trouble," Charlotte says, lowering her head.

"For playing outside?"

"No, for playing over there with—" Charlotte stops, quick, then says, "For going across the street without permission."

"Oh," I respond. Charlotte keeps looking at the ground instead of at my eyes, and I start to wonder if maybe Granddaddy was right bout these kids, and bout they momma. But I ain't got time to figure it out right now, cause I'm busy looking at her bike.

"Hey, can I ride your bike?" I figure she's gon' say no, but I ask anyway cause I need it.

To my surprise, Charlotte says, "Sure, long as you're careful." I start smiling real big and nodding too fast. "I have to go inside now, so just make sure you bring it back by the morning."

I don't know what made Charlotte decide to say yes, but I grab the handlebars and start pulling the bike closer before she can change her mind. "I will, I promise!"

Charlotte waves at me as she runs cross the street. I wave back, then climb up onto the seat—too short, so I gotta half stand—and start to pedal.

What the Fireflies Knew

Now I know I gotta come back, at least to bring Charlotte her bike. No matter what other people do to me, I ain't gon' break a promise to my friend.

Running away is harder than I thought it was gon' be. I realize now why Momma always be gettin' lost when we drive places. All the streets look the same, so I feel like I'm riding around in circles. I was gon' stop to try to find a map, but I don't even know how to read one. So, I just keep riding, hoping something gon' look familiar if I go long enough.

I think as I pedal of places I could go. Maybe a park, if I can find one, where I could eat at the picnic tables and sleep on the slide. But if it starts raining, I'm gon' get all wet. I stop at an orange flashing DO NOT WALK sign. Nothin' looks familiar, which ain't a surprise since nothin' here is familiar. I remember my plan at the beginning of the summer, to collect enough bottles and cans to get myself back home. I could maybe try to find my way to Detroit now, but I don't even wanna be there anymore. Not now, like this. Besides corner stores with people who know me by name and lottery pick, and a couple friends who started whispering bout me after my daddy died, I don't have a home in Detroit no more.

The WALK signal flashes on, with the little white light man telling me it's safe to go. I hop off Charlotte's bike and walk it cross the intersection, just like Momma taught me. I'm bout to climb back on when I see a big brick sign for a library. It's still early but looks like it's open cause a bunch of cars are parked out front. There's a bike rack near the door and I leave Charlotte's bike there, where it will be safe. Then I push through the double doors to a rush of chilly, air-conditioned air and the smell of fresh-turned pages. Finally, something familiar.

When we lost our house after Daddy died, there were days when we would sleep in the car, and we went to the library a bunch to use the bathroom and keep warm. I still don't know everything bout why we lost the house, but I think it had something to do with Daddy owing lots of people money, cause after he died, the phone kept ringing and the bills kept stacking up on the table til, eventually, we left our house for good. Sometimes we'd stay at the library all day, til one day when somebody asked Momma if we needed the phone number for a shelter. After that, we never went back again. I guess she ain't want them to know that some days the library was the only place we had to go. Eventually, we found the motel, but I liked the library much better. Funny that I'm here now, with nowhere else to go. But this is different, cause before stuff was always just happening to us, and now I'm making something happen.

In the young adult section, I resist the urge to sift through every page of every book. Instead, I find a seat in the back corner, where ain't nobody else around. I set my backpack down on the floor beside me to rest my shoulders, so I can think.

I try to remember those movies me and Nia used to watch with kids running away. They would always go to somebody's house, like a friend or a teacher. But I don't really know nobody here, cept for the people I ran away from.

What would Nia do? The thought pops into my head before I can stop it. Not long after Daddy's funeral, Nia tried to run away. She did run away, I think, for a few hours. Momma was yelling and crying and calling people on the phone. Turns out, Nia was at some boy's house. Momma whispered on the phone with the boy's momma and yelled on the phone with Nia. I pretended not to know what was going on. Then Nia came back home.

I think back to meeting Rondell at the swimming pool. Maybe if I ask somebody for directions to the swimming pool, then I can go back there, and maybe I can find him again. I bet if I do, he gon' be happy to see me. And maybe he can help me find some good places to run away to around here.

I stand up and stretch, then pick up my back-pack to leave. But first I pick up a book with a girl on the cover riding a horse. I went through all the trouble to run away; might as well do some stuff I like. I sit and read the entire book before anybody comes to stop me.

The swimming pool ain't nearly as packed as it was before. Probably cause it's not so hot today. Still hot enough for swimming, but cool enough to make different kinds of plans, too. I look around soon as I get there, hoping to see Rondell or his cousins. But I don't see them nowhere. In fact, I don't see nobody I recognize from the last time. Most of the people here today are old. And white. I think bout Bobby and Charlotte's momma, and I wonder if coming here was such a good idea.

I walk around pool chairs with Charlotte's bike at my side, being extra careful not to roll over any-body. I thought to leave the bike out front, but I was scared some kid might see it and steal it. There's a single chair at the edge of the pool in the back, and I head that way. Feels like everybody's staring at me as I walk by. Wonder if they can all tell I'm running away. I keep my head low and try to look like a kid who's obeying her parents.

What the Fireflies Knew

I reach the chair and sit down, leaning Charlotte's bike up against the pool gate. I look around, putting my hand up on my forehead to shield my gaze from the hot sun. Most of the people here are laying around the pool in chairs or on towels. Only a few are in the water, holding on to the edges like I used to hold on to Momma's ankles when she tried to leave. I count people to keep from noticing my grumbling tummy. Forty-nine, then I can't ignore it no more. I search in my backpack and find the apple, which I bite into greedily.

The only kid in the whole pool is a little girl, swimming with a man who I guess is her daddy. She looks younger than me, maybe bout seven. But even though she's small, she knows how to swim. Her golden head dips in and out the water as she slips and splashes past her daddy. They stop and play when she needs a break, tossing a soggy red ball back and forth with fast, wet breath. Whenever she paddles away to find the ball, her daddy watches her with a steady gaze and feet ready to move. If I had to guess what it feels like to have your daddy watch you like that, I bet it feels like being lifted so high up in the air it feels like flying, but being held so tight that no matter what happens, you know you ain't gon' fall. Kinda like it feels when Granddaddy holds my hands and listens to me talk, now that I think bout it.

I hear a familiar yell, and I know it's gon' be them before I even see the brown heads pop out the locker room door. I spot Dominique first, still yelling, then Porsha close behind her. The smallest boy comes after that, then the biggest. I still don't know either of their names. Then comes Rondell, laughing and yelling something to his cousins I can't hear. Seems like they all running from him, though, cause they hop in the water fast and start swimming away. Maybe another game of Marco Polo.

I wanna go in the pool, but my blue jean shorts ain't right for swimming. Plus, I don't want his cousins to see me and think I came back here just for him. Even though I did, but not like that.

I watch them play while I finish my apple. I don't think the game is Marco Polo, but I can't figure out what it is, either. Whatever the game, it's making all the old white people mad, cause Rondell and his cousins keep yelling and splashing. I giggle as I watch Rondell chase Porsha around the pool, heading in my direction, til she jumps into the water with knees tucked into her chest.

"Cannonball!" Porsha screams, so loud that everybody sleeping wakes up. I laugh and laugh and then I snort cause I'm laughing so hard. That's when Rondell looks up and sees me.

I don't think nobody else sees me, just him. He

don't wave, just offers me a tiny smile. I give him one back, then pretend like I was looking at something else. I'm still staring at the ground beside my chair when he walks up.

"Hey," he says, "what you doin' here?" I look up and pretend to be surprised to see him. His hair is in them braids again, like the first time.

"Hey," I reply, casual. "Just came for a swim." I realize after I say it that I sound silly. Surely he can see I ain't got on no swimming clothes. I'm sittin' over here, away from the pool, eating an apple with a bike and a stuffed backpack. Rondell looks at me real strange after my answer. I hide my apple beneath the seat, like that's gon' fix it all.

"Everything okay?" Rondell asks, as the half-eaten apple rolls from under my chair and toward the pool.

"Yeah, it's good." I wanna say more, but don't know where to start. Me and Rondell ain't known each other too long, at least not long enough for me to tell him I ran away and came to him. But I'm here now, so I guess it's too late for second thoughts.

"Sorry if I got you in trouble," Rondell says, then adds, "on your birthday." I was hoping he had somehow forgot all bout me showing him my underwear, but by the way he smirks at me, I know he ain't forget. I blush hard and lower my eyes.

"It's okay, I ain't get in trouble," I say, still not looking at him.

"I was hoping I was gon' see you again," says Rondell, scratching the back of his head as he talks. "We ain't get to finish our . . . conversation." Seems like both of us are feeling shy bout what happened at Pizza Land. I ain't even sure why I did it, cept that Nia was flirting so much it made it hard for me to see or think straight. I thought that taking control for once would help, but after, I ain't feel as good as I thought I would.

"Yeah, me too," I say, looking over at my packed backpack. I'm nervous that if I tell him I ran away, I'm gon' have to tell him why. That would mean telling him bout all the secrets and Nia with Jesse and the headshot that tore Momma and Granddaddy apart. It's too much to say, I know, cause it's too much to live. I wonder if there's any way to take all that stuff in my head and make it sound simple. "That's actually why I came here," I say finally.

"To the pool?" Rondell asks, looking back and forth from me to the water.

"To you." When I say the words, they sound serious, even to me. But I ain't mean it that way. I sound like one of them people in Momma's romantic movies that make her cry. I see Rondell's face start to look worried, so I know I gotta fix what I said.

"I ran away from my Granddaddy's house. And I don't know too many people here in Lansing." I talk fast. "So I was hoping you could help me figure out where to go." I tear at my nails as I talk, scrape dirt from under six before Rondell says anything.

"You ran away?" I can't tell if he's impressed or angry, cause even though his eyebrows frown, his mouth tilts upward like a half smile.

"Yeah," I say, lifting my head to look Rondell in the eye. Even if he don't like it, I feel proud of what I've done.

"Rondell!" Dominique's scream is a sharp knife that slices through our conversation. I turn before Rondell does. Porsha and Dominique are looking at us, but the boys are busy splashing. I can't tell if Dominique is mad, but she's standing at the edge of the pool with her hands on her hips, watching us like we stole something. I think Rondell's gon' go back to his cousins now, but he just chuckles and shakes his head.

"She always so loud," he whispers, then smiles at me. I smile back, cause I think he forgot bout being disappointed. "You wanna see something?" Rondell says, just like I said to him last time. I wonder if his belly is filled with butterflies like mine was when I said it.

"See what?" I ask, trying not to get tricked the same way I tricked him.

"I think I got somewhere you can go." He grabs my hand. His palm feels clammy against mine, still wrinkled from the pool. I ain't ever held hands with a boy, but this ain't quite holding hands. More like he wants me to stand up and is only grabbing my hand to help.

"Okay," I whisper, remembering to take my backpack. I peek back at his girl cousins as we walk away. Porsha has joined in the splashing with the boys, but Dominique's still standing there watching us. I wonder if we should go over and say something to her, but Rondell don't seem to care. He leads me past the pool, then past the locker rooms. We end up on the other side of the building, outside the gate. I suddenly remember Charlotte's bike, leaning against the pool gate where I can't see it no more.

"Where we going?" I ask anxiously, but he don't answer. Just squeezes my hand and keeps walking, like he knows I'm gon' follow him anywhere. Now we walking cross the half-empty parking lot. We get to the end, past the very last space. My hands start to tremble.

"You need somewhere to hide, right?" Rondell asks, and I nod yes, even though I ain't really put together running away and hiding. If Granddaddy showed up right now, I don't think I would hide. I bet I would hop in his Cadillac and try to pretend like none of this ever happened.

There is a giant green dumpster at the edge of the parking lot. I guess this is where Rondell been meaning to go. He walks me behind the dumpster like it's a fortress. 'Cept it smells like sour milk and mildew and flies buzz around like they're at home and I'm the intruder.

"What we doin' back here?" I look around with my hand pinching my nose. Rondell sits on a bunch of wood that I guess could be steps.

"You need somewhere to hide, right?" He says the same words again like it's a new argument. I don't know if I should just agree and smile or point out to him that a dumpster ain't no good place to take a girl, even if she needs to hide. But then he pats the spot beside him for me to sit, and I remind myself that he's tryna do a nice thing. Plus, I ain't got nobody else. I sit down and try to convince my senses to stop working, just for now.

"I know it's not really nice here," Rondell says like he can read my thoughts, "but it's quiet. And it's safe." He picks at his fingernails the same way I pick at my fingernails. I wonder if he's nervous bout something.

"You come here a lot?"

"Yeah," Rondell says, then adds, "I used to. Back when my Pops was alive, I used to come here all the time." He stares down at the ground, so I stare down at the ground.

After I count ten whole seconds of silence, I

finally ask, "Why?" I can tell Rondell's feeling shy, but I figure maybe he just needs someone to listen to him talk bout his daddy and the memories, just like me.

Rondell takes in a big breath, then lets it out in a loud sigh. "My Pops was a cool dude," he starts, staring off into nothin'. "He was real funny and could make everybody laugh. But sometimes . . ." His voice trails off, but I wait without speaking. Eventually, he starts back up.

"Sometimes, he would get mad. Real mad. And when my Pops was mad, everybody was in trouble. Especially me." Rondell shrugs, like he can shrug away the memory just by trying. "So I would come here, for some peace and quiet."

I don't speak, but I nod. Rondell's daddy was a lot like my daddy. As much as I loved Daddy, I also loved it when he was gone for hours or even days. That time, when he was away, was the only time it felt like we could stop trying so hard; when we could just breathe.

"So, why you run away?" Rondell asks, changing the subject. I sit there and think for a while. At first, I ain't know if I was ready to open up to Rondell. But now that he's opening up to me, I think maybe I should.

"Remember when I asked you bout your brother? And you said he don't talk to you much when his girlfriend's around?" Rondell nods. "Well, I got a sister. And that's how she acts, but all the time. She ain't even got no boyfriend, but she still don't talk to me."

Rondell shifts on the worn wood so that his face is right in front of mine. I swallow, hard, then continue.

"My momma left us here in Lansing, me and my sister, with our Granddaddy. And I like him well enough, but it just don't feel right to all be so far apart. Me and Nia and Momma and—" I stop, realizing that I almost forgot bout Daddy dying. "It's just not right, being here," I finish.

Rondell don't respond, just keeps staring at me. I start to feel uncomfortable cause his eyes are moving back and forth too quick and he keeps licking his already wet lips. Then he begins sneaking his hand toward the part of my thigh not covered by my too-short shorts. I cross my legs, quick, to make him stop.

"Can we go back to the pool?" I say. All at once, I realize how far away I am from everybody. Granddaddy's out on some lake, Nia's with that boy, even Porsha and Dominique seem real far from this dumpster with Rondell.

"Why you wanna do that?" Rondell asks, scooting closer. "I thought we was gon' have some fun." This Rondell, now, is different from the Rondell that just told me bout his daddy. And different in a way that's making me feel like I need to leave, fast.

"What you mean, fun?" I ask, tryna scoot away. But Rondell hooks his arm around my hips and pulls me back, even closer now. My body feels frozen.

"You know"—Rondell tilts his head—"fun like this." He leans in like he's gon' kiss me. I ain't ever kissed a boy, or even came close. Some of the girls in fifth grade said they started kissing boys when they was nine, but I don't believe that. Mostly cause boys our age act too scared to try stuff like that.

"How old are you again?" I ask Rondell.

"Same as you, remember?" Rondell smiles, sweet.

"Oh, you just turned thirteen, too?"

"Yeah, thirteen." Rondell starts creeping toward my thigh again, so I pretend to swat a fly, but I don't say nothin', cause if he lied bout how old he is, he gon' lie some more.

"I just remembered I gotta go," I say too loud, standing up too quick.

"Where you gotta go?" Rondell asks, then says, "Wait, ain't you running away? You ain't got nowhere to go." He grabs my wrist and pulls me back down, hard. I wince and pull away. I want him to stop. I ain't even pretending to be happy no more.

"I'm going home," I say, hoping he can't hear the shake in my voice. But I think he does, cause then he pulls me so close he can touch me like he wants. And he does. Touches me and touches me. I wanna scream, but I know it won't matter cause I ran away from anybody that might care. Instead, I watch a half-smushed fly, dying on the edge of the dumpster. The fly raises his wing, waves it at the other flies. But they all just keep buzzing around the trash, unbothered.

9

Rain splatters on my face, drip-drop, til I gotta wipe it away. My arms hurt when I lift them to my face. My face hurts when I wipe away the raindrops.

I been laying here a while. I don't count nothin', just lay here, doin' and feeling nothin'. When I don't count, time drags craters cross my mind that I try not to fill. Counting calms me down when things ain't goin' right. It gives me something else to focus on, besides my spinning thoughts. I started counting stuff the day after Daddy died and ain't stopped. Til now.

Rondell left when it was still sunny. After seeing my panties a second time, then shoving his hands up in 'em til I thought I would rip right in half. I'm scared if I look now, I'm gon' see blood.

I don't know why he left when he did. He kept

laughing and laughing and stabbing his fingers. I thought he wasn't gon' ever stop, but then he just got up and ran off, like he knew he was gon' get caught. But nobody ever came.

I'm happy for the rain, cause people leave from the pool in loud, laughing groups. Car doors open and close; motors rumble to a start, then fade away in the distance. Eventually, when all the noise is gone, I push myself up to sittin'.

My body hurts all over, even though he only touched me in one place. I hold the dumpster as I stand, cause my legs are soggy noodles. Still holding on, I peek out from behind the dumpster to the deserted pool. Seems like years since I left Charlotte's bike over there. Now it's gon' feel like years to walk all that way back to it.

I beg my legs to move, little steps that take me almost nowhere. But I gotta get to that bike, get home to Granddaddy's house. I think back to this morning, when I packed my bag and decided I was gon' leave. Cept I can't even remember now why I thought it mattered.

With every step, I can feel his fingernails digging in me again. But instead of seeing me, I see Nia, Jesse's hands in her panties. Touching and panting and pulling. Does Nia like the way that digging feels? The giggles and moans and pimple-faced boys? Or does she do it cause she ain't got no choice?

Finally, I make it to the black iron gate. Raindrops fall in the water and make puddles. I wonder how many raindrops it would take to make the pool overflow. I imagine the blue water spilling out over the top of the walls, swallowing everything in its path. The lounge chairs. The cart filled with clean, folded towels. The half apple I dropped on the ground when I still thought Rondell was good.

I drop to my knees on the hard cement deck. The raindrops ain't enough to overtake the pool. But more than enough to overtake me, with tears that topple, then overflow. I cry and cry, and I'm still crying as I pedal away on Charlotte's bike, to find my way back home.

* * *

It's black dark when I turn onto N. Rutherford. Ain't no streetlights on the block, so the only light comes from the windows of houses where families eat and play together. Granddaddy's house is nothin' but dark. Ain't even no fireflies to greet me.

I walk with Charlotte's bike beside me and my backpack hanging from the seat. I only rode for a couple blocks, til I hit a rock that made me bounce up on the seat. The shock of pain was a reminder of an aching part of my body I was working hard to ignore. So I walked the rest of the way, even though it meant being twice as tired and taking twice as long.

I look cross the street at Charlotte's house, bright with lights, and decide to wheel the bike to Granddaddy's and return it tomorrow morning, like she said. I park it in front of the porch, behind the bushes, where I know it's gon' be safe. Then I climb the steps and open the front door.

The house is even darker once I step inside, maybe on account of the silence. I flip on a light switch in the living room, then another in the dining room and kitchen. I go to Granddaddy's room and flip on the light there just long enough to put his money back in the shoebox where I found it, then I turn out that light and go back to the living room. I figured Nia wasn't gon' be here; what I ain't figure on was how much it was gon' matter to me, being alone.

I think back to the beginning of the summer, when I still thought I could fix everything. Me and Nia, Momma and Granddaddy. But now it's the end of July and the only thing I managed to do was make things worse. Nia is further away from me than ever before. I barely talk to Momma, and when I do, she don't even seem like Momma no more. Me and Granddaddy close, but I bet we might not be close no more if he knew bout what just happened, with Rondell.

My body goes weak, hot tears spilling down my face. I curl up on the couch with clothes and shoes still on, and my backpack at my feet. At night, I usually count into the hundreds before I can fall asleep. My mind swirls with so many thoughts that I gotta trick myself into turning 'em off. Tonight, my mind is empty. Everything that I could think bout, I already blocked from my mind for good.

I fall asleep before I can even count all the lights I left on.

When I wake up, it's still dark outside. I think I had a nightmare, but when I try to remember it, I can only see me and Rondell and that dumpster. I close my eyes to try to fall back asleep. But then I hear a noise, coming from the front porch. I sit up and wait to see if I hear it again. I do, this time even closer. My heart is beating loud and fast. I look around the room for something to grab. I spot Granddaddy's Bible and for some reason, it feels right. I grab it and hug it tight to my chest.

Then I hear a familiar giggle. Nia. Sure enough, the door opens a few moments later and in she walks with a smirk on her face. Pimple Boy's outline fades into shadow as he heads back to his car. I realize that it's only dark outside cause the sun is still rising, a sliver of light just beginning to peek through the trees. Nia stayed out all night with this boy, probably letting him do the same stuff Rondell did to me. I slam my eyes shut, quick, before Nia can tell I'm awake. I hear her footsteps get closer, then feel the weight of the blanket she lays cross my body before she tiptoes to the bedroom.

Once I hear the door shut, I get up and shuffle to the kitchen. I ain't ate nothin' since that awful apple. I find two old pieces of cheese pizza in the refrigerator and stack 'em on a plate that I put in the microwave for a minute and a half. Through the little window above the sink, the sun is heading up to the clouds, making the room brighter and brighter. The microwave dings and I sit at the table with my pizza, but it's lost all its flavor. Guess it has been a week since my birthday.

I jump up: today is Nia's birthday, one week after mine. I get to the bedroom door and think bout going in, but then decide to knock instead. It feels stupid, but no matter what Nia do, I can't help but come back to her. Even when deep down, I feel like she ain't ever gon' be my friend again;

not like before. Before, it was me and Nia on a team against everybody else. Now I'm on a team fighting all alone.

"Come in," Nia answers, sounding far away. When I open the door, she's in the closet, probably changing her clothes. I check the tiny alarm clock Nia keeps by the bed. Six thirty a.m. I wonder if she went to sleep somewhere sometime last night, or if she gon' sleep now that it's day. I start to ask, but say, "Happy birthday," instead, forcing my tired face into a smile.

She don't even poke her head out from the closet, just yells, "Thanks!" My shoulders slump and my gaze falls, but I stay planted in the same spot. Eventually, Nia emerges from the closet wearing a fresh outfit and a smile on her face. She sits down in front of the mirror and starts unbraiding her hair with quick fingers.

As I stand there in the middle of the room, watching Nia, I'm torn between wanting to be just like her and wanting to be nothin' like her. Some stuff bout Nia is the best stuff in the world—like how she can look at me and know just what I'm thinking, and how she's the only person in the world who shares all my same stories, all my same memories. But what I don't get is why she wants to let those memories go, when so much of them is bout us. Bout us as friends, as sisters, and as a family.

Before I turn to go, I take one last look at Nia in the mirror. My big sister, and probably the only person who could help me now, if she wanted to. I accidentally catch my own reflection in the mirror beside Nia. I'm surprised to see that after all that's happened, I still look the same.

I'm rinsing the pizza crumbs from my plate when Granddaddy comes home later that morning. He walks in and smiles at me from the door, which is enough to bring back the lump in my throat.

"Granddaddy, what you doin' here?" I say, smiling now. "I thought you wasn't gon' be back til later."

"I couldn't miss Nia's birthday!" He hobbles to the couch, sittin' down hard. I sit beside him, grab his hand, and give it a quick squeeze. I ain't been able to get through to Nia, so I'm happy Granddaddy came back for her. Even though she doin' a bunch of stuff I don't understand— sneaking out with boys and kissing cousins and not crying for Daddy—I still want her to be happy. Especially on her birthday.

"Granddaddy!" Nia's running from the bedroom, then turns the corner to find me and Granddaddy together on the couch and stops. For the first time, I wonder if I'm keeping Nia from being close with Granddaddy. I always felt like Nia was the reason I wasn't so close with Daddy, cause by the time I came around she was already his little angel. Whenever he had to pick just one of us to go with him somewhere, like on a walk to the store or a ride cross town to his barbershop, he would always pick her. Maybe this is like that.

"Happy birthday," Granddaddy says to Nia, patting the other spot beside him on the couch. Nia looks at me, hesitates, then accepts. We sit there, the three of us, without saying nothin'. I imagine how we look, Granddaddy and his girls. Maybe like a family, almost. Not like the kind you see on TV, but close.

Eventually, Granddaddy breaks the silence, looking right at Nia. "So, what does a big fifteen-year-old girl do to celebrate her birthday?" Nia blushes, then smiles.

"Well," she starts, "I was thinking maybe I could go with my friends to—"

I tune out the rest. Figures she wants to be with her friends. I wonder if Momma will call and sing my special birthday song to Nia, or if Nia will be too busy with her friends to even talk to Momma if she does call. I trudge past Granddaddy's fishing stuff, still beside the front door. I wonder if he caught any fish, but I don't see none. Maybe one day Granddaddy might take me fishing with him.

I bet it would be nice to sit there, quiet, nothin' but all that water to look at and listen to and enjoy.

The sun is full up now, but ain't nobody outside yet, nothin' moving. That's when I remember Charlotte's bike. Nia and Granddaddy still busy talking; they ain't even notice that I had the worst thing ever happen to me, so they sure ain't gon' notice when I leave. I gotta make sure I keep my promise to Charlotte.

Her bike is beside the bushes, right where I left it last night. Feels like years ago now. I hold the handlebars and roll the bike cross the street, thinking bout the whole summer, and when I put it all together, seems like Lansing been more bad than good. I thought I had already lost every-thing, then came here and lost even more. But I did meet Bobby and Charlotte. Besides Granddaddy, they bout the only bright spot in all of Lansing.

As I walk the bike cross the street, I wonder if I might tell Charlotte bout what happened with Rondell. It felt good to tell her bout Daddy, so maybe it will feel good to have somebody to talk to bout this, too. Before I reach the sidewalk, Charlotte is already running out her front door. I wave as I roll her bike up the driveway. That's when I notice her face don't look quite right. She ain't smiling, but it's more than that. Her face looks sad and scared, all at once. The screen door swings shut behind her, but then opens again, right away.

Her momma's face is bright red like the burner on the stove when it's turned up too high. She storms down the driveway looking straight at me. I bet I got Charlotte in trouble for keeping her bike too long. I look over at her to try to apologize with my eyes, but she won't even look at me.

"Give it back!" Charlotte's momma screams, and I turn my head to see if somebody is walking up behind me, but ain't nobody over here cept me.

"Give it back," she repeats, even louder now. I look at Charlotte's bike, then look at Charlotte.

"I'm here to bring Charlotte's bike back," I whisper, not sure what's going on. I meet Charlotte's momma in the middle of the driveway and pass the handlebars over to her.

"You better bring it back," Charlotte's momma screams, snatching the bike so hard it falls to the ground. Out the corner of my eye, I can see Charlotte cringe at the noise. "Don't you ever steal from us again!"

"Steal?" I ask, even more confused than before. I pull my fingers, one by one.

"Yes, steal!" She shoots fire at me with her eyes. I look back at Granddaddy's house, where him and Nia probably still on the couch planning her birthday. Somehow, I'm alone again, in another bad place.

But then Bobby comes racing out the front

door, and I'm saved. He's gon' stand up for me, even though Charlotte can't. I know she's just too scared to tell her momma the truth, that she gave me the bike to borrow.

"I ain't steal nothin'," I whisper, scared. "Charlotte told me I could use her bike if I brought it back this morning." I try to look at Charlotte and then Bobby, but they both staring at the ground.

"Liar," they momma screams. "She said no such thing!" She picks up the bike and holds it between me and her like a shield. "Right, Charlotte?" She turns to Charlotte, still on the porch with Bobby beside her. Charlotte hears her name and her whole face turns pale as a ghost. "Right, Charlotte?"

I see her watery eyes and I already know what she's gon' say before she says it. "Yes, Mama. That's right." Charlotte looks at the ground, then at her fingers, then at nothin' but air. Anything but me. My eyes rush to Bobby, cause I know he's gon' say something. He's gon' tell they momma that Charlotte is lying, that I'm their friend, that he knows I ain't steal that bike.

"Mom, this isn't—" Bobby starts, and a satis-fied look creeps onto my face.

"Robert Brian," his mother responds with lips in a tight, straight line.

I look away from her and back to Bobby. Wait

for him to say something else. But he don't. With his face turning bright red, he goes to stand beside Charlotte like a statue, not moving or speaking even once she starts to cry.

"I'm their friend," I say weakly, not even sure why I'm trying anymore. I think I want one of 'em to make my words true. Even though I'm starting to realize they won't.

"You're not their friend! You're a thief! My kids might be naïve, but I know your type. Dad on drugs, family loses their house, so now you come over here and steal from us?"

Before I can stop them, tears pour from my eyes. I look over at Charlotte, who finally looks back at me. I say to her with my eyes, **I can't believe you told**. But she don't respond.

"We don't want people like you around here!" Bobby and Charlotte's momma continues, screaming so loud she's turned red all over. I hear her last words repeat in my head over and over. **People like you.** I think bout what Granddaddy said, how they didn't like people like us, and how I ain't believe him. But now, with me standing stuck in the driveway and Bobby and Charlotte up on the porch, I see everything different. They been wearing masks all this time, so that they looked like my friends. But now they momma ripped the masks off, so all three of 'em are exactly who they are, plain. I start to back out the driveway, slow.

"What's the problem here?" Granddaddy's voice comes up behind me, strong and firm. I don't know how he got over here so quick, and without his cane. He stands in front of Bobby and Charlotte's momma, taller than I ever seen.

"What's the **problem**?" The momma moves toward Granddaddy as she yells, and I move to him, too, stand behind his legs. "I'll tell you what the problem is! Your granddaughter stole my daughter's bike." She lifts the bike up like proof. Her tone is so convincing that I half expect the bike to be covered in my fingerprints as she shakes it in the air.

"You need to keep her away from my children! She stole from them, and with her **family background**, it's no surprise." She says **family background** like they bad words, almost like the police officers on the day Daddy died, when they called him a fiend. All these words that other people use to label us, to decide who we are, who we gon' be.

I choke back the giant lump in my throat. "I ain't steal that bike, Granddaddy! I promise! Charlotte told me I could borrow it and I brought it right back." I look at Granddaddy when I talk but sneak a quick peek over at Charlotte when I say her name. Her face is still wet, but she's stopped crying. I can't tell if she feels bad for lying or if she's just scared of being in trouble with her momma. Either way, she told her momma my secrets. She betrayed me. I thought she cared bout me, but really, she ain't no better than Rondell.

"I know," Granddaddy says to me, then turns to the angry momma. "Don't you ever talk bout my granddaughter like that again," he says with an even voice. "She been playing over here with your kids all summer. They done all got to be friends, whether you like it or not." I'm surprised to hear this. If he knew all this time, why he ain't tell me to stop coming over, since he had already told me not to?

"Friends?" She screams the word like it's poison and she's gotta rid its venom from her mouth. "My children are not friends with **that** girl!" This would be the part in the movie where Bobby and Charlotte run over to me and grab my hands, showing they momma she was wrong. But they too busy acting like they don't even know me.

"Let's go, Kenyatta," Granddaddy says, taking my hand to cross back to our side of the street, but when we reach the sidewalk, he turns again to the momma, then to Bobby and Charlotte.

"Our children don't have to make the same mistakes we did." Granddaddy speaks, calm. "Let 'em decide who to be for themselves." Then we cross the street together, Granddaddy holding my hand and me wondering who I would be, if I could decide for myself.

Later that afternoon, Brittany pulls up in the front seat of her aunt's car, and they take Nia with them. I don't know where they're going, and I don't ask. Granddaddy sneaks a fifty-dollar bill into Nia's palm before she leaves, with a whispered "Happy birthday" special for her. She walks out the door with a smile big as Momma's, like I ain't seen on Nia's face in a long time. I'm happy to see Nia smile, but right now, I can't help but wish her smile was for me.

After sittin' in the bathroom awhile, not wanting to move, I take an hour-long shower and scrub my skin til it turns pink. No matter how hard I scrub, I still feel Rondell's touch there, like I been burned and scarred, even though there ain't no marks. I climb out and towel off, dressing in the oversized T-shirt and stretchy shorts I usually wear as pajamas, even though it's still afternoon. I don't feel much like going outside. Granddaddy sits in his wicker chair, reading from his Bible. I sit on the couch watching the muted TV. I wanna turn the volume up but don't wanna bother Granddaddy, so I watch the characters and make up in my mind what I think they're talking bout.

In the middle of a made-up story bout a little

girl that can read people's minds, Granddaddy asks, "You ever read the Bible?"

"No," I answer. "Momma don't let me touch her Bible and I don't have my own." I think for a second, then add, "I've read the Bible in the back of the seats at church, though. But I can't much understand what it's saying."

Granddaddy nods, then asks me, "Do you know why it's important to read the Bible?"

I shake my head no.

"The Bible is filled with stories, just like them books you always reading. But the stories are bout God, and they teach us how we should live our lives."

"Is that why you and Charlie read the Bible together sometimes?"

"Yeah," says Granddaddy, "that's called Bible study. God is happy when we come together to read His Word and pray and worship. That's what me and Charlie do when we have Bible study." Granddaddy stands from the rocking chair and joins me on the couch. Then he opens the Bible on his lap, so we can both see the pages. "You can have Bible study all on your own, too."

"But I wouldn't know how." I point at the page. "I barely know what all them words mean. And I don't know where I'm s'posed to start."

"You don't have to know." Granddaddy shuffles

the thin pages. "You just have to listen." I wonder if he's talking bout listening to him or listening to God. I watch as Granddaddy picks a page and scrolls his finger through the text til he lands on a spot. "See?"

The page he is on has a word at the top that I can't read. "What does this say?" I ask, pointing.

"Ecclesiastes," he says. I repeat it in my head over and over again after he says it, cause it's a hard word, but I can remember, cause it has a lot of **e** like **cheese**. "We're gon' read the fourth chapter"—he points at the bold number four in the text—"verses nine through twelve." I follow along closely, watching the words while he reads aloud.

"Two are better than one," he reads in a low voice, "because they have a good return for their labor: If either of them falls down, one can help the other up. But pity anyone who falls and has no one to help them up." He pauses to look at me. I nod to say, **Keep going**, so he does. "Again, if two lie down together, they will keep warm. But how can one keep warm alone? Though one may be overpowered, two can defend themselves. A cord of three strands is not quickly broken."

I sit there thinking awhile before I speak. I don't wanna disappoint Granddaddy by saying the wrong thing. "So," I finally begin, "God is saying He wants us to be together?" It's not much, but it's all I know for sure.

"Exactly." Granddaddy smiles, making me feel better bout my response. "God tells us that we can be stronger if we stick together. Even when it's tough, we gotta lift each other up." I think bout how he came to stand up for me outside with Bobby and Charlotte, and nod.

"You know, Kenyatta—" Granddaddy starts, but he's interrupted by the front door slamming open. Nia bursts in, face covered in tears.

"Nia!" I yell, jumping up. "What happened?"

"Nia?" Granddaddy's also standing now. But Nia ignores us both, running off to the bedroom and slamming the door. Me and Granddaddy stand there after she's gone, not sure what to do. Finally, Granddaddy goes to knock on the bedroom door. I hear him knock and knock, but Nia don't answer. He comes back to the living room and we both sit on the couch, doin' nothin'. Then Granddaddy turns the volume up on the TV, I think just to cover up all the silence.

After we barely pay attention to half an episode of **Jeopardy!**, Nia finally opens the door. I sit up and turn my head to look for her, but Granddaddy don't move. She walks by, now wearing stretch pants and a T-shirt, with headphones on her ears, and walks straight out the front door.

"Should I go talk to her?" Granddaddy asks, but I don't know what to do just cause Nia is my sister. I guess he ain't noticed she don't like me much no more.

"I don't know," I say.

Granddaddy hobbles over to the window. "I don't even see her no more." He's turning his head left to right and then left again.

Granddaddy starts to panic, so I start to panic. But then I get an idea and jump straight up. "I think I know where she is," I yell. "I'll be back!" I run out the front door and down the steps, and I find Nia a few moments later, beneath the house in that spot where I found her before.

"Hey," I whisper, hoping she ain't gon' be mad I found her, but when she looks up, she ain't mad, just crying.

"Hey," she sniffles, then wipes her nose with the back of her hand. Her headphones are laying on the ground, all tangled.

"Can I come in?" I ask.

"Sure," she says, scooting over. I tuck my knees into my chest, and we stay together like that for a while. It feels good.

"Do you wanna talk bout it?" I finally ask. Nia shakes her head no. I wanna give her space, but my mind is filled with bad thoughts bout Nia and boys and Rondell. Before I can stop myself, I yell, "Did one of them boys do something to you again? Cause I can go and find 'em—"

Nia stops me midsentence, her hand raised in the air.

"No boy did nothing to me," she says, then swallows hard. "No boy did nothing to me, cept tell me the truth."

"What you mean?" I ask, but Nia shakes her head, then jumps up fast and runs off to the house. I clamber out and follow, yelling, "Nia, wait! What you talking bout?"

Inside, Granddaddy is still in his spot on the couch. "Is it true?" Nia yells at him as she slams open the door. "Is it true that that crackhead is the reason we lost our house?"

I've heard the word **crackhead** plenty of times, usually in the same fights when Momma would use that other strange word, **fiend**. The way Nia says it, and the way Granddaddy reacts, I know it's bad. But I don't understand the last part, bout Daddy being the reason we lost the house. Momma ain't tell us everything bout why we lost the house, but what I know from listening is that Daddy owed some money to some people, and since we ain't pay it back, we lost the house. But when I heard Momma say it on the phone, she said it like it was just the normal kind of thing that happens when somebody dies. **The funeral is on Saturday at one p.m. We already have dinner for tonight. We lost the house because he owed some money to some people.**

"Where did you hear that?" Granddaddy's voice is stern.

"That doesn't matter," says Nia. "Is it true?" Granddaddy takes in a long, deep breath. I stand in the doorway still, not sure if I should move. I don't want them to notice me or they'll make me leave.

"Nia, this ain't a conversation we should be having without your momma," says Granddaddy, talking slow and careful now. "I ain't sure what happened, but maybe we should call her and—"

"I saw our cousin Jesse," Nia screams. "And him and some other boys got to laughing and saying my daddy was nothing but a crackhead. That he overdosed and died, and when I defended him, they said why am I defending him when he the reason I gotta live here now, since he sold our house for drugs?" Nia's talking so fast I barely realize she said she been with Jesse again. I wonder how she got to him when she left here with Brittany, but ain't no time to focus on that, with everything else Nia's saying.

"Nia." Granddaddy sighs. "You don't understand—"

"You're right!" Nia cuts in. "I don't understand, cause everybody's been lying to me. Including you!" And with that, Nia runs to the room and slams the door. Granddaddy drops his head, then just sits there all slumped over. I don't know if I should go to him or Nia. I wanna ask Granddaddy a bunch of questions, but as I think bout Nia alone and hurting, I know that now ain't the time.

I don't knock on the door, just walk in the bedroom and sit down on the edge of the bed, where Nia is laying with her face buried in the pillows.

"God wants us to be together," I finally say. Nia don't respond but shifts on the bed, so I know she's listening. "Me and Granddaddy read this chapter in the Bible earlier, E-cheese-e something, and it said we gotta stick together, even when it's hard. That's what's gon' make us stronger." Still no response from Nia. "I think that part of the Bible is for me and you, more than anything. Cause who else we gon' stick together with, if not each other?"

Finally, Nia turns over and looks at me. "E-cheese-e something?" she asks, then starts to laugh. So I do the same. We only laugh a couple seconds, but it's better than crying.

Once the laughing stops, I ask, "What's a crackhead?" I figure I should start there, with the easier question. Still, I don't think she gon' answer, but then she sits up and looks me right in the eye. Little lines of makeup are starting to run down her face.

"I'm sorry I said all that stuff in front of you," Nia says, smoothing my hair with her hand. It's the first time in so long Nia's touched my hair all soft like that. "I got real upset bout some stuff, but I ain't mean for you to hear."

"No," I say, "I'm happy you did. Nobody ever says anything in front of me. And they all lie to me, too. Bout Daddy and everything else." That lump's growing in my throat, all the questions swirling in my head.

Nia smiles. "You're right," she says, "we gotta stop treating you like a baby, cause you getting older and older every day." She turns serious again when she speaks. "Crackhead means"—she pauses here to think—"it means a person who uses drugs. Drugs are something bad that we ain't s'posed to have, but some people get 'em anyway." I know this already, but I don't interrupt. "And when you put drugs in your body, it makes you do bad stuff. Even to the people you love most." Nia stops talking. Her face clouds over with memories that must be sad, cause more tears spill down her face.

"Tell me more," I whisper, scooting closer. "What'd you mean bout Daddy? Who did he sell our house to?"

"It's complicated—" Nia starts, but I continue.

"And when he sold it, did he know we was gon' have to sleep in the car? Did he know it was gon' be some days Momma had to pick between giving us breakfast or dinner, cause we ain't have enough for both?" Nia's crying harder now, and I'm crying, too, but I can't stop. "Is that why you been mad all this time? Cause he did this to us, left us like this?" I pause, sniff. "Or did something else happen, something else you been keeping from me?"

Nia stops crying all at once and looks up at me.

"Is that it?" I ask, cautious. "What did he do to you, Nia?" I'm scared to know, but I been chasing secrets too long to stop now.

"He . . . he . . ." Giant tears puddle in the corners of Nia's eyes.

"You can tell me," I whisper, pulling Nia's hand into my lap.

Nia half smiles, then lets out a big sigh that sounds like letting go of everything she was holding in for so long. "Before Daddy died, me and him got in a fight. I had been hearing stuff about him at school from one of the kids whose dad was a cop. He told a bunch of people about that time Daddy got arrested. He was calling Daddy a dirty druggie. He kept saying it all day— **dirty druggie, dirty druggie**—to me and anyone else who would listen."

I stroke Nia's thumb with my finger when she pauses. She shrugs her shoulders and continues.

"I guess I was mad or embarrassed . . . probably both. I came home early that day and decided I was gon' confront Daddy. I was looking for him all over the house and couldn't find him, then realized, of course, he was on them stairs. So, I went down there." The discomfort of the image she remembers darkens Nia's eyes. "I remember him like that now, when I think of him. All hunched over and frantic. It didn't even look like him."

Nia's voice drags off. I try to see the image she describes, but it's one memory of Daddy that's only Nia's, not mine.

"I was just so mad!" Nia starts again. "Daddy was sitting there doing the exact thing I was busy tryna defend him about. I was so"—Nia clenches her teeth—"angry."

"So what you do?" I ask, voice shaking.

Nia's gaze is stuck on the closed door now, like she can see Daddy sittin' over there. "I ran down the stairs so fast I almost tripped. He was right there in the middle—not at the top or the bottom of the stairs. Right in the middle." Nia's eyes flutter as she speaks. "His back was to me, but he must've heard me coming. He must've . . . But he didn't turn around. Made me run all the way down to the bottom and look up at him. He ain't even stop . . ."

Nia pauses so long this time, I don't know if she's gon' finish. I squeeze her hand to say, **Keep going**, and finally she does.

"I just started screaming at him. Screaming bout how he didn't love us enough. Asking how he could choose drugs when it was killing him.

322

Killing us." Nia clenches her eyes shut as she talks now. "At first, I wasn't sure he could even hear me, because he didn't stop. I walked up the steps, got right in his face. And called him that name."

Tears squeeze out from Nia's still shut eyes. "What name?" I whisper.

Nia laughs, but it ain't a real laugh. More like a cry trapped in a laugh. "I got up in Daddy's face, waited for him to finally look at me." Nia takes a deep breath and, as she exhales, whispers the words, "Dirty druggie."

I lower my head quickly, before Nia can see the anger that rushes onto my face. "It's not your fault," I eventually say, even though I ain't sure I mean it. "Them kids was saying that stuff and gettin' all in your head. You ain't mean it."

Nia rolls her head back, lifts her face to the ceiling. I wait for her to say something, but she don't.

"You ain't mean it," I repeat, "right?"

"Do you wanna know what Daddy did after I said it?" Nia asks, her voice barely a whisper now. I nod, slow. Her voice stays even, distant. "It was like he ain't see me til right that moment. His eyes locked on mine, but they wasn't Daddy's eyes. They looked . . . wild. Lost." Nia pulls her hands from my lap and hugs her shoulders, rocking back and forth, slow. "He just looked at me like that. Didn't say nothing. And then he . . ."

Nia is rocking and rocking, but not speaking. "He what, Nia? What did Daddy do to you?"

"He ain't mean it," Nia whispers and rocks. "He ain't mean it."

"Did he hurt you?" I ask. Nia slowly starts to nod, then faster and faster. The faster she nods, the more my heart breaks.

"He hit me so hard, it knocked me down the stairs. I landed flat on my back." Nia breathes deep, the air again escaping from her body. "He ain't even stop. He ain't even **stop**." Tears are running down Nia's face, past her chin. "I was just laying there, crying for him. Crying for him to help me . . ." Nia's voice cracks, then melts into sobs.

"It's okay. It's okay. You're okay." I cradle Nia in my arms like a baby. She lays her head in my lap and I rub her hair, whispering, "Shh-shh," into the silence. I try to think through what Nia just told me, but I ain't even sure where to begin. All I know for now is that Nia needs me. We might not be the perfect family, but we the kind of family that's gon' be there when you need 'em. Just like Momma and Granddaddy, I suddenly realize. They ain't even been talking all these years, but when Momma needed him, Granddaddy was there. That's what family does.

"Hey, you remember that time we all went to Chicago?" I ask Nia, still stroking her hair. She nods, then settles back in my lap. The memory fills the room, but I don't speak, so Nia don't speak. We don't have to use words to make it come alive, cause it lives in both our minds forever, the same.

Daddy said, **Sometimes you gotta give up something you want to get something you need,** and I finally know what he gave up that weekend in Chicago. And I know I gotta do the same, for me and for Nia. I clear my throat before I speak again.

"Something happened yesterday," I begin, and then I tell Nia bout running away and Rondell and the dumpster. Halfway through, Nia lifts her head and holds my hand as I talk, guarding tears at the rim of her eyes. I tell Nia bout Rondell lying and pretending to be my friend, and then touching me again and again. Bout how somebody I thought I could count on betrayed me. Hurt me. As I talk, I know Nia's thinking bout what happened between her and Daddy. She shared her secret with me, so I'm sharing my secret with her. This way, we ain't gotta be alone. I confess and cry and rub Nia's hair. Soon she's crying and rubbing my hair, neither of us speaking. We lay there like that, both remembering and crying, til we can forget.

"I wanna apologize to you," Nia says once we're quiet again.

"For what?" I sniffle.

"Well, even though I ain't mean for it to, I think you got the worse end of everything I've been dealing with." Nia folds her hands and tucks them under her chin. "Honestly, it's hard to talk to you sometimes, cause you always wanna talk about the past, and I just wanna forget it." Nia sighs. "I mean, ain't it hard for you to remember all that stuff? Even remembering good stuff about Daddy makes me feel like I'm ripping in half." Nia's voice cracks as she finishes.

I take some time to think before I answer, twisting my hair around my pinky finger. "It's hard for me, too," I eventually respond, "but it feels like I gotta do it. You and Momma don't wanna talk bout Daddy, so it feels like if I don't, then he's really gon' be gone forever. Even if he did some bad stuff, he was still our daddy. He still made you laugh harder than me or Momma ever could. And when he would dance with Momma"—I pause to imagine them there, dancing in the room beside us—"I never saw Momma happier than when she was in his arms."

Nia smiles so big her teeth show. "Yeah," she replies. "I remember."

"I'm so scared I'm gon' forget all that stuff. That I'm gon' lose him." I cry again, but this time it feels like it's coming from somewhere deeper, somewhere I ain't even know was there. Nia wraps her arms around me, and I sob into her chest. But instead of feeling sad, I feel safe.

Daddy's gone. Momma's gone. But Nia's still

here, with me. She lifts my head, offers me her version of an ice cream cone smile. I'm eleven years old and I've lost so much, but here with Nia, I know I still got some important stuff, too. It's like I'm standing in a field full of fireflies, struggling to catch 'em all, when really, I just gotta slow down and catch one.

PART III

August 1995

10

Once we reach the middle of August, I'm almost positive Momma ain't gon' ever come back. It's been three weeks since Nia's birthday, since me and Nia finding our way back to each other. She still don't play with me all the time, but sometimes she helps me find caterpillars or rocks. And last week, she even surprised me with a new book.

"What's this?" I asked when she handed me the bag one night after dinner. Nia ain't answer, just smiled. I looked over at Granddaddy and he was smiling, too. Weird.

I opened the bag and inside was a book with a girl on the cover who looked just like me. She was younger than me—missing two front teeth—but besides that, she was just like me. Same eyes and nose and smile. She even wore her hair in two ponytails with braids and bows, just like I used to wear, before I changed my hair to be like Nia.

"I know it's below your reading level," Nia said as I turned to the back cover, "but I thought it would be nice for you to read a book about a girl who's just like you, for once."

I read the title again, **Amazing Grace**. "What's it bout?" I asked Nia.

Nia smiled. "Well, it's about a girl named Grace, who loves to use her imagination." I turned the page and found Grace dressed in battle gear, and on the next page, positioned like a spider. "Grace loves to pretend like she's other people in other places, and she's really good at it," Nia continued. "But one day, one of Grace's classmates tells her she can't audition for the role of Peter Pan in the school play."

"Why does he say that?" I asked, following along with the colorful illustrations.

"Well, he didn't think Grace could be Peter Pan because she was Black."

I looked up from the book and frowned. "Well, that's not true. Right?" I peered at Nia, then Granddaddy. Granddaddy started to stand up, but Nia shook her head.

"Of course it's not true," Nia said, wrapping her arm around my shoulders. "Grace could do anything she wanted to do, be anybody she wanted to be. That was her gift." Nia pulled me in closer. "It's your gift, too."

"Me?" I flipped to the end of the book, watched as Grace went from sad to triumphant.

"Yes, you. When Grace is told what she can't do, who she can't be, that's what helps her discover who she really is. Grace realizes that she can do anything she sets her mind to. Just like you." Nia turned my shoulder til I was facing her. "You can do anything, KB. You're the smartest person I know." Then Nia hugged me, tight.

I hug the book tight to my chest now from my spot on the porch. From the moment I said thank you to Nia for the book, I already knew it was gon' be my new best book. Mostly cause I ain't gotta learn no new words or talk no different. Grace is just like me, exactly as I am, and that's what makes her special. I guess that's what makes me special, too.

"KB!" Nia's voice calls from inside the house.

I perch my book on the steps carefully before responding. "Yeah?" I answer, wondering if I'm gon' have to go inside. I think it's still too early for dinner, but maybe we gon' eat early today.

Before I stand up, Nia is already outside and standing in front of me. "Granddaddy says we can go out for dinner tonight, if you want."

I dip my head and smile. It feels good to have

Nia check in on what I want, instead of just being bossy and mean all the time. "Yeah, I wanna go," I reply coolly, not wanting to seem too anxious. "Where we gon' go?"

Nia shrugs. "Granddaddy said we can pick." I nod, then wait for her to pick. Even with us gettin' along now, Nia's still the one who makes decisions for us. I'm okay with it, though, cause I bet Nia gon' pick something I like, too.

"Maybe we can talk to Granddaddy tonight," I say, then whisper, "bout the plan." After me and Nia made up, I told her everything I knew bout Momma and Granddaddy. Bout Granny dying when Momma was ten. Bout the headshot and the fight. Then I told Nia bout my plan to fix Momma and Granddaddy, so we could go back home. She ain't seem as convinced as me that it could work, but she ain't call it stupid, either.

"What do you think we should say?" Nia asks quietly, sittin' down beside me on the steps.

I shrug. The only thing I ain't told Nia bout yet is Momma being at the treatment facility. "Have you talked to Momma since we been here?"

Nia shakes her head no. Looks like if Momma did call Nia on her birthday, Nia ain't talk to her.

"Why not?"

This time, Nia shrugs. "I guess it was weird to talk to her since I ain't wanna tell her bout what happened with Daddy. I was so mad at him, and it made her mad at me, I think." I reach over and pat Nia's knee to say, **I understand**. "And even if it wasn't for that, I was mad at Momma, too. For leaving, you know?"

I nod. "Yeah, I was mad, too. But then, when I talked to her, I started feeling kinda different."

"Different? Why?"

"Well, Momma ain't been sounding like herself since we been here. I started thinking maybe something else was wrong with her, besides just being sad bout Daddy dying."

"I don't know, KB, I think Momma just sad—"

"There's more," I interrupt.

Nia laughs. "Of course there is. What else you got?"

"Well, one time I heard Granddaddy and Charlie talking," I start quickly, "and I think they was talking bout Momma."

"Mm-hmm," Nia says, with a face like she trying not to laugh.

"I know, I know, I'm s'posed to stay outta grown folks' conversation. But this was important!" I ignore Nia's laughter and shaking head. "They was saying something bout Momma being in some kind of treatment. So, I asked Granddaddy bout it—"

"Wait, you talked to Granddaddy about this and not me?"

I lower my head and whisper, "Yeah." Then

louder: "I'm sorry, Nia, it was before we started talking again! I thought you would just say it was stupid and tell me to leave you alone."

Nia wraps her arm around my shoulders and pulls me in close to her. "You're right. I'm sorry. Keep going." We smile at each other, quick, before I speak again.

"Granddaddy talked to me bout it, and told me that Momma needed some extra help right now, cause she been so sad. It's more than just sad, though. He said Momma been depressed."

I wait for Nia's reaction cause I ain't sure if she knows what it means. But the scared and shocked look on her face lets me know that she understands exactly. Probably even more than I do.

"Okay," Nia eventually says, "I think we need a new plan."

I stand up, quick. "Why? You don't like my plan?"

"Shh!" Nia whispers, pulling me back down to the steps. "I do like your plan! It's just . . . what if the best thing for us right now is staying, instead of trying to leave?"

I sit there for a while, thinking bout what Nia said. "But," I stammer, "you don't wanna be back with Momma again?"

Nia shakes her head. "Of course I do. But what if we ain't have to leave?" Nia leans in closer. "What if instead of tryna get back home to

Momma, we try to get Momma to come and live here with us, with Granddaddy?"

As soon as the words are out her mouth, a giant grin spreads cross my face. "Does that mean you like the new plan?" Nia asks, and I nod enthusiastically.

"I love the new plan," I say, realizing for the first time how much I ain't wanna leave Granddaddy. Maybe he started out like Marilla Cuthbert, but turns out, he was a Matthew all along. And the truth is, Marilla loved Anne, too. Some people just got a funny way of showing it.

"Okay," Nia says, popping up, "I think we should start the plan tonight!"

"What we gon' do?" I ask, standing up beside Nia. She starts to walk down the porch steps, and I follow.

"When we go to dinner," Nia says, leaning up against my tree, "we should get Granddaddy talking about what happened with him and Momma. I bet if we can get him talking about it, he might realize that he's been silly all these years for not talking to Momma."

"But what if it's Momma who ain't been doin' the talking?" I ask, thinking bout Granddaddy's sad eyes when he told me bout the big fight.

"Even better!" Nia reaches down and picks up a tiny caterpillar from the base of the tree. "If Granddaddy is ready to talk, then all we gotta do is get Momma here." Nia lets the caterpillar crawl over the back of her hand, then her palm.

"And how we gon' do that?" I ask, once I get tired of watching.

"The same way we get Momma to do anything," Nia says in a sneaky voice. "We just gotta make her think we need her; then, I bet she gon' be here."

"Okay," I reply quietly.

"What, you don't think it's gon' work?" Nia asks, hands on her hips.

I nod, even though I ain't so sure. But it's worth a try, especially if it's gon' make Nia happy, and maybe even make Momma and Granddaddy happy again, too. "But I think it's one thing we gotta do first."

"What's that?" Nia asks.

I step away from the tree and dust dirt off the back of my shorts. "We gotta call Momma."

Nia's face wrinkles. "Why?" She crosses over to the post at the edge of the porch and leans against it, taking a bit of her hair between her fingers.

"Why you say it like that?" I ask. "You don't wanna talk to Momma?"

"I mean, I do. Kinda." Nia starts to chew her hair, which she only does when she's nervous bout something. "It's just . . . been awhile, you know?"

"I know!" I exclaim, jumping up excitedly. "That's why we definitely gotta call! You ain't talked to Momma all summer. I bet she gon' be so happy to hear from you."

"Okay," Nia says, but her voice trails off like she ain't convinced.

"Plus," I continue, "it's gon' be the perfect way for us to get goin' on the plan. Once we get Momma on the same page as us, it's gon' be easy to get Granddaddy on board!" I move closer to Nia, brushing my shoulder against hers. "Come on, Nia, don't you miss Momma at all?"

"You know I miss Momma," Nia says, pushing me away. "It's just complicated."

"It **is** complicated," I say, scooting back close to Nia, this time forcing my arm around her shoulders. "And that's exactly why we gotta talk. How else we gon' get through it?"

"Okay, okay." Nia sighs. "Let's call Momma."

I try to hide my giant smile as Nia opens the door and heads inside.

"There's just one thing," I say, once we get to the kitchen.

Nia turns to look at me and rolls her eyes. "What?"

Now that I got the old Nia back, I can't help but laugh at her rolling her eyes and pretending to be mad. "I'm sorry, I'm sorry!" I squeal. "It's just that I ain't sure if Granddaddy wanted me to tell you bout the treatment facility. So let me be the one to ask him to call."

Nia cocks her head to the side, but I rush off before she can say anything else. I find Granddaddy at the back of the house, just bout to head into his bedroom.

"Granddaddy!" I shriek before he can close the door.

He turns around real quick, then stares at me. "Well, what's so important that you almost scared an old man straight outta his skin?"

I giggle and say, "Sorry, Granddaddy," before continuing. "Me and Nia wanna call Momma before we go to dinner. Can you dial the number for us?"

"Now, Kenyatta—"

"It's gon' be fast, Granddaddy, I promise! It's just that Nia ain't talked to Momma since we been here, so she just wanna say hi right quick." I bat my eyelashes, hoping Granddaddy ain't gon' notice I'm up to something.

Seems like my plan works, cause Granddaddy starts his slow walk back to the front of the house. I tiptoe behind him, tryna seem calm when I'm jumping for joy on the inside. Once we get to the kitchen, Granddaddy picks up the phone and begins to dial.

"Make it quick," he says once he's done, handing the receiver to Nia. "Once I get my clothes on, it's gon' be time to go." And with that, he ambles back down the hallway, leaving me and Nia alone to talk to Momma.

It feels different this time, watching Nia hold the receiver and wondering what Momma's doin' on the other end. After a few seconds, Nia's eyebrows raise, but she don't say nothin'. I figure that means Momma's on the phone by now, so I nudge Nia.

"Hey, Momma," Nia finally says. Soon as she says it, she's got tears in her eyes. I don't know what Momma says next, but Nia don't talk for a while, just listens and cries. Finally, Nia speaks again.

"We bout to go to dinner with Granddaddy," she says, "but it's something we wanted to talk to you about first." Then she don't talk again for a while, cept saying "mm-hmm" and nodding, then eventually finishing with, "Yeah, she's right here."

Nia hands me the phone and I take a breath before saying, "Hello." The last two times I talked to Momma ain't go exactly as planned, so I'm hoping this time gon' be better.

"Hey, KB," Momma says, her voice sweet and drippy like syrup.

"Hey, Momma," I say back. "How you been doin'?"

"I been good, baby. Real good, actually." And Momma sounds good, too, for the first time in a long time. Seems like whatever she's doin' at the treatment facility is working.

"That's good," I say, watching Nia wipe her eyes, "cause we got something to talk to you bout. See, the thing is—"

"I need to talk to you about something, too," Momma interrupts.

My stomach flips like when I'm bout to be in trouble. "You do?"

"I do." Momma chuckles. "But don't worry, you're not in trouble." Momma takes a quick breath. "I wanted to apologize to you. I shouldn't have snapped at you when we talked before."

"It's okay," I say, quick, cause it's strange to have Momma apologizing to me.

"No, it's not okay. It's just that you were asking me about a memory that's hard for me to remember. And with everything else going on . . ."

"Because of Daddy?"

"Yes, because of Daddy. But not just that. When your daddy died it was . . . do you know the expression 'the straw that broke the camel's back'?"

"Yes," I say, even though I ain't quite sure what it means.

"What happened with your daddy was the straw that broke the camel's back for me. I had already been through so much—and came out on top. But this time . . ." Momma's voice trails off.

"Why was that memory with Granddaddy so hard to remember?" I ask, still stuck on that part. I think back to the weird stuff Javon was saying bout what Granddaddy did to Momma after the headshot, how he wouldn't describe it as **little**. Maybe there's more to the story than what Granddaddy told me.

"What exactly did your Granddaddy tell you?" Momma asks, like she's also wondering which parts of the story he held back.

"Well, he told me bout the headshot, and how after he ain't let you get it, you got it done anyway, by some guy at the mall. But then when he saw it, he told you he ain't wanna hear nothin' bout it. Then he left."

"Then he left?"

"Yeah, he said he threw down the picture, then he left."

Momma is silent for a long time, but I can still hear her breathing, so I know she's there. Finally, she clears her throat.

"When I met your daddy, I was only sixteen years old. Just a year older than Nia is now." I look over at Nia when Momma says this; try to imagine Momma that age and meeting Daddy. "It's hard to believe I was that young," Momma continues, "because I felt like I knew everything about everything back then." Momma chuckles and I listen without speaking, just enjoying the sound of her laugh.

"So yeah, I was young. And I was mad at your Granddaddy. When I met your daddy, it was right after that fight. In a way, I started dating him just to make your Granddaddy mad. But then somewhere along the way, I realized it was more than that."

Nia goes and sits down at the dining room table. I twist the phone cord around my finger as I listen, hoping Nia ain't mad that we talking so long.

"The first moment I knew I loved your daddy was when I told him about the fight with your Granddaddy. It was our first real date, and he took me to see a movie. About halfway through the movie, he realized I was crying. And the movie was a comedy! So, he took me outside and asked me what was wrong." The line is silent for five whole seconds before Momma speaks again. "I told him the truth, about how me and my daddy had just got in a big stupid fight over a headshot. How I felt like my own daddy didn't even love me anymore, because when he saw the picture, the picture that made me feel so beautiful, like a woman . . . he slapped me and said I looked like a whore."

The first thought that flashes cross my mind is **not Granddaddy**. I don't say nothin', though, cause I ain't sure what to say. Momma ain't ever even used that word, **whore**, when talking to me. I'm surprised she told me all of this now. I'm surprised Granddaddy **ain't** tell me.

"I'm sorry, Momma," I finally say. "Granddaddy ain't tell me that part."

"And he shouldn't have," Momma says, "because you're still a little girl, KB, even though you want to know everything the adults know. But we just want you to enjoy being a kid. Being all grown up is a lot harder than it seems."

"Yeah," I say, fighting away images of that dumpster and Rondell.

"And besides, your Granddaddy is so happy to have you and Nia there. He loves you girls so much! I think it's good for him to have you there. Almost like it—"

Momma stops, so I finish. "Almost like it makes up for what he did to you?"

"Almost," Momma whispers.

We both stay silent after that. I think bout what Momma just told me, then think bout what Nia told me, bout her and Daddy. Two different daughters, both hurt by they daddies. I bet if Momma knew what Daddy did to Nia, she might go easier on her. I bet if Nia knew what Granddaddy did to Momma, she might understand differently what Daddy did to her. But for now, I'm the only one who knows everything. I wonder what it means bout our family that this has happened to Momma and to Nia. I wonder what it means bout Momma that even after it happened, she sent us here, to live with Granddaddy. And I wonder what any of this means now that I love Granddaddy and think he's bout the best man that's ever been in my life.

"KB?" Momma finally says. Her voice is shaky, like she either been crying or trying not to cry.

"I'm here," I say.

"I just want you to know that . . . nobody's perfect. Not even the people who you want to be perfect. **Need** to be perfect. Even those people are going to make mistakes. And it's up to us, the ones who get hurt, to decide what's going to happen after that."

"But what if you don't wanna forgive 'em?" I ask, looking at Nia.

"I'm gonna tell you something that's taken me a long time to learn," Momma says. "In life, we're going to get hurt. If we stay focused on that hurt, and nothing else, then we won't ever be able to heal. But if we focus on the healing, well, then we'll start to notice that hurt disappear. It's all a matter of what you choose to focus on."

I nod, then remember Momma can't see me, so I say, "Yes, ma'am."

"Have fun at dinner."

"I love you, Momma."

"I love you back, KB." Momma hangs up, but I keep the phone up to my ear a few seconds longer.

"So," Nia says, breaking the silence, "looks like you ain't get to tell her bout the plan, either." I shake my head no and we both stare at each other for a second before breaking out into giggles. "Same ol' Momma," Nia says.

"Same ol' Momma," I say back.

We decide to go to a Mexican restaurant for dinner. It's the perfect choice cause I love the chips and cheese they bring out to the table when we first sit down, and chicken quesadillas are Nia's favorite food. Seems like Granddaddy happy with the choice, too, cause he eats almost all of the first basket of chips before I can.

After our failed conversation with Momma, me and Nia decided we would go back to the original plan, trying to convince Granddaddy that we should all live together in Lansing. And since Nia don't know everything I know, my other secret plan is to get Granddaddy to apologize to Momma. At first, I was nothin' but mad at Granddaddy. But then I remembered everything he told me bout how much he loved Momma; how scared he was after Granny died. When I put that together with what Momma said—**if we focus on the healing, we'll start to notice the hurt disappear**—I decided that it ain't bout me knowing and understanding what happened; it's bout Momma and Granddaddy doin' that for themselves.

"So, Granddaddy," Nia starts up before our food even arrives, "we've been thinking."

"Is that so," Granddaddy says, smirking as he takes a sip of his water. "And what have you been thinking about, exactly?"

"Well, summer is almost over. And we still haven't heard anything about when exactly Momma is planning to come back. Have you talked to her?" Nia innocently stirs her ice cubes around with her straw.

Granddaddy shifts in his seat, then clasps and unclasps his hands two times before speaking. "We ain't talked much. But your momma got other stuff to worry bout right now."

"Like what?" Nia asks, sneaking a glance at me. I pretend not to notice, cause I don't exactly want Granddaddy to know that I told Nia what we talked bout. It don't make much sense for me to know and not Nia, but still, I ain't sure if I was s'posed to tell.

"It's not my place to tell your momma's business," Granddaddy answers with a sigh, "but all you need to know is that she's taking care of some stuff, and she gon' be back soon as she can." Granddaddy looks at Nia, then looks at me. Now I know he knows that I told her.

"Can you tell us bout what Momma was like when she was our age?" I say quickly, tryna change the subject before Nia gets too impatient or Granddaddy gets too mad. And it seems like it works, cause Granddaddy's face softens, and even Nia perks up to listen.

"She was just like the both of you, rolled into one." Granddaddy smiles as he gazes off at the image of young Momma that lives in his mind. "Beautiful and tough. Funny and serious. Smart as a whip and determined to do whatever she said she was gon' do. And always asking too many questions," Granddaddy finishes with a wink.

As I listen, I put an image of young Momma together in my mind, adding pieces from me and pieces from Nia. I wish I could know her that way, cause I bet we would be best friends. Momma now ain't much like the Momma that Granddaddy describes.

Seems like Nia thinking the same, cause then she asks, "How come Momma so different now?"

Granddaddy sits up, just a little. "What you mean, different?"

"Well, she's still beautiful and smart for sure. And I get the serious part, definitely. But funny? Tough? That don't sound much like the Momma we know."

"Well, she can be funny when she wanna be," I

cut in, remembering the funny notes she wrote on that homemade wrapping paper years ago.

"Hold on nah, you don't think your momma is tough?" Granddaddy asks, now sittin' all the way up. "After all that she's been through, I'm surprised she's still standing."

"What has she been through?" Nia takes the opportunity to ask. "You just mean what happened to Daddy, or something else?"

Granddaddy looks at me again, this time with a face that says, **See what happens when you tell secrets?** "Nia—" Granddaddy starts, but just then, our food arrives. We all sit there quiet while our waiter sets down full, hot plates in front of each of us. Once he walks away, Granddaddy talks again, not even bothering to look at his food.

"What is it that yawl girls want?" We don't say nothin', but Granddaddy ain't easily fooled. "C'mon now, I know yawl want somethin'. I could tell from the minute we got here that yawl had a plan. So gon' 'head. Spill it." Granddaddy takes a big bite of his food and chews slowly while he waits for us to talk.

Nia stuffs a bite of quesadilla in her mouth and looks at me. I look back at her and shrug. Maybe it's time to just tell Granddaddy the truth. Nia's still looking at me, so now I nod.

"We want to stay here," Nia whispers once she

finishes chewing, not making eye contact with Granddaddy.

"Speak up, girl," Granddaddy replies. "You know I can't understand you when you mumble."

This time, I jump in, louder. "We wanna stay here, with you, Granddaddy."

"In Lansing," Nia finishes, then we both look at Granddaddy at once.

"Oh," Granddaddy says eventually, like maybe we caught him off guard. "But what about yawl Momma?"

"We want her to live here with you, too," Nia says quickly. "We think it would be perfect for all of us!" Nia pauses mid-excitement. "That is, if you have enough space, and want us to stay and stuff." Now Nia looks back down at the table. Granddaddy reaches cross the table and places his finger underneath her chin, tipping her head up so she's looking right at him.

"Of course I want you to stay." Granddaddy smiles, Nia smiles, I smile. "It's just"— Granddaddy leans back into the booth—"I don't know if your momma is gon' want to stay here, with me."

"Don't worry, Granddaddy," I say, "we have a perfect plan to get Momma here. And once she's here, the first thing you gotta do is apologize." I give Granddaddy a look that I hope says, **I know**

what you did. "I know you can make her forgive you, I just know it."

"How do you know that, huh?" Granddaddy asks, voice strained. "I really hurt her. I don't know if she's ever gon' be able to forgive me. I don't even know if she should."

This time, it's Nia who reaches cross the table and lifts Granddaddy's dipped chin. "She'll forgive you," Nia says. "Daddies make mistakes, but it don't change that special thing between a daddy and his daughter. Ain't nothing that can change that."

I rest my hand on Nia's thigh and squeeze, just a little, to let her know I'm proud. Maybe she ain't get her chance to forgive Daddy, but now she got a chance to keep Momma from making the same choice. Nia's right—daddies make mistakes. And the hurt they cause, that can't be undone. But how they try to make up for those mistakes is important, too. Like Granddaddy, being here for Momma when she needs him. As I think bout all that Granddaddy's done for us this summer, I realize, it looks a whole lot like working hard for her forgiveness.

Granddaddy eats the rest of his food without talking, so me and Nia eat our food without talking. Finally, after Granddaddy finishes his whole plate of food—and me and Nia finish half of

our own, then box up the rest to take home—
Granddaddy speaks again.

"I'll talk to your momma," he says. Me and Nia
squeal excitedly. "I ain't makin' no promises, nah!
But I'll talk to her." Granddaddy tries to look serious, but mostly, he just looks happy.

While we wait for the waiter to deliver the bill,
I close my eyes and think of all the things I'm
grateful for. But then I open them again when I
discover it's too many to count. Instead, I enjoy
what it feels like to be in this moment—squished
in the booth beside Nia, smiling at Granddaddy,
tummy full with chips and cheese and tacos,
laughing so hard til my face hurts.

Momma is back. The air is cooler now and lifts my
hair as I run to her, grinning hard. She pulls in the
driveway so slow I am already at her car before she
can park. She climbs out and hugs me so tight that
I cough and cough til it turns to laughs.

Momma came back, just like I knew she would.
I ain't sure what Granddaddy said or did to get her
here, but he did it. Momma is here and looking
better than ever. She pulls back from our hug,
gives me first one wink, then blows two kisses. I

catch the first and kiss it, catch the second and blow it back into the wind. Our special thing, just me and Momma.

Soon, Nia is there, too, and Momma wraps us both in a hug that feels complete, like ain't nothin' missing. Then she stoops low to look us both in the eyes and asks, "Guess what?"

Me and Nia wait without speaking.

"We have a house!" Momma's voice squeaks that last part, from either excitement or emotion, I can't tell. She waits for me and Nia to be happy, but we both stand there, quiet. I turn and look at Granddaddy, standing silent beside the porch. Nia and Momma turn to look at him, too, so Granddaddy comes over and stands between me and Nia, then clears his throat.

"It's okay, girls. Me and your momma done talked. And we both decided that it's gon' be best for yawl to go on back to Detroit, get your life back on track there."

"What does that mean?" I ask.

"It means," Granddaddy replies, "that we tryna work things out. And we still got a ways to go to get back what we lost"—Granddaddy looks at Momma—"but I'm gon' do everything I can to get there. Starting with getting yawl back together." Now Granddaddy looks at me and Nia again. "I helped yawl Momma out with a down payment on your very own house."

"But what about our plan?" Nia stammers, taking the words out of my mouth.

"Plans change," Granddaddy says with a smile. "Yawl are ready to go home now. All of yawl." He looks at Momma when he says this last part and winks.

I watch Momma and Granddaddy, then watch Nia. She takes a big breath, then lets it out as she rushes into Momma's arms. So I rush into Momma's arms, too. Momma wraps both of us into a tight squeeze and we jump up and down together like kids. We stay there like that long as we can, til we hear Granddaddy start to walk back toward the porch.

"You girls gon' in and pack up your stuff. And don't worry," Momma says, "we'll be back." She smiles and it's her best ice cream cone smile yet, cause this one ain't sad in none of her secret places. Nia walks quick, but I walk slow so I can grab Momma by the arm. When she turns to look at me, I pull her in for what seems like a hug, but then I whisper in her ear, "You should tell Nia bout what happened between you and Granddaddy. She needs to hear it." Then, before Momma can respond, I follow Nia to the house.

As we climb the porch steps, Momma approaches Granddaddy. She don't try to hug him this time, just walks up to him, still smiling. But he takes her hands in his, and as I walk past them into the house, I hear him whisper, "How's my star?" And this time it's Granddaddy that goes for the hug, and after a couple seconds, Momma hugs right back.

I smile my biggest smile, then run inside before my looking makes the hug go away. A daddy hug is something special that you don't even know you need. I swallow the lump in my throat quick, cause even though my daddy's hug is gone for good, Momma got hers back. I think bout all me and Nia had to go through this summer, to find our way back together, so I know this hug is just the beginning. But still, it's a start.

Momma and Granddaddy wait on the porch while we pack our small bags. Nia is quiet, so I am quiet, too. Plus, I ain't got much to say. I am happy to see Momma, but I am sad, too, bout all that I gotta leave behind here. My tree. Granddaddy. I think back to the beginning of the summer, the things that mattered along the way. Ain't gon' be nobody to catch all them magical fireflies once I'm gone.

I stuff my rainbow jacket into the bag and then struggle to get it zipped. Nia finishes first and leaves the room without a second look. But not me. I sit down on the edge of the bed and put my eyes on everything that matters. The mirror that Nia always looked in. The dresser that held my books and the bed that held my dreams. The crack in the ceiling that reminds me of my life now. A little bit of bad that can still be good, if you look at it just right.

I walk out to the porch. Granddaddy sits on the steps with both hands in his lap. Momma and Nia already in the car, so I know it's time for my good-bye. I sit next to Granddaddy, and for minutes, neither of us speaks.

"I'm gon' miss you," I finally say, looking down at my hands in my lap.

"I'm gon' miss you, too, Kenyatta. My favorite **Wheel of Fortune** partner." Granddaddy nudges me with his shoulder and I can't help but look up at him and smile. "You promise to visit your lonely old granddaddy sometimes?"

I nod. "Every summer," I say with a big smile, hoping it's gon' be true. Granddaddy smiles back before his face turns thoughtful.

"You know, when I was your age, I lost somebody, too. My big cousin, James." Granddaddy's voice breaks, but he clears his throat and continues. "James was my hero. I did everything he did and liked everything he liked. When I lost him, it was almost like losing me."

I nod, cause I don't know what to say.

"I been watching you this summer, Kenyatta, and I know you hurting. You done seen stuff that a kid your age ain't s'posed to see. And you lost somebody that left a big hole, right here." He taps his finger against my shirt, right above my heart. Just like he did on my birthday, when we talked bout Daddy. I told myself I wasn't gon' cry today, but now my eyes feel pretty itchy.

"I really miss him," I finally whisper. "Things just ain't the same without Daddy, even if he did do some bad stuff." I sniffle, but Granddaddy surprises me by smiling.

"I know you miss your daddy, Kenyatta. But that's not who I'm talking bout. You lost someone else this summer, too." Granddaddy turns his head to Momma's car and looks right at Nia, in the back seat with her headphones.

"Nia?" I ask.

"Remember what I said. When I lost my big cousin, it was almost like losing me." Granddaddy squeezes me in a quick hug, then slowly stands to head back inside the house.

"Granddaddy," I call out, just as his hand touches the screen door. He looks at me, and I can't tell if his eyes look happy or sad. "You got it wrong." I stand now, too, but don't move closer. "I ain't lose Nia this summer." I turn around and spot her in Momma's back seat, still with headphones on, but now watching me through the smudged window. She smiles, so I smile, too. "I found her." I duck my head before Granddaddy can respond, then wave good-bye.

I walk to the car, quick, and climb inside. As I

get settled in my seat, I realize that just like Granddaddy said, I been scared to lose Nia this whole time, cause losing Nia felt like losing me, too. The part of me that laughed til I snorted and threw snowballs. The part of me that had a daddy. But I ain't lose Nia. Not yet, and if I'm lucky, not ever.

"All buckled?" Momma glances into the back seat at me and Nia, and we both nod. But then I remember something I almost forgot.

"Momma, wait," I yell, unsnapping my seat belt. "My mayonnaise jar!" I'm already out the car before Momma can ask any questions, but I see the confused look on her face as I run back to Granddaddy's porch, where I hid the jar beneath the steps.

After a whole summer finding caterpillars, I only got one left. I don't know if they died or turned to butterflies, cause they are just gone. I wonder if Granddaddy found my jar and hid the dead bodies, so I wouldn't have to find 'em.

I watch the last caterpillar crawl along the bottom of the mayonnaise jar. Momma once brought home a book from the secondhand store bout a hungry caterpillar who ate everything he could find. I thought it was a funny book, cause back then I only knew the little-kid version of that story, where the caterpillar hatches one day from an egg. Eats and eats til he is longer, fatter. Then, one day, once he's had enough, he stops eating and hangs himself upside down from a twig, spins a cocoon, and in that silky covering, the caterpillar magically transforms into a butterfly, shedding all the versions of himself cept that very best one.

But the truth bout the little orange caterpillar crawling around the bottom of my jar is that he will have to give himself up completely before he can become something new. When he climbs into his cocoon, there won't be nothin' magic bout him digesting himself, then dissolving all his tissues til he's nothin'. Only then can he become something else.

The caterpillar pushes against the edge of the jar. I wonder if he hates it in there. All the grass that me and Nia put at the bottom is brown and filled with holes now, and the jar looks cloudy on the inside. He probably hates it, but it's been his home. He ain't have no choice bout none of it, just ended up there and had to make the best of it.

I turn the jar over in my hands, think of all that was there before and all that is gone now. And then I know what I gotta do.

I twist the lid off the top of the mayonnaise jar and sit it back on Granddaddy's porch. Maybe the caterpillar will keep living inside, but maybe he'll find a way out, instead. I want him to have a chance, so I gotta let go. The second lesson I learned from Daddy; the one he ain't follow, in the end.

I run back to Momma's car, dreaming of butterflies. I take one last look cross the street and find Bobby and Charlotte sittin' on their porch. Charlotte starts to stand when she sees me, but then sits down quick, like she just remembered something. I look away, cause I know them white kids can't be no different, even if they wanna. Or maybe they can, and just won't. But then, just as I open the car door, Bobby calls out.

"KB!" I turn back, and he offers a tiny wave that's already gone before I can return it. I dip my hand in my pocket instead, count the lumps of rock there that he gave me back when none of us knew better. One, two, three. I climb in the car and Momma drives away.

At the end of **Anne of Green Gables**, Anne had to say good-bye, too. The whole book was bout Anne settling into Green Gables—her first real home and real family. A happy story that you figure would have a happy ending. But in the end, Matthew died of a heart attack, and Anne gave up her own dreams to stay in Green Gables with Marilla. Our ending here in Lansing ain't like that ending, cause ain't nobody died, cept Daddy, which somehow feels like a long time ago. And instead of staying, we gotta leave. But even though it's hard to leave, it's probably for the best like Granddaddy said. He already tried holding Momma back once; now it's time for him to let her go. And who knows, maybe this will be our own version of a happy ending.

As N. Rutherford fades away in the rearview mirror, I worry that I ain't ever gon' see this house again. I think back to the beginning of the summer and wonder if Momma was right when she said we'd be thankful. There was a lot of bad this summer, but a lot of good, too, and I think I needed it all. Just like Anne, I done lost a little and gained a lot more. I look out the window and try to memorize everything I see. It's daytime, so ain't no last firefly for me to learn by heart. Everything that happened here is only a memory now, but I finally understand that that don't mean it's gone for good. The memories always come back to us, right when we need 'em. At the beginning of the summer, I ain't even know how to catch a firefly. I smile to myself, cause now I can catch a firefly, and I can hold on, too.

I look over at Nia, still with headphones on her ears. She sees me looking and pulls 'em off, then hands 'em to me with a smile. I smile back, then cross my eyes and stick out my tongue to make her laugh. Just like our **Good Times** nights, before Daddy took that TV away. Before them stairs and all them secrets. And before me and Nia almost lost each other. Nia snorts, a habit now, then we both giggle. We laugh and laugh, cause finally, we can.

ACKNOWLEDGMENTS

When I was a little Black girl growing up in Detroit, I had a ton of questions all the time, and thought I could fix everything, just like KB. I spent a lot of time obsessing over what I thought a "perfect" family should look like. I wondered why my life didn't look like the lives of the people in the stories I read. For a long time, I thought something was wrong with my life. Now I know that there was something wrong with those stories.

This book was born from a desire to show Black girlhood at its best, at its worst, at its most dull and most exciting. It was written and revised over the course of six years, beginning as a short story in a fiction workshop during my MA at Belmont University in 2014. I am thankful to the people and places who were a part of the origin of this story, whether they meant to be or not.

Acknowledgments

Much gratitude to my wonderful agent, Ayesha Pande, who sent me such a beautiful letter after reading the manuscript for the first time and has been convincing me of my talents ever since. Thank you for always fighting for the things you know matter most to me. You and everyone at APL make me feel so welcome and loved, and it is more than I dared to expect at the beginning of all this.

Many, many thanks to Amber Oliver, who is the fierce and passionate editor I always hoped for. Whenever we're together, the #blackgirlmagic is overflowing. I'm so grateful to have worked with you, learned from you, and been a part of your Tiny Rep journey. And speaking of . . . I am forever grateful for and fangirling over the one and only Phoebe Robinson. Your vision and dedication to the imprint impresses me daily. The entire team at Tiny Reparations Books has regularly made me feel seen, valued, and empowered. And a special thank-you to the folks who helped make this book happen—Christine Ball, John Parsley, Stephanie Cooper, Amanda Walker, Jamie Knapp, Katie Taylor, Tiffani Ren, Samantha Srinivasan, LeeAnn Pemberton, Susan Schwartz, Kristin del Rosario, Tiffany Estreicher, Kaitlin Kall, Dominique Jones, and Ryan Richardson.

The best thing about the four years I spent in the PhD program at Western Michigan University

Acknowledgments

was the people I met there. Beginning with my mentor, Thisbe Nissen, who has been fighting fiercely for me since before we met. Thank you for encouraging me, teaching me, loving me. I am immensely better for having met you. Thank you to the folks I workshopped with, my first real readers, and especially Nicole, Chad, Cody, Deb, Ariel, Tim, and Samantha. I am also thankful for my faculty mentors—John Saillant, Meghann Meussen, Staci Perryman-Clark, and Allen Webb—for being the advocates and allies I needed.

I am blessed to have my very own ride-or-die bosom buddies. Christina, Sydney, and Marissa, thanks for being the type of friends who will show up for me, tell me when I'm wrong, and love me through it all. To my HWW Doctianas—Suban, Sophia, Lisa—as soon as we met, I knew y'all would be squad for life. And my Face Off sisters: thank you for being there during the toughest and most exciting parts of my journey and celebrating me along the way.

Special thanks to: Leah, for helping me find my way (and find the right opening for this book). Corri, for the motivation and friendship. Al, for being the first person to read the entire book and encouraging me to tweet during #PitMad. Meg and Audrey, for reading my work and letting me read yours. Teya, for the love and support. Annette

Acknowledgments

Sisson, for the encouragement and leadership, and Gary McDowell, for the bolstering friendship. Ali Herring, for being the first agent to believe in me and this book. And last but not least, the WTFK Street Team, for holding me down!

I must pay homage to my literary inspirations: Toni Morrison, Maya Angelou, Jesmyn Ward, Zora Neale Hurston. Without you, there is no me. Thank you for showing me the way. Nicole Dennis-Benn and Danielle Evans, thank you for personally welcoming me into the club. Much love to Laura Pegram at **Kweli** for believing in this story (and me) from the beginning. I am also grateful to the folks I met as a VONA/Voices fellow, and especially Faith Adiele.

I am thankful for my family, and for everyone who has been family to me. My mom and sister plus me are the three musketeers, always sticking together through everything. And when I was growing up, there was nothing better than having cousins. No matter where we are in the world or in our relationship, I am always rooting for all of you. And to my darling nieces: Tia loves you!

At the heart of this story is loss, and while KB's loss looks different than mine, we both know it all too well. Daddy, I miss your laugh. Hearing you sing. Watching you cook. A decade later and I still can't find enough to fill the hole. Granddaddy Grady, I miss our summers with you in Lansing,

Acknowledgments

catching fireflies and telling jokes. I hid pieces of both of you in KB's heart. I haven't felt so close to the two of you since you were here with me on earth, and I will forever be grateful to this book for that.

Being a "momma" to my three daughters has been one of my life's greatest joys. Kailah, Makenzie, and Zuri, everything I do is to make you proud, to make you strong, and capable, and confident. It took me forever to realize that maybe, just maybe, I could live my dreams. I promise to do everything I can to help you three live your dreams even sooner, even fuller.

And finally, my husband, partner, and forever friend. Chris, you give my life meaning and joy. I hear that living with a writer isn't easy, but you make it look effortless. You give me so much love and comfort and happiness. Thank you for giving me the kickstart I needed back in the day to become the person I am now. You da best.

My childhood had trauma, but it also had joy. In the end, I laughed more than I cried. Still, I used to wonder why I couldn't just have an ordinary childhood, and it's only now, after writing KB's story that I've realized that my childhood was an ordinary childhood. Black girlhood is girlhood. Black stories are universal. Black lives **are** lives, and we matter. Telling our stories matters. I hope that by reading this book, someone feels

Acknowledgments

seen. I hope someone else will open their eyes and begin to see. But if nothing else comes of this, I know that the little girl I used to be is so proud of the woman I am now. She might even catch an extra special firefly, just for me.

ABOUT THE AUTHOR

KAI HARRIS is a writer and educator from Detroit, Michigan, who uses her voice to uplift the Black community through realistic fiction centered on the Black experience. Her work has appeared in **Guernica, Kweli Journal, Longform**, and the **Killens Review of Arts & Letters**, among others. In addition to fiction, Kai has published poetry, personal essays, and peer-reviewed academic articles on topics related to Black girlhood and womanhood, the slave narrative genre, motherhood, and Black identity. A graduate of Western Michigan University's PhD program, Kai was the recipient of the university's Gwen Frostic Creative Writing Fiction Award for her short story "While We Live." Kai now lives in the Bay Area with her husband, three daughters, and dog, Tabasco, and is an assistant professor of creative writing at Santa Clara University.